D0466815

THE AUSTIN AFFAIR

A NOVEL

FIC
POLLO
12/15/07

THE AUSTIN AFFAIR

D.J. Pollock

NORTH LOGAN CITY LIBRARY
475 East 2500 North
North Logan, UT 84341
435-755-7169

Guild Bindery Press
Memphis, Tennessee

Copyright © 1994 by D.J. Pollock

All rights reserved. Written permission must be secured from the publisher to use or reproduce any part of this book, except for brief quotations in critical reviews or articles.

PUBLISHED IN MEMPHIS, TENNESSEE
BY GUILD BINDERY PRESS, INC.

Library of Congress Cataloging-in-Publication Data

CIP
94-60504

Pollock, D.J.
        The Austin Affair / D.J. Pollock
        p.   cm.

ISBN 155793-041-4
Fiction

Printed in the United States of America

1 2 3 4 5 6 7 8 9
First Edition, 1994
Second Edition, 1995

ACKNOWLEDGEMENTS

During the research and writing of this novel, I met so many warm and gracious people it would be impossible to list all of them. I would, however, like to take this opportunity to extend a sincere 'thank you' to all for the words and letters of encouragement.

I would like to give special acknowledgement to Mr. Tye Hochstrasser of the Driskill Hotel and Mrs. James (Annetta) White, co-owner of the Broken Spoke, both of Austin, Texas, for giving me a tour of their establishments.

Finally, I would like to express my deepest appreciation to my loving and supportive husband, without whom this work would probably never have been completed.

D. J. Pollock

To my husband, George Dean Pollock, III, M.D.

CHAPTER ONE

The funeral director ushered Louis Hamilton and his executive secretary, Beth Wagner, to the visitation room of April Nicole Crafton. They stopped at the door and Beth signed both names on the visitors' registry. The intense fragrance emanating from all the floral sprays placed around the coffin reminded them of the sweetness and beauty of her young body.

Beth stepped close to the coffin and placed a warm hand on the dead girl's arm. "Oh April, April. What am I going to do without you?" A tear slid down the right side of her face as she dabbed her eyes with a tissue. No one had counted on this, and no one would ever know exactly how hard it would be to replace her...in more ways than one. "Look at her, Louis. Isn't she beautiful?"

"Yes, she is. One of the most beautiful girls we've ever hired," he whispered. "It's so hard to believe this has happened. April was such a good, loyal employee."

"There'll never be another April, Louis."

"You're right about that."

He took Beth by the arm and led her to an empty space along the paneled wall. She glanced around the room. It was filled to capacity. She dabbed the tears from her eyes again and noticed that the people sat motionless and were staring at them. Maybe they think we're responsible for April's death, she kept thinking. Maybe they've heard something.

Maybe she was getting paranoid. She dabbed a thin line of perspiration that had formed along her upper lip.

"Beth, are you okay? Come on, let's step outside. You look like you could use some fresh air." He led her outside the funeral home and stopped under an oak tree near the edge of the well-kept lawn.

"What happened? You turned pale as a ghost in there."

"Nothing. Really, I'm okay, Louis."

"I wonder who the little lady sitting next to the tall cowboy was?" he asked.

She fumbled in her purse for a small mirror and checked her mascara. "I don't know," she said. "According to our records, April didn't have a family. They certainly didn't appear to be her class of people."

"Well...they both looked pretty upset."

She placed the mirror back into her purse and crammed the damp tissue in a side pocket. "April's gone, Louis, so I guess it's no longer important."

"You think we should go back in and say something to them? Maybe find out who they are?"

"No. I don't really want to get involved. There's no telling who they are."

"It just seems a little cold to walk out and not say something."

"Let it go, Louis. It's the way April would have wanted it."

"I guess you're right," he sighed and looked at his watch. "Seven o'clock. "Are you hungry?"

"A little."

"Why don't we go someplace and get a bite to eat."

"Okay. There's a place just a few blocks away."

They drove the five blocks to the Candlelite Inn, parked Louis's black Mercedes and went inside.

The dining room was softly illuminated by chandeliers hanging from the ceiling and large white candles on each table. The tables were dressed with elegant lace placed over white linen tablecloths. The solid cherry chairs were polished to perfection.

The waitress came immediately and handed each a menu. "Would you care for a glass of wine?" she asked.

Beth looked at Louis, then answered, "Yes, a glass of white wine would be nice."

"Make that two."

She returned shortly with the wine, took their orders and disappeared into the kitchen. A small man with thick horn-rimmed glasses, presumably the Candlelite's owner, walked femininely to the microphone and announced the lead singer. "Ladies and gentlemen, please welcome Miss Ashley Denton."

The large crowded room became vibrant with audible cheers and whistles. The overhead lights dimmed and the pianist began to play softly as a beautiful, tall, red-headed girl entered from a side curtain and glided smoothly to the microphone placed near the edge of the first row of tables. She smiled and began to sing.

Louis Hamilton settled back in his chair and folded his arms across his chest. After a few seconds, he lifted his head and became totally enthralled as the clear, beautiful voice came over the loudspeaker. The waitress arrived and stood between them as she set the plates on the table. He was beyond surprise and sat motionless, hardly noticing the food. He bent his head and placed his mouth close to Beth's ear. "What'd he say her name was?"

"Ashley Denton."

"I want you to find out about her. She might just be the one I need to replace April. Go call our investigator and tell him I want a full report on my desk first thing Monday morning."

"But Louis, it's Wednesday."

"I know what day it is." He smiled.

She knew what the 'I know' and the smile meant. She slowly worked her way through the tables to a pay phone where she placed the call to Jacob Hughes, the firm's investigator.

✿   ✿   ✿

Monday, 9 a.m. The report on Ashley Denton was placed on Beth Wagner's large cluttered desk. She pressed the intercom button to Hamilton's office. "The report you requested is here."

"Bring it in."

She picked up the report, her cup of fresh coffee, sauntered into Hamilton's office and seated herself.

"What do we have?" he asked.

Beth pulled the contents from the brown envelope.

"Ashley Nicole Denton. Twenty-four years old, 5'8" tall, 120 pounds, and, as you saw Wednesday night, long, very thick red hair."

"I've never seen such natural beauty before," Louis added with a smile.

"Control yourself, Louis. You're old enough to be her father."

"Where does she live?"

"1429 South Vine Street, Apartment 6. That's over in the Hyde Park area."

"Uh-huh," he muttered. "Is she married?"

"Let's see." She read for a few moments. "No, and she lives alone."

Hamilton placed his elbows on his large antique desk and began massaging his temples with eight fingertips. "Any boyfriends?"

"Only one made mention of -- a young pathologist, Dr. Christopher Michael Burns, employed by the State Crime Lab. Been there two years."

"Hmmm." Hamilton pulled a cigarette from his heavily starched shirt pocket and lighted it eagerly. He inhaled and held the smoke in his lungs for the maximum effect. "What about her family?"

"No brothers or sisters. Both parents were killed in a hurricane while they lived in Gulfport, Mississippi.

"She was out of town when they died. She then lived with friends who were transferred here to Austin eight years ago, shortly after the hurricane."

"Education?"

Beth took a sip of coffee and shuffled the papers some more. "Ah, here we go. Graduated from Austin Central High School six years ago in the top five percent of her class. Completed two years at the University of Texas. Looks like she's planning to major in computer science. Apparently hasn't had the funds to finish the last two years."

"All right, that's perfect," Hamilton said as he leaned back in his chair. "Has she worked any place other than the Candlelite?"

"No, she's been there four years."

"Does the report list a salary?"

"Uh, yes." She flipped back two pages of the report. "Eight hundred ninety-three dollars a month, plus a few tips. That's take-home pay."

"Beth, my dear, I think we may have a replacement for April. Go see her and set up an appointment. The more I think about it, the more I want this girl on my staff."

"But Louis, she doesn't have any computer experience."

"You have a degree in computer science, Beth. Train her yourself."

"Okay." She paused for a moment. "I just hope you're not biting off more than you can chew."

"Let me worry about what I can chew." He smiled.

"Are you sure this is what you want?"

"Trust me, Beth. I've been in this business for 20 years. Have her in here tomorrow morning."

Beth parked her white Corvette in front of Ashley Denton's modest apartment. She ambled past the dark green Chevy parked in the driveway and noticed that it had a flat and a bald front tire. She walked slowly up the one concrete step and lifted her hand to knock on the badly weathered door. For several minutes she waited for an answer, then knocked again.

Ashley rolled out of bed and grabbed her chenille bathrobe, one of the last new items she had been able to afford before moving out of the Baxter home four years ago. The dark blue color had succumbed to the brutal beatings in the heavy-duty washer at the laundromat, and tiny rows of holes in numerous places revealed its age. She had left the Baxter home on good terms, feeling it was time to leave the nest. Their only daughter had already graduated from law school and had accepted a position with a large firm in Dallas. Even though they had tried persuading her to stay, she felt it was time to give this gracious couple some privacy of their own.

She stumbled to the door and peered through the diamond-shaped glass at the top. She clicked the dead-bolt, another lock with a chain and opened the door. "Yes?" she asked, squinting into the blinding sunlight.

"Ashley Denton?" Beth smiled.

"Yes, I'm Ashley."

"I'm Beth Wagner from Hamilton Medical Services. May I come in?"

Ashley stared at her for a moment, then nodded her head in the direction of the sparsely furnished living room.

"First I want to compliment you on your performance last Wednesday night. My employer, Mr. Louis Hamilton, and I visited the Candlelite and were quite impressed with the meal and your singing, especially your singing. You have a beautiful voice."

"Thank you." This was it, this was finally the break she had been waiting for. Someone from the music world had appreciated her talent and had come prepared to offer her a contract. She closed her eyes and, for a moment, dreamed of sports cars, fancy clothes, countless bank accounts all over Texas and long tiresome tours all over the world.

"Ashley?"

"Oh! I'm sorry. I was about to ask if you're in the recording business."

"Oh no, better than that." Beth chuckled.

The chuckle fell on deaf ears. What could be better than the recording business? But, what difference would it make now? There would be no deals made here today. She adjusted the front of her robe and pulled a hard knot in the belt.

Beth cleared her throat and spoke softly. "We're Hamilton Medical Services. We do computerized billing for a conglomeration of physicians all over Texas, Oklahoma and parts of Arkansas."

"Excuse me if I seem a little out of focus here, Miss Wagner, but I don't understand why you're here to see me."

Beth grinned sheepishly. "Mr. Hamilton checked you out and he's interested in you. One of our computer operators was killed in a car accident last week, and we're looking for a replacement."

"What do you mean, checked me out?"

"Please don't be offended, Ashley. All our files are strictly confidential, and we do a routine background check on any prospective computer operator. You have an excellent record, and we're prepared to make you an offer."

"I don't have any computer experience. I'm working on my degree in computer science, but I don't have any 'on the job' training. So far, every employer has wanted experienced operators."

She paused a moment. "What kind of offer?"

"Mr. Hamilton will tell you if you'll agree to an interview."

"When would he like to see me?"

"Would in the morning be convenient? Say around 10:30?"

"That would be fine."

"We have 19 other girls working for us and none of them had experience either. We train our own girls." She half-lied and smiled.

"Sounds good to me."

7

"Great! I'll have a driver pick you up at ten in the morning. Looks like you've had some bad luck with your car."

"Yeah, 'fraid so. The mechanic a couple blocks down the way wanted three hundred dollars to fix it, with no guarantees." She flashed a smile revealing perfect white teeth. "Unfortunately, it's not worth that much."

"Well," Beth smiled, walking to the open door and pointing to the white Corvette, "come to work for us and you may be able to afford one of those."

"Nice set of wheels!" Ashley smiled. "But I'm afraid it'll be a long time before I could be in the market for one of those."

"You never know," Beth said as she waved from the doorstep.

Tuesday, 8:30 a.m. Big Ben danced on Ashley's nightstand. She reached over, shut off the alarm and placed her fatigued feet on the floor. Her hours at the Candlelite were from 7:00 p.m. until 1:00 a.m., but visions of the white Corvette kept interrupting her blank mental screen, preventing much sleep.

She stood in front of the long mirror attached to the inside of the bathroom door that hinged out instead of in, and took a deep breath. What a mess, she thought. Her nose was shining, and her hair looked like a homespun mop. She undressed and stepped into the shower, hoping that the hot soothing water would melt away the tension and butterflies in the pit of her stomach.

At precisely 10:00 a.m., the office boy from Hamilton Medical Services sounded the horn of Beth's white Corvette. Ashley rushed through the door, secured the lock and walked briskly to the car. He opened the door on the passenger's side, and she seated herself in the plush blue velvet seat.

Ashley lost track of time as they drove. The radio blared as the young office boy tapped his fingers on the steering wheel to the beat of the rap music. He flipped on the blinker light and exited the expressway. They drove a few minutes more, made a couple of left turns, then the impressive oak and mesquite trees blocked the view of the highway. They stopped in front of a modern, blond-brick building with a drive-through canopy over the front entrance. She noted the inscription, 'HAMILTON BUILDING, constructed in 1982', on the concrete block embedded in the brick next to the front entrance.

The office boy opened her door and she stepped out onto the brick drive and waited as he parked the car.

They entered the spacious foyer on the ground floor of the three-story building. Large, fluted columns, topped with an arrangement of mixed flowers, accented each side of the room. A guard sat at the end in a glass cubicle, heavily equipped with television monitors, intercom systems and a large panel of switches. He electronically opened the large door to the right and motioned them in.

The office boy pointed out Beth Wagner's office on the right. She smoothed her pale yellow sun dress and knocked.

"Come in. The door's open."

Ashley entered. "Good morning, Miss Wagner," she said.

"Ashley! How are you?"

"Fine, thank you."

Beth straightened a stack of papers and placed them back in the file. "Come on, we'll start with a tour and you can meet the rest of the girls."

Ashley followed her out of the office and through a solid steel door that required the insertion of a plastic coded card in a small box on the wall to the right.

"Why all the security doors?" Ashley asked.

"When I explain the operation, you'll understand." They stopped at the first office on the left of the long hall. "This floor houses ten offices, eight computer operators, my office and the owner, Mr. Louis Hamilton. There are 12 offices on the second floor. Each office in the building has a computer with a modem. Do you understand what a modem does?"

"Yes I do," she answered.

Beth continued. "As I was saying, each office is equipped with a computer. Each computer has a modem that connects the system to a telephone line. This allows us to communicate with another computer in another building, or even across the country."

Ashley smiled and nodded affirmatively.

"We have 410 physician accounts from all over the states of Texas, Oklahoma and Arkansas, and each patient is registered by computer. The service they receive is entered when the visit is completed, and at the end of each day, all transactions are forwarded to our computers. Do you follow me so far?"

"I think so. It's very interesting."

"Each operator has 21 accounts, equally distributed, of course. We don't want to overload our girls. We enter each patient on their own spreadsheet, and at the end of each month, statements are mailed. Their insurance is filed on a daily basis, direct to the insurance companies through the fax machines."

"I'm very impressed."

They stepped briefly into each office, Beth making introductions, Ashley smiling and trying hard to remember as many names and faces as she could.

As they walked down the hall, Ashley noticed a large breakroom with several vending machines, soft drink machines and a microwave oven. It was furnished with glass tabletops mounted on Corinthian-column bases and then complemented by chairs of white cast iron. Lion wall fountains and oversized mirrors adorned the walls.

At the end of the hall, they entered the elevator, after using a code card in the code box, and went to the second floor. The same ritual...smiles, introductions, names and faces.

10

Back in the elevator, Beth asked, "Well...what do you think? Pretty neat operation, huh?"

"Yes it is."

"Now, let's go down and meet the big boss."

Beth knocked. Hamilton mumbled, "Yes?"

"Ashley Denton's here."

"Fine. Send her in."

He stood and extended his hand. "Good morning, Miss Denton. I'm Louis Hamilton. Have a seat." He paused until she was seated comfortably. "What do you think of our operation?"

"I'm very impressed."

"Let me give you a bit more history. I organized this company 20 years ago and started with ten accounts. Since then we've grown, from those accounts and one computer, to over 400 accounts and 20 computers. I pay my employees well and offer them hospital and life insurance, a dental plan, profit-sharing and a nice bonus for Christmas." He waited for a response.

"Sounds ideal so far, Mr. Hamilton." Ashley smiled.

"It's a nice package." He put on his reading glasses. " Now, let's talk salary. How does $6,000.00 a month, plus overtime for social functions, sound to you?" He smiled, knowing damn well what her present salary was, and looked up over his reading glasses in time to see her repeat the figure inaudibly.

"Six...thousand...dollars...a...month...plus?"

"That's right, Ashley." He repeated the figure again. "Plus a sizable raise at the end of six months if your performance is satisfactory." He sensed Ashley's interest. "If you accept my offer, you'll only have 11 accounts. Your duties will include more public relations than the rest of the girls, and your time will be limited as far as accounts go. Would you excuse me a moment?"

He removed his reading glasses and deliberately left the room to give her some time to think.

Ashley Denton was very independent and practical. What's the deal here? Why such a fabulous salary for an untrained worker who wasn't even close to a college degree? She had never intended for the job at the Candlelite to be a career and neither had it been much of a living. Just an existence. There was one thing she had noticed during the tour of this firm; all the female employees looked healthy and happy with no visible signs of abuse. There was really nothing about this place that frightened her at this point, and she felt her uneasy mood was temporary and would soon pass.

A few moments later he returned and sat on the edge of the desk, just a few inches from her chair. "Have you made a decision or do you need more time to think it over?"

"Well, Mr. Hamilton, there's one question I'd like to ask, if you don't mind."

"Certainly. I'll do my best to answer it."

"Why such a large salary for an untrained worker?"

He looked stunned and paused a long moment. "It's a long story, Miss Denton. If you come to work for me, you'll find out. If you turn me down, it wouldn't be important, would it?"

"No sir, I don't suppose it would."

"One more important issue." He wrinkled his forehead. "What about boyfriends?"

The shock of that question hit her full force, feeling like a bomb had exploded in her stomach and then spread upward. By now, she had grown accustomed to male advances, and her first inclination was to tell him to kiss her ass, take this high-paying job and shove it.

She stared at him and finally broke the silence to say: "To be perfectly honest, Mr. Hamilton, I don't think my personal life should be any of your concern."

"I didn't mean to offend you, but there'll be numerous socials you'll be required to attend with me. I simply wouldn't want a jealous boyfriend complicating matters."

"What kind of socials?"

"Political socials mainly. Simply a matter of public relations."

A hunger pain gnawed its way through her stomach with the reminder that there was only five dollars left between her and the next paycheck three days away. She couldn't afford to be too cocky. "That shouldn't be a problem, Mr. Hamilton."

"Good." He winked. "I think we'll get along just fine, Miss Denton."

"Thank you, sir."

"I need an answer as soon as possible. I can't afford for one of my computers to be down too long. It makes it hard on the other girls."

She allowed several seconds of silence before answering, "Your offer's very generous, Mr. Hamilton, and I accept the position."

"Good. I think you'll like it here. By the way, I'm told you're in dire need of transportation. True?"

"Yes, sir," she answered, feeling the color of her face turn from pink to a crimson red.

"Tell you what. I'll rent you a car and have it delivered to your apartment. Use it as long as you need to get squared away. Beth also told me you'd need to find another apartment."

"Yes, sir. I plan to start looking right away."

"Oh, I almost forgot. A wardrobe will be furnished for all the socials you'll have to attend with me. Beth will get with you later on that. Can you come to work Monday?"

"I really should give two weeks' notice at the Candlelite. I wouldn't feel good about myself if I didn't."

"I admire your loyalty, but let me take care of that for you. I'll have Beth call them and explain. You'll need the rest of the week to find another place to live. I'll also have her fix you a $3,000 check to help you out. Okay? I'll see you Monday. The hours are from 9:00 a.m. till 5:00 p.m. Goodbye, Ashley."

Beth had reminded Louis Hamilton of his eleven o'clock

13

meeting at the Chamber of Commerce. She watched from her office window as he drove through the oak and mesquite trees until he was well out of sight. She picked up her phone and dialed. After several rings, a male voice answered, "Hello."

"Louis hired that redhead I told you about. I'm afraid she could be a problem."

"Why?" he asked.

"I've been around long enough to know she's not a product of poverty. She's too smart for our own good, and there's something else about her that worries me. She's already asking questions."

"What's wrong with a new employee asking questions? Are you sure it's not just jealousy or a fear of losing your own job?"

"Listen. None of the other girls ever asked about the security system here or why we pay such high salaries. You need to pay more attention and start looking past the curves."

"What do you think you can do about it?"

"That's why I called you."

"To do what?"

"I need a few days to find someone else for the position. Is there some way to delay her first day of employment for a week or two?"

"You said Louis had already hired her."

"I can handle that. He's aware we need someone now."

There was a short pause from Beth's male friend. "Yeah, I think I can handle that."

"Then do it. There's one more thing."

"What's that?"

"Find out more about her. I don't think Jacob Hughes has told us the whole truth."

"The whole truth about what?"

"That's what I want you to find out."

"What's her name and address?"

"Ashley Denton. 1429 South Vine Street, Apartment 6."

"No problem. I'll take care of it."

"Good, and I'll thank you later."

Back in her apartment two hours later, Ashley was awakened by a loud knock on the front door.

"Yes?"

"Miss Ashley Denton?"

"I'm Ashley." She had spied the emblem of Austin Car Rentals on the driver's shirt sleeve before she unlocked the door.

"Here's the rental Hamilton Medical Service asked us to deliver." He handed her a clipboard and asked her to sign where the red check mark had been placed. She signed and handed it back. "Thank you," he said, dropping the keys into her hand.

Ashley stood staring in disbelief at the shiny blue and white Buick parked in the driveway behind the old rusty Chevy. At that moment, the phone began to ring. She ran back inside and picked up the receiver.

"Hello"

"Hey, Carrot Top. What are you doing up at 2 p.m.?"

"Hi, Chris. I've been up since early this morning."

"Are you sick or something?"

"I may be."

"What the hell are you talking about?"

"Can't tell you over the phone."

"Well then...have dinner with me tonight so you can fill me in on your mystery."

"Okay. But I'm not working at the Candlelite anymore."

"What happened?"

"I can't tell you over the phone."

"I'm working late, so meet me at the Old San Francisco around 7:00 p.m."

"Sounds good to me. See you then."

CHAPTER TWO

Ashley parked the new Buick at the Old San Francisco restaurant and rushed inside. The maitre d' escorted her to Christopher Burns's carefully chosen table in the rear of the large dining room and seated her politely.

Chris flashed an alluring smile. "You look absolutely beautiful. Why don't we just skip dinner and go back to my place."

"Very tempting, Chris, but I haven't had a chance to eat all day and I'm starved."

"New dress?"

"Uh-huh. Do you like?"

"Very pretty."

"Thank you, Doctor." She snatched the white napkin from the water glass, popped it in the air and laid it across her lap.

"Well, aren't you going to ask?"

"Ask you what, babe?"

"About my new job."

"I have a feeling you'll tell me anyway."

"This is not just a job, Chris. It's an opportunity."

"What have you done, hon, joined the Navy?"

"No, you idiot. Look at me."

"I'm looking and I like what I see."

"You are looking at the newest computer operator for Hamilton Medical Services."

"Are you serious?"

"Would I lie? Have you ever heard of them?"

"Of course I have. What doctor in Texas hasn't?"

"Are they that big?"

"You bet. How did you find out about it?"

"Well...actually, I didn't find it, he found me."

"What do you mean, he found you? And who is 'he'?"

"Mr. Hamilton. He owns the place. He and his secretary saw me at the Candlelite."

"And?"

"I've already been for an interview and they hired me. It's really a very unique operation. They process insurance claims and handle patient billing for over 400 doctors here in Texas, Oklahoma and Arkansas."

"Damn." He closed his eyes and used a heavy index finger to calculate in space. "If they charge each doctor $1,000 a month, that's over 400,000 bucks. Hell, maybe I'm in the wrong business."

"It's a huge place. There are 20 other girls, two security men and an office boy there."

"Twenty-one females. Hey, maybe I could get a job there."

"No way, handsome. They could turn out to be man-eaters."

"Tell me something, Ash. Why would they need security guards?"

"I asked the same question and was told that they have millions of dollars in accounts and computers."

"I guess they offered you a much nicer salary than the Candlelite and better hours too. Right?"

"Six thousand a month."

"Whoa! Run that figure by me again."

"Six thousand a month."

"For a computer operator?"

"And a little social work at night."

"At $6,000 a month, I'll just bet there's a whole lot of social work at night."

"Why are you being such an ass? I thought you'd be proud

17

of me."

"I'm very proud of you, Ash, but...we need to talk a little more about this social work. Did your new boss give you any specifics?"

"I was so nervous, I can't remember if he did or not."

"Think, Ashley."

"You said you'd heard about Hamilton Medical. Have you ever heard anything bad?"

"No, I can't say that I have."

"Then why are you getting all bent out of shape?"

"Ashley, I've been through college and medical school and I've been around, know what I mean?"

He shifted in his seat, slowly sipped his glass of wine, and watched the expression change on her face. He knew what she was thinking and knew she was right. It was common knowledge that most medical students were as wild as March hares, indulging in beer busts and wild games with the girls most weekends. On one occasion, one of the bashes had gotten out of control and pictures of the rowdy students had appeared on the front page of the morning paper, followed by a stiff reprimand from the dean. Chris had flown to D.C. for a weekend visit with his parents and was fortunate enough to have escaped that embarrassing scene.

"What I'm trying to say is this, sweetheart. Working at the crime lab, I've seen a little bit of everything. It's not always the wonderful world you think, and sometimes you can't trust everybody."

"Don't lecture me, Chris. I'm not a child, and I haven't exactly been an angel either."

"Bull. You've lived in such a clean, protected world, you don't know the half of it, and that's one of the things I love about you. End of lecture. When do you start your new job?"

"Monday."

"Are they expanding or did someone quit?"

"No to both questions. I'm replacing a girl who was killed in an auto accident. I think her name was April Crafton."

"What did you say?"

"I said I'm replacing..."

"No, what'd you say her name was?"

"April Crafton. Why?"

"I assisted Dr. Sulcer with an autopsy on a young lady by that name a few days ago. I wonder if it was the same girl?"

"Chris! Stop lying to me."

"I'm not lying to you, babe. We think she was murdered."

"Oh God, I hope it wasn't the same girl."

"I'm talking out of school here, so please don't say anything about this. The police commissioner picked up the report as soon as we were finished. Apparently he has some suspicions of his own, or they wouldn't have requested an autopsy."

"You mean it's not routine for the commissioner to pick up a report?"

"No, not unless there's foul play suspected."

The conversation was placed on hold until the New York strips and baked potatoes were served. The waiter refilled the wine glasses, removed the salad plates and left.

"You know, Chris, now that I think about it, there were a couple of things that caught my eye today during the tour of the Hamilton building."

"What were they, Ash?"

"First, when we arrived, I noticed that the building had three floors, but the elevator only showed two."

"Could be a private elevator or stairway to the top floor. That's probably where the so-called social part of the job takes place, and that worries me. What was the other thing you noticed?"

"All the girls were dressed to kill, and I wondered why they would need an extravagant wardrobe to work in such a secluded place?"

"Did you ask about this before you agreed to take the job?"

"No. I didn't think it was important, and Mr. Hamilton

didn't mention it either. Stop worrying, Chris. I'll be okay. I really need this job."

"I know you'll be okay. None of us have any guarantee of safety on our jobs."

"Then what do I have to lose?"

"I don't guess you have anything to lose. I've seen so much crap in the crime lab, I have a tendency to over-react sometimes. Hell, if it feels good, go for it. Speaking of jobs, I got some good news today, too."

"What?"

"Let's dance and I'll tell you."

The music was soft and soothing. Chris took her in his arms and held her close. "The director of the lab will be leaving in three months, and I've been appointed to take his place."

"Congratulations, Dr. Burns. I'm very proud of you."

"What do you have planned for tomorrow?"

She moved in his arms and braced her forehead against his chin. "I have to find a new apartment. Why?"

He waited a few seconds. "The apartment next to mine's vacant. Why don't we go over and rent it tonight? Then we can go pick up your things."

"Tonight? It's nine o'clock, Chris."

"I know the manager real well. She won't mind."

Ashley bit her lip thoughtfully. "She?"

"Yeah, she. And...she is in her fifties."

"Why the rush? I can do that tomorrow."

He lifted her face, smiled and looked deeply into her green eyes. She pressed against his very strong, masculine body. After a few moments, he gently broke the embrace and led her back to the table.

"I have a few days off, and you don't have to report to work until Monday. Why don't we move your things tonight and fly down to Orlando and spend the next four days at Disney World. If you won't move in with me, at least I can keep an eye on you if you're next door."

Ashley shrugged. "Why not?"

"How did you get here, a taxi?"

"No, Mr. Hamilton rented me a car."

He looked shocked. "The hell you say! Did he give you the money to rent an apartment too?"

"As a matter of fact, he did, Chris. And don't start lecturing me again."

"I'm sorry, Ashley. You didn't deserve that. I guess I'm a little upset because you wouldn't let me buy you a new car or help you rent a nice place to live. You've always been so hung up on the words 'obligation and self-respect.' I hope you're not getting yourself in debt to this man."

"Please, Chris. It was just an advancement on my salary and that 'man' is in his fifties, too. Are you getting jealous?"

"Well, what do you think? I love you Ash, and I don't want to see you get into something over your sweet head. Let's go," he said and stood up from the table. "Follow me over to my place."

She nodded and he led the way to the cashier's desk. His words had left her profoundly frustrated. Never, in the past year since they started dating, had he ever displayed such signs of jealousy and concern. Of course she could keep things under control, if there was anything to keep under control. She wasn't worried about that. She was only interested in two things -- a good paying job and getting out of the dismal existence she had tolerated for the past two years.

Chris woke the apartment manager and Ashley rented the apartment next to his. She collected the key, and they rode the elevator to the third floor. As she entered her new apartment, tears filled her eyes as they roamed around the plush living room.

She gazed in awe at the modern furnishings, which had been chosen with exquisite taste. She turned to Chris with a wide smile. "My furniture's prettier than yours. Who was your decorator, Dr. Burns?"

He grinned. "Obviously, not the same as yours, sweetheart. Why don't you look at the rest of the apartment."

She ran to the bedroom and opened the double doors. Her eyes sparkled at the beauty of the bedroom. She stood for a long moment admiring the large bath that adjoined the bedroom. She ran in circles with her arms outstretched.

"I take it you're pleased with your new home," Chris said, finally breaking the silence.

"I love it. I feel like I've gone from rags to riches."

He motioned. "Come on, let's go to my place. I need to change clothes before we go get your things."

Chris changed from his pin-striped suit to a pair of denim shorts and a polo pullover, then went next door and borrowed his neighbor's pickup, with the camper on top, to move Ashley's belongings.

The van rolled slowly down South Vine Street and pulled to a stop across from the run-down building numbered 1429. Blade Henderson sat staring in the direction of Apartment 6 and after a few seconds mumbled, "Damn you, Beth Wagner. This can't be the right address." He reached for his cellular phone and dialed her number.

"Hello."

"Are you sure you gave me the redhead's right address?"

"What did you write down, Blade?"

"1429 South Vine Street, Apartment 6."

"That's right. Where are you?"

"I'm here at that address, but it just doesn't seem to fit what you told me about the girl."

"There seems to be a lot that doesn't fit. That's why you're there."

"Ten four, see you later."

He reached behind the seat for his utility bar and stepped out of the van. Looking in all directions, he crossed the short stretch of sidewalk that led to the building. He stepped up on the small porch and approached the door of Apartment 6.

Looking over his shoulder, he pushed with brute strength against the door and slid the tool in the narrow crack.

Within seconds, he pushed the door open and stepped quietly into the front room, pausing a moment to listen. The penciled beam of his flashlight traveled over every inch of the tiny apartment in all directions. "Now, let's see what we can find out about this little lady that she might not want us to know."

Hurriedly, he searched. The front room, the kitchen, the bathroom. Nothing. What a disappointment. So far he had found nothing.

As he stepped into the bedroom, he heard muffled young voices coming from just outside the window. He extinguished his flashlight and for a few moments stood motionless. After allowing his eyes to adjust to the darkness, he stepped around the small bed to the window. He slowly pulled the curtain back and looked outside.

"Oh, hell," he mumbled as he watched two young boys stick their long, white cigarettes into the match flame, puff vigorously and cough as they tried to inhale.

The wait seemed much longer than it actually was. After the cigarettes were puffed down to the filter and the whispering, coughing and giggles subsided, the two boys scampered off into the dark street. A woman's voice rang out in sharp reprimand. "Where the hell are you kids? Get your little asses home, and I mean now."

Blade replaced the curtain and turned his attention back to the bedroom. From the scattered pile of personal belongings he had emptied from the dresser and chest of drawers, he picked up a Bible and thumbed through the pages. He carefully opened the envelope that had been placed in the back and began to read. "Holy shit," he mumbled as he read. Fumbling awkwardly, he refolded the letter, stuffed it back into the envelope and placed it back where he had found it.

Chris and Ashley entered the expressway and drove in

silence for a few minutes. "Penny for your thoughts, Carrot Top."

She chuckled. "I was just wondering what your father, the Honorable Senator Brandon J. Burns, would have thought of my old apartment?"

Chris smiled. "My mom would probably have summoned the butler to bury his tailor-made suit pants." They laughed heartily, then fell silent once more.

Ashley wiped her perspiring hands. She could not remember when she had felt so exhausted. She rubbed her eyes; they felt as though someone had thrown a bucketful of sand in her direction.

Suddenly, the lights of the Austin Aviation Service sign glared in her face. Her old apartment building would soon be in full view.

Chris parked the borrowed pickup behind the old green Chevy and opened Ashley's door. "What are you going to do with your old car?"

"The mechanic down the way offered me a hundred dollars for it. I'll get in touch with him when we get back from Florida."

By this time, they had reached the front door of her apartment, and Chris noticed that the door was ajar.

"Get back, Ashley!"

"Why?" she asked, stepping backwards down the step.

"The door's broken! Someone's been here!"

Chris reached around the open door, felt for the light switch and turned on the living room light. Gradually his eyes focused, and he began searching the apartment.

Ashley stood by the front step, trembling. Finally, she could wait no longer. Cautiously, and holding her breath, she stepped inside. "Chris! Where are you?"

"In the bedroom, Ash."

Ashley entered and looked down at the floor. Her face suddenly became completely without color. Everything she owned was scattered on the floor and all over the bed. "How could they?" she cried. "What in hell could they have wanted?"

"That's a good question. Call the police."

Twenty minutes later, Ashley's heart beat noticeably faster as she followed two burly policemen through each room.

"Have you noticed anything missing?" one of the officers asked.

"No sir. So far, nothing."

"Do you live by yourself?"

"Yes sir."

"I don't advise you to stay here by yourself tonight."

"I had planned to move to another apartment across town tonight. Will it be okay?"

"Yes, ma'am. I'll make a report and send someone over here a little later to try to lift some fingerprints. We probably won't find anything, so don't expect too many answers. By the way, where can we get in touch with you if we need you?"

"I'm going to be out of town for the next few days."

"When you get back, you can check with the precinct to find out if we came up with anything."

Ashley placed her wardrobe in the spacious closet of her new apartment and distributed her toiletries and groceries to their designated places. She then picked up her box of memorabilia and emptied the contents on the bed. It contained her report cards from her junior and senior years in high school, a few graduation photos of classmates, her diploma and a large King James version of the Holy Bible, presented to her by the Methodist minister on the day of her parents' funeral.

Most of her memorabilia of the first 16 years had been destroyed in the hurricane that had taken her wonderful parents. They had been avid church attenders, and her father

25

had always carried his Bible to every service. 'Felt naked without it,' he'd say. They had been strict, but at the same time, had allowed an unforgettable childhood. She missed them terribly, and tears filled her eyes as she picked up the Bible and slowly thumbed through the pages. Near the back, she found a letter-sized envelope. "Oh, my God, Chris!"

"What is it, Ash?"

"I remember picking this up at the post office the day I returned the box key. It's from First State Bank to my father. Two days after the funeral, I moved to Austin with the Baxter's, and this letter's been in my Bible for six years."

"Well...open it, Ash."

She flipped the letter over. "It's already open, Chris."

"Maybe you opened it and don't remember."

"Well, of course not. If I'd read it, I'd know what it's about and I don't. Someone else has opened it."

"What are you waiting for? Read it."

"I'm afraid to, Chris." She handed the envelope to him. "You read it, please."

Chris removed the letter and silently began to read. He gasped and looked down at Ashley with a blank expression on his face.

"Is something wrong?" she asked.

"No," he answered bluntly, and his attention was drawn back to the letter. He finished reading and sat limply on the bed next to her. Suddenly, she saw one of the most incredible, sedating smiles she had ever seen.

"Get packed, Ash. We're going to Mississippi tomorrow. You have a date with the president of Gulfport First State Bank. Disney World can wait."

"What is it? Chris?"

"I'll just keep this letter and let you find out tomorrow when we get there. You've waited six years. One more night won't kill you."

      ❀   ❀   ❀

At the airport terminal, their flight was called for the last time. They walked down the boarding ramp in silence and boarded the plane. Ashley yawned and her shoulders jerked. After being up most of the night and the morning chaos at the airport, trying to get tickets to Gulfport, it was not odd that she was exhausted. She sat tensely as the jet rumbled down the runway and lifted smoothly into the air. As soon as the seat belt light was extinguished, she unbuckled and slumped in her seat.

After a Coke and a bag that contained exactly 14 honey-glazed peanuts, Chris inaudibly reread the letter while Ashley dozed. So far, the flight had been smooth and very relaxing, and she needed the rest. He folded the letter and placed it in the inside pocket of his suit coat. He felt like a first-class heel for withholding the information, but he thought the news should come from the bank president. He glanced at Ashley and studied the sweet innocence of her face. She was incredibly beautiful, even with her mouth gaped open and eruptions coming from her throat sounding like Mount St. Helens.

Chris tapped Ashley gently on the shoulder. "Wake up, Helen."

"Helen? Who's Helen?" she asked with a puzzled look on her face.

There was a gleam of humor in his eyes. "Oh...you wouldn't know her. You sound a lot like her, but you wouldn't know her."

"Sometimes I worry about you, Chris."

He smiled. "Buckle up, Carrot Top. We'll be landing in Memphis in about 20 minutes."

"I wish we had time to tour Graceland. I've always wanted to see where Elvis lived. They say it's beautiful."

"Someday soon we will. I promise."

"I want to see Beale Street and the Pyramid too."

"You're on, babe."

She smiled, rather pleased. "Gonna hold you to it,

27

Christopher Burns."

She fastened her seat belt and sat limply. Her life at Gulfport seemed so far away. She shivered and deliberately shoved all her childhood thoughts of wonder and magic aside and replaced them with hard realities. What would she find at the bank? Had she been adopted or were there old debts that were six years past due? Suddenly, she realized she was trembling.

The jet landed gracefully at Memphis International Airport, and they deplaned at 10:15 a.m. There would be a 55-minute layover, then they would take a smaller plane on to Gulfport, arriving there at approximately 1:00 p.m.

"All-in-all, a pretty nice flight," Chris said conversationally.

They rushed downstairs to retrieve their luggage, then back upstairs to get information about the small aircraft that would take them on to Gulfport. They located the short line and sat their bags down. A few more passengers got in line and, likewise, sat their bags down to hurry up and wait.

Ashley turned around and glanced down the waiting line. A woman smiled and a man, who caught, and held, her eyes and all of her attention for a few seconds, turned and began to gaze in the opposite direction.

He was a small man, brown thinning hair on top, chopped close to his rounded head. He had an unusually full, heavy mustache that looked out of place with such a short haircut on the sides. He was about 50, and his large brown eyes, with a childish brightness, seemed to be always laughing. She had seen those unforgettable eyes somewhere, but she was exhausted, and her ability to retrieve something from her mental computer had shut down. They began to walk down the boarding ramp, and he escaped her thoughts.

They wandered through the sparsely loaded plane and agreed on two seats near the rear. Chris picked up a book, left in the seat by the last passenger, and began to read. Ashley buckled herself in, leaned back and resumed her rest.

CHAPTER THREE

The sign above the Gulfport First State Bank registered the time, 1:33 p.m., and the temperature, 90 degrees. It was mid-July, and the gentle breeze from the ocean lent a freshness to the air that settled on the skin like a cool, soothing mist.

With a firm hand on Ashley's elbow, Chris urged her along. They entered and Ashley, looking around the vast bank, saw Josh McPearson, the bank president. She started smiling and began to walk in his direction.

Seeing Mr. McPearson again, Ashley was suddenly gripped with nostalgia. One of the nicest things she remembered about him was his devotion to the youth choir at the Methodist church, the same church she and her parents attended every time there was a service. He was minister of music and had spent countless hours with her, preparing her for a career in music, which he was confident she could have.

He came down the short flight of steps in the lobby -- a short man, handsome, carrying his 60 years with noticeable ease. His attire had not changed much, still wearing light summer suits, a white shirt and floral tie, the famous *Matlock* style. His thick wavy hair had more grey than she remembered.

He looked momentarily shocked as he walked briskly in her direction. "Ashley? Ashley Denton? Is it really you?" He took her hands in his and said graciously, "What a pleasant surprise. I'm so glad to see you."

"Mr. McPearson. This is my friend from Austin, Texas, Dr. Christopher Burns."

Chris extended a hand and they exchanged 'glad to meet you's.'

"Come to my office," Mr. McPearson said. "We have lots to talk about. Again, Ashley, it's so good to see you."

The conversation continued while they both were feeling the loss of all the years. Chris followed close behind, trying hard not to feel ignored, and from time to time would smile or nod his head.

Finally Mr. McPearson led them into his large office near the front of the building. His walnut desk was lined with computer printouts and folders in neat stacks. Nothing had changed. One massive, wall-sized tinted window allowed a breathtaking view of the Gulf, with only the highway and beach-front parking between them.

Mr. McPearson motioned toward two navy plaid wingbacks and said. "Have a seat. Could I get you something to drink? Coke or coffee?"

"No, thank you, sir," they both replied.

He then seated himself in his large leather chair, leaned forward and flipped on his intercom. "Tina, bring me the folder on Mr. Lowell Denton, please."

"Where would I find it, sir?"

"Never mind, I'll get it myself," he said and flashed a smile at his guests. "She just started working here Monday, and she's green as a gourd. Excuse me, I'll be right back."

Ashley nervously walked to the large tinted window and looked in the direction of the oceanside parking lot. Her face grew pale, and she called to Chris. With a wave of her hand, she motioned him to the window.

"What is it, Ash?"

"See that man leaning against the car in the parking lot?"

"Yeah, what about him?"

"Now I remember where I saw him. He was on the plane

from Austin to Memphis and on to Gulfport. I wonder if he's following us?"

"Well...there's one thing for sure," he answered. "We'll find out, if he's still there when we leave this bank."

At that moment, Mr. McPearson entered the office with the folder, and they returned to their seats. He opened the file and revealed the numerous attempts he had made to contact her.

"Where are you living now, Ashley?"

"I moved to Austin, Texas, with the Baxters two days after my parents' funeral."

"Oh, yes. I remember Tom and his family. Nice folks."

Chris retrieved the letter from his pocket and handed it to Mr. McPearson. "Ashley found this last night while she was moving to a different location. That's why we're here. Her new address is 3013 Clark Towers."

Mr. McPearson reached for the letter and said, "Thank you." He read it, laid it aside and offered no comment. He then opened the file and thumbed through the pages. Finally he looked directly at Ashley. "As I pointed out earlier, I made numerous attempts to contact you and, as you know, without success. I'll try to start from the beginning. If you have any questions along the way, don't hesitate to interrupt me."

She nodded nervously and smiled.

"This letter was mailed two days before the hurricane destroyed most of Gulfport. I sent the letter to inform your father that it was time to reinvest his Treasury Bills."

"Treasury Bills?" Ashley frowned.

"Yes, Ashley, your father was a very successful businessman, and was the best manager Gulfport Realty ever had. He can never be replaced, and he, along with you and your mother, has been greatly missed in our community."

Ashley suppressed the tears that burned behind her eyelids. "Thank you, Mr. McPearson."

"Now," he continued, "I'll start with the details." He paused for a moment. "Your father made me the executor of his estate until you reached the age of 21, then I became the co-executor. I've tried to carry out his wishes to the best of my ability." He picked up a sheet of figures and began. "Each year, he bought a substantial Treasury Bill, then at the end of every other year, he invested the earned interest in other wisely selected areas. Over the past 20 years, he has built up quite an estate. As it stands now, the interest from all the investments amounts to just a few dollars over 10,000 a month. Since I had failed to locate you, I reinvested the interest in several other areas. Are there any questions so far?"

Ashley sank back against the cushioned chair, her mind racing. His compassion had brought back painful memories of her parents, and her eyes filled with tears. Chris reached for her hand. "Are you going to be all right?" With her emotions finally under control again, she nodded. "I'm sorry, Mr. McPearson, please go on."

He looked deeply into her eyes with a tender smile on his lips. "When you're ready, my dear."

"I'm okay now, really."

He smiled again with relief. "Your father also owned a life insurance policy in the amount of $150,000. Another policy, on the house and its contents, was for $125,000. I invested the proceeds from those two policies in what I thought was the safest place with the highest yield." He paused to catch his breath. "I deducted the attorney's fee of $6,000, to execute the will, from the two $10,000 automobile policies, leaving a balance of $14,000, which I placed in a special account for you in your name. I certainly hope all of my decisions have met with your approval."

Ashley nodded quickly. "Of course it has, Mr. McPearson."

"Now...I'll have some papers for you to sign and get you all fixed up for your deposits on the first of each month. The bookkeeper will add up the exact figure, and we'll wire it to your bank tomorrow. Your first deposit will be somewhere in the neighborhood of $30,000. Is all of this agreeable to you?"

Her initial gaze of shock was replaced by one of gratitude. "Yes, sir. Thank you for all you've done. I'm beginning to realize how smart my father was."

"We're all guilty of that. When I was growing up, I thought my father was a total idiot. Now that I have five children of my own, I'm convinced he was a brilliant man."

"You're very kind. Again, thank you, Mr. McPearson."

"It's been my pleasure, Ashley, and if ever you need anything, please don't hesitate to call me."

She signed the necessary documents, witnessed by two bank employees, and handed the clerk one of her deposit slips that contained her account number at the Austin bank.

Mr. McPearson stood up from behind his desk. "You certainly look well and healthy, Ashley. This young man must be taking good care of you."

Chris smiled. "I do my best, sir."

Mr. McPearson guided them to the front door. "Don't wait so long to come back for a visit." He smiled at them both. "And remember, I'm here if you need me, Ashley. Nice meeting you, Dr. Burns. Take care, now."

They looked in the direction of the parking lot across the highway. The stranger was still waiting, now standing in the shade of a small tree, smoke drifting slowly up from his cigar.

"Act normal, Ash. Pretend you don't see him," Chris muttered from the corner of his mouth.

They strolled to the rental with their arms outstretched, filling their lungs with the wonderful ocean air. Chris unlocked the door, and Ashley slid in from his side of the car.

"Don't turn around. I'll watch from the rearview mirror."

He started the engine and pulled out onto Oceanside Drive. He drove slowly, as though they were lost, watching the street behind in the rearview mirror.

The stranger crushed his cigar with his heel and hurried to his car. He drove out of the brief crescent-shaped drive and entered the highway behind them.

"You were right, babe. He's right on target."

"What does he want?"

"Don't know, but I intend to find out. Didn't we pass an amusement park just off the highway coming from the airport?"

"Yes, a couple miles back."

"Good, but first, I want to be positive he's on our tail."

Chris made a sharp right on Main, a quick left on Eastern Avenue, back right on McClure Street, straight across Mardis, Longcrest, Dogwood, and entered the highway again. They drove the speed limit to the amusement park entrance.

The little man, in his rented Volvo, stayed about four car lengths behind.

Chris drove through the parking lot of the amusement park and located the perfect parking space. He had laid out his plan to Ashley, and she knew her job. They parked and strolled nonchalantly toward the park entrance. He glanced around, but the stranger was not yet in sight. They raced to a grove of hardy bushes that bordered the edge of the grounds.

Suddenly the stranger appeared through the brick entrance. His short strides were as quiet as a leopard's as he moved in their direction. He walked slowly, looking around interestedly at his surroundings. As he grew closer, his steps grew shorter and more deliberate.

When he was close enough, Chris and Ashley stepped from behind a small tool shed that housed the lawn mower and yard equipment and began to walk beside the stranger. Chris on the right, Ashley on the left, elbow to elbow. The walkway was deserted.

Slowly, Chris slipped his large hand between the stranger's side and forearm, closing his fingers in an air-tight grip. "Don't even think about running," he said softly. "I want to know who you are and what the hell you think you're doing."

Out of the corner of his eye, the stranger could see the 6'2", 200-pound linebacker's nostrils flare and drop with his breathing. He had little hope of out-running or out-muscling this tower of strength, hardly a match.

Suddenly the stranger stopped, his brown eyes bulging and keeping his smile, he answered. "Jacob Hughes, Private Investigator. Austin, Texas."

"Well...what a coincidence, Mr. Hughes. What are you doing down here in Gulfport?"

"That's privileged...."

Chris put more pressure on his hand that still rested on the investigator's arm.

"Who are you working for?" Chris asked sharply.

Left with no alternative, Jacob Hughes began to speak. "I work for Hamilton Medical Services. I investigate all new employees. Mr. Hamilton likes to know if they can be trusted."

"Trusted for what?" Chris asked.

"The diagnosis and treatment on each patient, that comes from their physician, is strictly confidential. One slip of the tongue could warrant a lawsuit against Hamilton Medical Services. He has to know who he is hiring, and if they can be trusted with this information."

"Did you break into my apartment?" Ashley asked.

"No. I don't break the law in any of my investigations."

"Is Hamilton Medical Services a legitimate company?" Chris asked.

"Yes, a very legitimate and prestigious organization."

"Why did you follow us to Gulfport?"

"Miss Wagner was not pleased with my investigation. She wanted more family background, and she pretty much runs the show."

"Pretty thorough, aren't you, Mr. Hughes?" Chris added.

"I try to be. Thank you."

"What do you know about a girl named April Crafton who worked for Hamilton Medical Services?"

"Nothing."

35

"I don't believe you, Mr. Hughes." Chris folded his large strong hand into a fist.

"All right! All right! You know she was in a car wreck, but I suspect she may have been murdered. Notice...I said suspect. I don't have any evidence, and if you mention this conversation, I'll deny every word."

"Did you kill her?" Chris frowned.

"Oh, come on, do I look like a killer?"

"I don't know, Mr. Hughes, what does a killer look like?"

"I can't answer that question. I've never killed anybody."

"If you think this girl was murdered, why do you continue to work for Hamilton?"

"I have to find a way to get inside information. For personal reasons, I just can't let go until I know the truth."

"Was Louis Hamilton involved with her?"

"It's possible," Hughes spoke quickly.

"What do you base your suspicions on?" Chris's eyes narrowed.

"Not anything concrete. It's just a gut feeling."

"And I have a gut feeling you're not telling everything you know. Right, Mr. Hughes?"

"I'm working on some leads."

"Well...I'm sure you've found out who I am and who my father is, haven't you?"

"Yes. As a matter of fact I have, Doctor. As you said, I'm very thorough."

"Then I strongly suggest when you turn your report in on Miss Ashley Denton, you'll make it look good. I'd hate like hell for you to turn up on my slab."

"My report will be accurate, Doctor Burns."

"Now...get out of here. I don't want to see you around unless you have something I need to know. Understand?"

"I get the message." He turned to Ashley. "Sorry about your apartment, Miss Denton."

"Thanks, Mr. Hughes. I don't live there anymore."

"Where'd you move to, Missy?"

"That's none of your business," Chris snapped. "Now get back to Austin and file your report before I change my mind and choke you to death."

The investigator wiped his mouth with the back of his hand and muttered, "You drive a hard bargain, Doctor." He retrieved the dead stump of a cigar from his pocket, lighted it, then began to edge his way along the grove of bushes to the park exit.

Ashley's eyes blazed. "That little shrimp certainly had his nerve!"

"How's that, Ash?"

"Following us all the way to Mississippi."

"I wouldn't worry about it."

"Why not, Chris?"

"I think he's harmless. He's just trying to do his job. In a way, I kinda like him. Come on, Ash. We'll fly back to Austin tomorrow and find you a new car. I'll just bet I can get you a good deal on a new Porsche. What do you say?"

She moved her head to one side politely. "I say you drive a hard bargain, Doctor."

CHAPTER FOUR

The noise and constant clacking of shoes against the hard floor of Austin's Robert Mueller Municipal Airport was deafening. Chris grabbed Ashley's hand as they hurried through the crowd to the front entrance.

They strolled through the parking lot and, as they approached Chris' car, noticed a young Mexican boy leaning against the driver's door with an envelope clutched in his hand.

"Are you Doctor Burns?" he asked.

"Yes I am."

"This is for you." He handed Chris the envelope.

"Thank you." Chris gave him some coins from his pocket, and the lad disappeared among the cars.

Ashley listened carefully as Chris read the contents of the note. "Meet me at Sugar's on Highland Mall Boulevard at 3:00 p.m. Very important. Jacob Hughes, P.I."

"Wonder what he wants now?" she asked.

"I don't have a clue. I told him in Gulfport I didn't want to see him around unless he had something I needed to know. So ... let's go find out what he has. It's 2:30 now, and I'm not exactly sure where this place is located."

Chris seated Ashley in his white Cadillac sedan, and she sank low in the leather seat. She watched admiringly as he pulled off his sunglasses and began to rub them with the bottom of his white polo. He looked fresh and wide awake, even though there had been little rest in the past 48 hours. So much had happened since Tuesday. She had suddenly gained great wealth, and the future seemed full of promise. She felt that she had died and awakened in a different world, in a new time zone. For one terrible moment, she resented the past four years of needless poverty on Vine Street, not exactly the ideal place to go jogging after dark. But the experience had been one of extreme value. She had learned to be self-sustaining, not to mention her education in street survival.

Chris folded the letter, returned it to the envelope and dropped it down the side of his seat. He started the engine and pulled out onto Manor Road. After they had driven a few moments, he blew his breath out in a satisfied gust and whispered, "How does it feel to be rich?"

Ashley curved her lips into a seductive smile. "Ask me again tomorrow, after I've had a good night's sleep. At the moment, I'm numb."

Chris turned the car onto Highland Mall Boulevard and spied Sugar's. He drove slowly by the building and noticed all the parking spaces were occupied. He parked the car at the next available space, and then they walked back and stepped into the narrow corridor. Double-tinted doors let them into the small restaurant.

Jacob Hughes, sitting in the back booth wearing a brown hat that was half a size too small, motioned to Chris and Ashley. They seated themselves and Jacob waved to the waitress. She came to their booth and all three ordered coffee.

Jacob sat silently brushing his mustache with a thumbnail, collecting his thoughts.

Chris stared at him with level eyes. "Well?"

Jacob's eyes glittered through cigar smoke as the waitress served the coffee. She left and he spoke in a low tone. "A friend of mine, who works for the homicide division, slipped me a copy of the autopsy report on April Crafton. The cause of death was listed as a cervical fracture, sustained on impact.

There was no mention of foul play, and I have to know if we're talking about the same April Crafton." He reached into his shirt pocket, withdrew a photograph and handed it to Chris. "Is this the girl?"

Chris sat his coffee cup abruptly on the table. "Yes, I assisted Dr. Steve Sulcer with that girl, and I know what we found."

Jacob knocked cigar ash on the floor and returned the cigar to his mouth. "Who made out the report?"

"I have to assume Dr. Sulcer did."

"What do you know about him?"

Chris frowned. "Not much. In his sixties. His wife died a year ago after a long illness and he was pretty upset about that. Basically, he's a loner."

Jacob made a modest grimace. "Do you think he would falsify the report?"

Chris drew his lower lip in between his teeth and sat silently for a few moments. "I couldn't say. I don't know him that well. He's retiring in three months. I suppose it's possible, but why are you telling us all of this?"

Jacob's voice was low in his throat. "For several reasons. I thought perhaps you could get some information at the lab as to who changed the autopsy report and why. Your sweetie, here, will be starting to work for Louis Hamilton on Monday, and she could keep her eyes and ears open there. Also, your father, being a senator, could pull some weight with the FBI, should the need arise."

Ashley sat silently running her slender fingers through her tousled hair. "Do you think Mr. Hamilton could be involved in her death?"

Jacob leaned forward, took off his hat and tossed it aside on the table. "At this point, I don't feel he's involved with murder. I think he's only guilty of wanting a professional-looking staff and the best qualified computer operators to attract prospective accounts. As far as personal involvement with any of the employees, I couldn't say. It's possible, but that's no crime. He's a wealthy, good-looking single man, and most young girls could be tempted."

Ashley said slowly, "I don't need this job, Mr. Hughes, and I don't relish the possibility of placing myself in a situation that could endanger my life."

"I did make a few inquiries before I left Gulfport last night, and I'm well aware that you don't need this job or any other job. I found that your father was a very successful man and left you a comfortable living."

Chris's eyes snapped. "You've done your job quite well, Mr. Hughes. Do you know how much 'comfortable' means?"

"No, I didn't feel that was any of my business or anyone else's for that matter. I try to be thorough, but at the same time, I know just where to draw the line."

"Thank you, Mr. Hughes. I suddenly feel my life has been placed under a microscope," Ashley said.

"I'm sorry. I had no intentions of making you feel that way, but I feel you're my last resort. Would you please consider the job with Hamilton Medical Services? I desperately need someone on the inside."

"I'm afraid not, Mr. Hughes. I have no experience, none whatsoever, in the detective line of work."

"Miss Denton," Jacob continued, "I don't feel you would be in any danger during the working hours with so many people around. The danger could be in the after-hour socials, and I would be right there to guide you and see that you're not harmed. What do you say?"

"No, Mr. Hughes."

Jacob flashed a smile that had nothing to do with pleasure. "But you must. April Crafton is not the first girl to die mysteriously while working there. Another one died two years ago. Supposedly suicide."

"That's too bad, Mr. Hughes."

"I'm positive that something's going on." Jacob frowned.

41

"I just never could prove anything. You and Dr. Burns would be in a perfect position to help me find the truth. If my suspicions are valid, other young women could be in danger."

Ashley withheld her reply for a thoughtful moment. "Okay, Mr. Hughes. I won't make any promises, but give me a couple of days to think about it. I'll let you know."

Jacob's face lost its hard lines. "Of course, my dear. What about you, Chris?"

"What's in this for you, Mr. Hughes?"

"Personal satisfaction. I had a daughter who would be about Ashley's age, had she had the chance to live. We'll leave it at that. Okay?"

"I'm sorry," Chris replied and thought for a long moment. "Where can we get in touch with you?"

Jacob fumbled in his back pocket and handed both a card. "Call the first number during the day. My secretary will get in touch with me immediately. Call the second number at night."

Chris swallowed dryly. "I hope you're wrong about this."

Jacob's jaws tightened as he pulled on his cigar. "Far from it, I'm afraid. Call anytime you need me, I'll be waiting." He stood, picked up his hat and walked quickly out of the restaurant.

The restaurant was empty except for an older couple and a black-haired man with dark, piercing eyes. He was tall, slim, long faced and well dressed in a double-breasted suit. Not a muscle in his face moved as he ate, and he made eye contact with no one seated in the small dining room.

It was 4:00 p.m., and, having missed breakfast and lunch, Chris suggested a meal; Ashley readily agreed. He motioned for the tall, gangly waitress, whose greying hair testified to her 60-something years. He sat pushing his fingers, from front to back through his thick hair, as the waitress scribbled their order and left. With their faces very close, he asked, "What are you going to do?"

42

She leaned back in the booth and looked up slowly, her face pale and blank. "What do you think I should do?"

"I don't know, Ash. This has to be your decision, but whatever you decide, I'll support you."

She stared at him, biting her bottom lip. "My better judgment says no, but in my heart, I know that this desperate little man will not take no for an answer. There's just something I can't put my finger on. I don't think he's told us everything. How do you feel about all of this? You haven't said much."

"I feel like you. This is not just a case of two females mysteriously dying. There's some deep personal involvement here with Mr. Hughes, and I don't think he'll let it rest...or us."

The waitress came with a plate in each bony hand and set them on the table. She left and returned in a few seconds to refill the coffee cups.

Chris stared at Ashley. "Whether we're willing to admit it or not, we're already involved in this dilemma. I know the autopsy was changed, and that automatically puts me in a dangerous position. We have some serious thinking to do and a decision to make. We're both exhausted, so let's go home and get some rest. We'll figure this out tomorrow."

"That sounds good to me."

Chris looked at his wristwatch. "Damn, it's five o'clock. I need to go by the supermarket and pick up a few things."

She leaned forward, slid her hand up the back of his head, running her fingers through his hair. "How about a nice bottle of wine to celebrate my newly found fortune?"

"Are you buying?"

"You bet."

"You got it, babe."

They rose from the booth and left Sugar's. They strolled arm-in-arm back to the car. The supermarket was only 15 minutes away. Chris started the engine and whipped out of the parking space. He began to weave in and out of the traffic

43

as though it were an obstacle course. As he approached the next stoplight, a man driving a pickup truck sat waiting on the opposite side of the intersection for the light to change. At 50 miles-an-hour, Chris sped down 51st, a heavily traveled street. At that moment, the traffic light changed to green, giving him the right-of-way to proceed. No one saw the dark brown station wagon swerve around the pickup and out into the intersection.

Without slowing, Chris tried to veer to the left. Too late. He stood on the brakes and heard the tires screech. Suddenly the brake pedal lost its hold and slammed against the floor. He gripped the steering wheel with one hand and grabbed Ashley's arm with the other. "Oh hell!"

There was a crash of glass...a deafening roar of metal against metal. Seconds later, the cars came to an abrupt stop.

Chris sat stiffly in his seat, mopping his bleeding nose with the back of his hand as the drops fell fast and thick down the front of his white sweater. "Ashley? Are you okay?"

Ashley sat limply, her chin resting on her chest. She didn't answer. Chris could not see her breathe. The shock nearly caused him to faint. His heart pounding, he cried, "Oh God, no!"

Both doors of the car were ajar. He unfastened his seat belt and began to examine Ashley's injuries.

Ashley's breath shuddered in and her eyes fluttered. "Chris?" She wrinkled her brow. "Chris? Where are you?"

"I'm right here, Ash. I'm fine. Are you okay?"

"I think so."

A young man in a summer jogging suit approached the car and asked, "Anyone hurt?"

"I think we're okay here. What about the man in the station wagon?"

"He's okay," said the young man. "Just had too much to drink. Probably feel worse tomorrow from a hangover."

Chris limped as quickly as he could manage toward the

driver of the station wagon, who by this time had staggered out of the car. He was grossly obese and very intoxicated. He could not have walked three feet without falling on his face.

Chris became furious. Contempt for the 60-year-old driver was in his eyes. "Can't you see, old man?" he asked with coldness in his voice.

The man's thick shoulders stiffened, and a thin mocking smile crossed his lips. "I hit you, didn't I?"

Chris moved closer to the car and the man. "I really ought to kick your ass until you sober up."

The man in the jogging suit summoned Chris. "The lady in your car's passed out!"

Chris groaned aloud, "Oh, God!" and ran back to the car. At that moment, he heard the howling of sirens. The sight of red flashing lights from the patrol car and ambulance brought a number of people to the sidewalks. The intersection was littered with debris. It was a tangled mass of glass and metal, battered hubcaps, strips of chrome, a rearview mirror and other objects knocked free from the cars on impact.

Two policemen stopped, got out of their patrol car and began to survey the accident. One of the officers signaled and two EMTs came forward, lugging their equipment and a stretcher. After several minutes, Ashley was gently placed on the cot and into the back of the ambulance.

One of the hospital EMTs recognized Chris. "Dr. Burns, would you like to ride with us to the hospital?" He nodded and climbed into the back of the ambulance as it wailed away.

The officers placed the old driver spread-eagle against the side of the station wagon as they searched him. He protested and asked, with a thick tongue, what was going on. One officer instructed him to remain silent. "You're in enough trouble as it is," he snarled.

At Holy Cross Hospital, Chris was X-rayed, treated for contusions of the left leg and released. After an extensive examination, Ashley was admitted to the hospital. Dr. Ted Billings studied the series of skull X-rays and returned to her room. "Well, Miss Denton, you're a very lucky young lady." He folded his tall frame and sat down in the chair next to her bed. "Your X-rays are completely negative. Looks like you had a mild concussion. I do feel you should stay overnight, strictly for observation. That's usually routine. I don't feel you'll have any complications, but I like to be on the safe side. I'll probably let you go home in the morning, and you'll be good as new in a couple of days. Any questions?"

"Yes, sir. Will I be well enough to start a new job Monday?"

"I'd suggest you wait a couple of days before you take on the stress of a new job. You took quite a hard blow." He scratched his bushy gray head. "I'll say Wednesday. Come by and see me Tuesday, and we'll see. Okay. Any more questions?"

"No, sir. Thank you very much."

"Good." He stood, picked up the chart and placed it under his arm. "I'll see you early in the morning."

Chris sat on the side of the bed. "Is there anything I can do for you or anything I can get?"

"I'd like for you to call Jacob Hughes and tell him I'll take the job with Hamilton."

"Don't you want to think about this later, when you're feeling better and have had some rest?"

"No! That's all I've been able to think about since we were brought to the hospital. I suddenly realized how fast I could have died, and I won't be able to rest until I give Jacob an answer. Would you make the call for me, please?"

"You're positive this is what you want to do?"

"I'm positive."

"I'd be glad to make the call for both of us. Is there anything else?"

"Yes, you can call Mr. Hamilton if you will. Tell him what's happened."

"It's done. Be right back. Try and get some rest."

The waiting room next to the nurses' station was filled to capacity. Chris left Ashley on the second floor and caught the elevator to the ground floor lobby to place the calls. There were three pay phones on the wall to the left. Chris stepped to the middle phone, dropped a coin into the slot and dialed his number.

"Hello."

"Mr. Hamilton?"

"Yes."

"This is Dr. Chris Burns, a friend of Ashley Denton's. She was in an auto accident this evening and has been admitted to the hospital."

"I'm sorry to hear that, Dr. Burns. Was she seriously injured?"

"No, sir, just a mild concussion. She's going to be fine, but her physician has suggested that she should wait a couple of days before starting a new job."

"No problem. Tell her to take her time and not to worry. The job can wait. Is there anything I can do?"

"No, sir, thank you for asking."

Chris dug in his pocket for the card, shoved the second coin in the slot and dialed the first number. No answer. He dialed the second number on the card and waited.

A male voice answered, "Jacob Hughes."

"Jacob, this is Dr. Chris Burns. Ashley and I had an auto accident this afternoon after we left you, and Ashley's been admitted to Holy Cross Hospital."

"Oh, my God! Was she seriously hurt?"

"No. She had a mild concussion, but she's going to be fine."

"What happened?"

"A drunk driver pulled out of the intersection, and my brakes failed. He hit Ashley's side of the car, and her head shattered the side glass."

"Your brakes failed?"

"Yes, they worked fine when we left Sugar's. All of a sudden, they went to the floor."

"I don't want to scare you, but I don't like the sound of this. I'll check it out. Where did they take your car?"

"The wrecker carried it over to McHaney Motor Company."

"Fine. I know the owner well. I'm going to go over there now and take a look."

"I think Ashley's beginning to worry. She asked me to call and tell you that she would be taking the position at Hamilton."

"Good! Good! I feel at last we'll get to the bottom of this. Tell her I'm very grateful."

"You can count me in, too. All the way."

"This is the best news I've heard in a long time. I can't tell you how much I appreciate this."

"I hope we can get to the bottom of this thing in the shortest time possible."

"I share that same feeling. You take good care of Ashley and we'll talk soon."

"Fine. Goodbye, Jacob." Chris hung up the phone and returned upstairs to Ashley's room.

The man in the double-breasted suit, sitting in the ground floor lobby, lowered the newspaper from his face and ambled to the phones. His dark, piercing eyes carefully surveyed the empty room, then he quickly retrieved the concealed listening device from under the booths and dropped them into his coat pocket. "Good work, Downs," he muttered and smiled. He pushed a coin into the slot, dialed the operator and placed a credit card call.

A voice answered, "Hello."

"Sir, this is Downs. I have some very interesting news."

"What's that, Downs?"

"The red-haired singer has agreed to take the job with Hamilton Medical Services."

"When does she start?"

"I'm not sure, probably Wednesday."

"Why Wednesday?"

"She and the doctor had an auto accident a few hours ago. I'm here at Holy Cross Hospital, and the girl has been admitted.

"How bad are her injuries?"

"Not bad, but the real problem is this. She and the doctor have agreed to work with the private investigator, Hughes. Will this man be a threat?"

"I don't think so. We'll just have to watch him and find out what he's up to and how much he knows. In the past, he's only investigated new employees for Hamilton. Hughes can't do much by himself. The girl and the doctor could be a problem, especially if they stumble onto the truth about the autopsy and the redhead finds out who the dead girl was involved with. If this happens, I'm afraid we'll have to make other arrangements for them. Are the bugs still in place at the dead girl's apartment?"

"Yes, sir, I haven't had a chance to remove them yet."

"Just leave them for the time being. Let's be sure her roommate is still in the dark. Understand?"

"I understand, sir."

"Good, keep me posted."

Downs placed the phone back on the hook and walked down to the vending machines at the end of the lobby. He fumbled in his pocket for the correct change and dropped the coins into the slot. He picked up his coffee, walked to the window and stood watching the evening traffic. After a few moments, he returned to his seat, picked up his newspaper and again made himself comfortable.

Chris tiptoed into Ashley's room and seated himself next to her bed. She opened her eyes and gave him a weak smile. "Did you make the calls?"

"You bet. Everything's taken care of. Mr. Hamilton said take your time, the job can wait. I left Jacob on cloud nine. Now close those big green eyes and get some rest. Think some pleasant thoughts, and you'll drift off."

Ashley closed her tired eyes and began to make plans. She would return the rented Buick and spend money for a new car and new clothes. She would buy thick, very thick, steaks and have a candlelight dinner with Chris. Everywhere she would go, everyone would know how good she was feeling. So good it would show in her eyes, her face and her movements. She laughed and hugged her chest. She opened her mouth to shout but, realizing where she was, changed her mind. She sighed and pulled the covers up around her chin.

Chris, by now, was mentally and physically exhausted. He slid down in the large hospital chair, propped his feet on the bed rail and, likewise, fell fast asleep. They were awakened the next morning as Dr. Billings stepped into the room to discharge Ashley from the hospital.

CHAPTER FIVE

Ashley's two days of recuperation passed with dreamlike rapidity. Chris rented a car, and she bought a fully loaded yellow Honda Accord, complete with a sunroof. Then they embarked on a modest shopping spree for clothes, lingerie, etc. Ashley was intoxicated with the feeling of freedom, the strangeness of money in the bank, and the conviction that she was deeply in love.

Wednesday, 8:30 a.m. Chief of security, Blade Henderson, was sitting with his back to the lobby entrance when Ashley entered the Hamilton Building. He was listening attentively to a recording on a portable tape player and didn't seem to notice her. He stubbed his cigarette and lifted his coffee cup to his lips.

Ashley stood at the small window in the glass cuboid and watched him intently. He was a tall, raw-boned man with brown, curly hair and a dark tan. He was a big man and, judging from his size and stature, had probably once been a football player. If he hadn't, she thought, he should have been.

Suddenly, as if he had felt the eyes of someone staring, he whirled around in his leather chair. His large brown eyes, with lashes that mopped his cheeks, met hers. As he rolled his chair toward the window, a playful, mocking smile slowly spread over his face. His voice purred, "You must be Ashley Denton."

"Yes, I am." She smiled. "Is Miss Wagner here yet?"

51

"She sure is. I'll tell her you're here." He rolled his chair back to the intercom system and announced her arrival, then opened the steel door and motioned her in.

Beth was waiting in the hallway. "Good morning, Ashley."

"Good morning, Miss Wagner."

"Please, not so formal. Call me Beth. Miss Wagner sounds cold. I was so sorry to hear about your accident. How are you feeling?"

"I'm fine, thank you," Ashley replied.

"Come on in my office. I have some paperwork to do for you before we get started, and also, I need to make you a code card so you can get through the security doors."

Ashley seated herself and Beth went over the necessary papers in detail, then rolled her chair over to a small machine at the back of her office and printed a code card. "Insert the card in the box to the right of the door and wait for a click. The door will automatically open for you. Okay?" She handed the card to Ashley and said, "Guard this card with your life."

Next she punched the intercom button and asked, "Blade, would you come to my office, please?"

"I'll be right there," he replied.

"Blade Henderson is our chief of security."

He entered her office and stood next to Ashley's chair.

"Blade, this is Ashley Denton. She'll be filling April's position."

"I kinda figured that. Pleased to meet you, Ashley."

He stood looking intently at her with a practiced smile on his face and a hungry gleam in his eyes. She shuddered as his eyes swept over her from head to toe. It was obvious that he was excited by her beauty and that the prospect of working with her aroused him.

Ashley instantly decided that she neither liked him nor trusted him. Her feelings must have shown on her face because Beth instantly seemed to be aware of the tension that was forming between them. She waved an impatient hand toward the door. "That'll be all, Blade."

He released a long gush of pent-up breath, brushed against the back of Ashley's chair and slammed the door as he left the office.

Beth forced a thin smile and her deep blue eyes blazed. "Don't mind Blade. Sometimes he forgets his manners. That's off the record, of course. Come on, I'll show you to your office."

Ashley shrugged away the momentary uneasy feeling caused by Blade's behavior and followed Beth out of the office. She inserted her code card in the box and the huge steel door opened. Their footfalls on the tile floor made loud, lonely sounds as she followed Beth down the long hall to the fourth office on the right.

Beth opened the door and flipped on the light switch. The panelled office was large and furnished with two brass-studded leather chairs, a polished mahogany desk, a built-in bookcase filled with office supplies and two large wood-grain file cabinets. Royal blue drapes adorned the large picture window, and the plush carpet was of the same color. A computer sat on the desk, and a telephone was located on the small table behind the desk and chair.

Beth opened the top file cabinet drawer, retrieved two large stacks of patient accounts and placed them on the desk next to the computer.

"These are April's accounts that need to be entered and brought up to date. I'll help you get started."

Ashley sat down and turned on the computer. She listened attentively as Beth went over the instructions of the spreadsheets. She began to work with speed and accuracy, impressing Beth, who leaned over her shoulder and silently watched.

After half an hour of observance, Beth finally spoke. "You're good, Ashley. You're a natural at this. I can see you'll have no problems."

"Thank you, Beth, I hope you're right."

Beth opened the top drawer of the desk and handed Ashley a black folder. "This is a menu from the Shady Grove restaurant. We have our lunch prepared there. By the time you fight the traffic downtown to find a place to park, your lunch hour's over. I'll come back about ten-thirty this morning and take your order. You can pay the office boy when he delivers. All the girls eat in the break area across the hall. It'll give you a chance to get to know them. Any questions before I get back to work myself?"

"No, I can't think of any."

"Very well. If you need me for anything, my number's on the list by the telephone. Just pick up, punch intercom, and dial."

"Thanks Beth." She watched as Beth's tall, slender figure gracefully exited through the doorway, her thick blond hair, swaying with each movement of her head, always falling gently back in place. She stopped in the hall and walked back to the door. "There's coffee in the breakroom. Get yourself a cup if you like."

"Thanks, I think I will."

Ashley's muscles began to tighten from strain as she walked down the hall to the breakroom. She had an uncomfortable feeling that the Hamilton Building could become a trap from which she could not escape. For four years she had lived on Vine Street, a rough neighborhood, without an ounce of fear. Suddenly, however, she felt the need to be looking over her shoulder every second.

She returned to her desk, put down her cup and seated herself again. She began to punch keys on the computer and soon lost herself deep within the spreadsheets.

After what seemed to be only a few minutes, she looked at her watch and saw it was already 10:30. At that moment, Beth entered her office without knocking and startled her.

She looked up with a weak smile on her face.

"What would you like for lunch?" Beth asked softly.

"A salad would be fine."

"Good girl, we have to watch our waistlines around here." She smiled and left abruptly.

Ashley's mind began to tumble. She leaned back in her chair to collect her thoughts and pull herself away from questions she could not answer, not yet, anyway.

Her thoughts were interrupted by a noise coming from the office directly overhead. It sounded as though someone was pacing slowly back and forth, back and forth. In her mind, she tried to produce a sketch of the offices on the second floor as she had seen them the week before. Instinctively she walked down the hall counting the number of steps from her office to the elevator. She pushed the button and glanced over her shoulder. She stepped in and prayed for the hall to remain deserted while she waited for the doors to conceal her presence. On the second floor, she counted the same number of steps back down the hall and stopped.

In the office above her own, she quietly observed a girl, almost as tall as her own 5'8". Her full figure suggested that she had a constant battle with her weight. She was standing near the window with her back to the door, her long dark hair hanging down to her waist in permed ringlets. She turned as Ashley approached, revealing a pretty face that looked like that of an innocent child, vulnerable and almost fragile. Her dark green eyes were filled with tears.

Ashley started to speak but was quieted by a shake of the young woman's head as she picked up a pencil and jotted on a piece of paper: *Will talk to you at noon. Save me a seat in the breakroom.*

Ashley nodded and tiptoed out of the office, looking over her shoulder along the hallway back to the elevator. If she were seen, it might be difficult to explain her presence there.

She stepped quickly into the elevator and returned to her

office unnoticed. After only three hours working in the Hamilton Building, the atmosphere was beginning to give her the creeps. For a few moments, she wished that she had followed her first instinct and refused Jacob's plea. But she had made an agreement, and she would see it through and help if she could. Even though, at the moment, she was very uncertain as to what she would be looking for.

Ashley walked around the desk and stood at the window surveying the grounds around the building. As far as she could see, tall cedar trees were swaying in the gentle breeze. No other buildings were in sight. It was quiet, peaceful and lonely.

She felt an urgent need to see Chris, but he was out of town on business until later that night. She looked at her watch and wondered where he was. It was noon and she suddenly realized that she was hungry.

She walked down the hall to the breakroom and chose a table near the back by one of the wall fountains and waited for the girl from upstairs. She looked around and could see no possibility of being overheard.

The girl arrived just as the delivery boy brought lunch. They ate for a time in silence.

"I'm Savannah Page," the girl finally said.

"I'm Ashley Denton."

"Yes, I remember the day Beth brought you around. It would be hard to forget your beautiful red hair."

"Well, thank you, you're very kind."

"I tried to call you several times, but didn't get an answer."

"I had to take care of some business out of town. Why were you trying to get in touch with me?"

"I thought maybe you might like to go out for dinner and we could get acquainted since we'll be working together. I'll be helping you from time to time on your accounts."

"Yes, of course, I'd like that."

"Good."

"How long have you worked here?"

"Four years."

"Do you like it?"

"Yes. It's a nice job. It's been a little difficult since April Crafton's death."

"Did you know her well?"

"Yes, she was my roommate and best friend."

"Why couldn't you talk to me in your office?"

"Mr. Hamilton was down the hall going over some accounts with Wanda." Savannah paused. "I miss April so much." Her chin quivered as if she might start crying again.

"I'm sure you do," Ashley said. She thought for a few moments. "Why don't I pick you up around seven tonight and let's take in a movie. What do you say?"

"Sure, that'd be great." She dug in her purse for a pen and scribbled on a table napkin. "Here's my address and phone number. It's been a long time since I've been to a movie."

The days and nights for the next two weeks seemed to melt together. Ashley was making good progress on the delinquent accounts that had stacked up since April's death. She had put special emphasis on speed and accuracy and by now had become half hypnotized by tons of figures and the constant clicking of the computer keys. The days had proceeded smoothly and without incident.

She placed the next stack of accounts on the desk and sighed. She closed her eyes and felt a gentle warmth creep over her. She daydreamed of a wedding that everyone in Austin would talk about for months, a two-week honeymoon someplace in a deserted and beautiful part of the country. For 14 wonderful days and nights, she would be loved and pampered. It would be wonderful to spend money without worrying that a $20 purchase would wreck her budget. Wasn't that every American girl's dream?

In vain, she tried to concentrate on her duties.

She was extremely pleased with the friendship and closeness she had developed with Savannah over the past two weeks. On several occasions, Ashley had felt sure there was something Savannah had wanted to say but couldn't find the courage. Then she reminded herself there was no rush and no use taking risks. She had thought when she accepted this position that she was being overpaid, but now she was beginning to feel that the stress of simply maintaining her sanity was worth every cent. Suddenly, she felt a soft hand clamp over her arm.

"Are you going to take a lunch break?" Savannah asked softly.

"Is it lunch time already?"

"Yes, let's go. I'm starved."

They picked up their lunches and seated themselves at their favorite table. Ashley ripped open the package and dowsed her salad with Thousand Island. "When does your vacation start?" she asked.

"Next month. Two glorious weeks. After you're here five years, you get three weeks. April and I went to Las Vegas last year."

Tears welled in her eyes. "It's so hard to believe I'll never see her again."

"It takes time to get over something like that, Savannah. And believe me, it won't happen overnight. I lost both of my parents suddenly when I was 16. That was eight years ago, and I still have my bad days."

"I'm sorry about your parents. I didn't know."

Ashley picked at her now-wilted lettuce, tossed the plastic fork in the Styrofoam bowl and pushed it aside. "Let me ask you something, Savannah."

"Sure."

"Have you had any problems since you've been working here?"

"No. Just the loneliness since April's death. She was like that little sister I never had."

"I'll bet it is tough, working here where she worked, then having to go home to an empty apartment."

"Yeah. If it wasn't for the security I have here, I'd try to find a job someplace else, maybe in Dallas. But you get used to nice clothes, a nice car and plenty to eat. You know, the works. It's probably the highest-paying job I could find in Texas."

"So that's what Mr. Hamilton was talking about."

"Pardon me?"

"Nothing. Just thinking out loud. What happened to April? Did she go to sleep and drive off the highway?"

Savannah put down her fork and grew silent. She took a pen from her purse, got a napkin from the stack in front of her and began writing. Then she gave Ashley the napkin to read. *I meant to tell you the other day that this building is full of bugs and Blade listens to everything we say. They want to know everything that goes on, for security reasons, they claim. I don't know if all the other girls know this or not. Blade told Michelle, and she told me. Just between you and me, I don't think her death was an accident at all. I think she was murdered.*

"What makes you think that?" Ashley asked.

Savannah took another napkin and wrote: *She told me she was pregnant. One day she was in the ladies room vomiting, and Beth came in and caught her. She must have put two and two together. Anyway, a couple of weeks after that, April was found dead.*

Ashley took the pen and asked the question: *Why would a pregnancy prevent her from working here?*

A pregnancy wouldn't. I think the father of her unborn child was the problem, Savannah replied on the other side of the napkin.

"She told you his name?"

Savannah nodded fearfully.

Ashley took a few more bites of the wilted lettuce. "Can you tell me?"

"Yes, but I think you'll have a hard time believing it."

"Well...go ahead. Try me."

Savannah took yet another fresh napkin and wrote in capital letters: *VICE PRESIDENT DREW RAMSEY.*

Ashley stared at Savannah. She flipped over the napkin and scribbled *Vice President Drew Ramsey, like Vice President of the United States of America?"*

"One and the same."

"Are you sure?"

"I'm positive."

"Where on earth did she meet him?"

"Here in Austin." She wrote the rest: *He came to several political functions, and, according to April, they got involved after their first meeting. Sometimes she'd go out of town to be with him.*

"Did you ever see them together?"

No, but he called our apartment regularly.

A couple of minutes passed before Ashley took another napkin and wrote: *If she was murdered, who do you think was responsible?*

I don't know. For some reason, I feel Beth Wagner's involved, but I could be wrong, came Savannah's printed response.

"Did she tell the father?"

"That I don't know for sure."

What about Michelle Ingram? Ashley wrote.

Savannah hesitated a moment. "Where did you hear about her?"

Ashley simply wrote the name *Jacob Hughes.*

"Sure. He does a lot of work for Mr. Hamilton."

Ashley smiled to herself. "I found that out before I started working here."

Savannah took the pen and wrote: *Michelle was his daughter.*

Ashley rolled her eyes toward the ceiling and released a long sigh. "I've been such a blind idiot. I should have known."

"Yep. She was his little darling. She slipped off and married when she was 19 but only stayed married six months."

"Poor man."

"Oh, that's not all." Savannah hastily began jotting down

background information. *Her husband went to prison for drug dealing, and she divorced him just before she came to work here. After she'd been here for a while, she fell in love with Blade Henderson and started dating him. He was a lot older, but she didn't mind.*

It suddenly became crystal clear to Ashley why Jacob Hughes had such an interest in this case. The details Savannah had given her had answered a lot of questions that had been bothering her.

Still scribbling, Savannah offered one more piece of the puzzle to ponder: *A couple of months after April came to work here, she found a letter Michelle had written to Blade, but had never given to him. Apparently, Michelle's computer manual had fallen behind the file cabinet. The letter was inside the manual. She wrote him that she knew he was in love with Beth Wagner and was going to dump her, and she didn't want to live without him.*

"What happened to the letter?"

"I don't know. I couldn't find it when I moved April's things out of the apartment."

"Maybe it's for the best," Ashley said as she looked at her watch. "It's almost 1:00 p.m. We'd better get back to work."

Savannah gathered up all the napkins they had used and made a purposeful detour to the restroom on the way back to her office.

Ashley sat down at her computer and tried to work, but her mind wouldn't settle back into a routine. Twice during the morning, Blade had wandered by her office and smiled with a slow, almost devilish smile. There was so much she wanted to know, but she was afraid to exhibit her curiosity where it might not be welcomed. She thought of terminating her employment with Hamilton, but a born and bred stubbornness silenced the idea. She forced her mind back to her work, making false motions until it was finally time to go home.

She left the building with the rest of the girls and fought the traffic 14 blocks to her apartment. She had hoped that Chris would be home, but he had not returned from his business trip. She was anxious to tell him of her conversation with Savannah.

It was after eleven when Ashley returned home from the late movie, and, after a long, hot bath, she sat on the side of the bed brushing her hair. A knock on the door made her jump. She snatched her robe from the bed. A second knock.

"Ashley?"

"Chris!" she called out.

She opened the door, threw herself into his arms and bathed his face with kisses.

"Man, I think I'll leave again tomorrow."

She ignored his statement. "I have lots to tell you, Chris, and you're going to find some of it hard to believe, but first, let's order something to eat. Are you hungry?"

"Yes, I'm starved, but we've got to talk first. Jacob Hughes was waiting for me downstairs when I got home tonight. He talked to the mechanic at McHaney Motors, and someone definitely tampered with my brakes. A damn sloppy job, but that's the way it stands."

"What does that mean, Chris?"

"It means, Carrot Top, that we are in this now whether we like it or not, and it's for real. Someone wants us dead, and even if we mind our own business from here on out, there's no guarantee they won't still be trying to kill us."

"Chris, how do we know we can trust Hughes? He hasn't told us everything. I found out at work today that Michelle Ingram was Hughes' daughter. What if he tampered with your brakes just enough to scare us into becoming involved in his own private vendetta against whoever he thinks killed his daughter? And that's not all. When April died she was pregnant and the child was Drew Ramsey's. That's right, our vice president. Did Dr. Sulcer omit that little fact from his bogus autopsy report as well?"

Chris was stunned enough by the news to lose his composure. "I doubt that Jacob would harm us, but you're right, Ash; ultimately, we can only trust each other. It's crazy. I go to work at the lab, and the conspiracy is waiting there in the form of Dr. Sulcer and the autopsy he allegedly falsified. I come home to you, and, immediately, Hamilton Medical Services rears its ugly head. You could have been killed. Dammit, Ashley, I love you, and I'm tired of living like this, in two separate places."

"Christopher Burns! Is that a proposal?"

"As plain as I can make it. What do you say, Ashley, will you marry me?"

"Conventional wisdom would dictate that we wait until all this is over before we make a decision like that, Chris. But I don't want to be conventional. I don't want to be rational. I may not live long enough for that. You're right, darling, it is crazy. My answer is...yes!"

He grinned and she jumped into his arms. They began squealing and wrestling on the floor like two young children. He pulled her close and began kissing her slowly and sweetly. Suddenly he held her at arm's length and said, "Oh...by the way, my parents are coming this weekend for a visit."

"That's nice." By the time the words had left her lips, a worried look covered her face.

"Don't worry, Ash, they'll like you, but...if they don't, it'll be their loss. Besides, they won't be living with you...I will."

"Do you want to marry me for my money or my mind?"

"Neither, you magnificent redhead. I'm going to marry you for your body."

"You're not much, but at least you're honest."

CHAPTER SIX

The next morning, sunlight flooded through a crack in the blinds. Chris rolled over, opened one eye and looked at the clock on the nightstand. It had ceased to function at 4:00 a.m. He grabbed his wristwatch. It was nine o'clock and he was two hours late for work. He remembered his father's sermons when he was a child, "Get where you're going on time and don't be late." Now his father was a United States senator, and on lots of days, the senator didn't make it to work at all. No one noticed. No one cared.

Without a shower or shave, Chris quickly dressed and, as soon as his shoes were tied, promptly slammed the alarm clock to the floor and stomped on it until there was nothing left that resembled a clock.

By the time he arrived at the crime lab, he was out of breath. He grabbed his lab coat and pulled it over his broad shoulders. He looked curiously at his 45-year-old blonde secretary as she stood behind her desk. Tears spilled down her cheeks and her mascara ran, leaving dark tracks on her face.

"Jeri Lynn, what's the matter? Has Luther split again?" Luther was her boyfriend who, on a monthly basis, came up missing for days at a time. She'd throw him out, but two weeks later he'd show up on her doorstep, offering that sad bassett hound look. Every time, she'd melt like butter and take him back again.

She covered her mouth with her hands, but the sobs escaped

through her fingers. "You mean you haven't heard?"

"Heard what?"

She licked her dry lips. "Dr. Sulcer was found dead this morning."

"The hell you say! What happened to him?"

"I don't know. When he didn't show up for work this morning, I called his home. I tried again about ten minutes later, thinking he might be in the shower or something, but still didn't get an answer. So then I called his neighbor. The police called back about 20 minutes ago and said Dr. Sulcer had apparently died in his sleep."

"Was he sick yesterday?"

"No, or at least he didn't appear to be. He did get a telephone call that seemed to upset him."

"Who from?"

"I don't know. I did hear him change his retirement plans. As you know, he had originally planned to retire in October, but after he got off the phone, he told me he wouldn't be retiring until the end of the year."

"I'm sorry, Jeri. I know you loved him."

"Yes, but he didn't even know I existed."

"Maybe he did. There was always Luther, you know."

"Luther's just something that's better than nothing. At my age, you can't be too choosy."

"Now, Granny." He always called her Granny when she talked about her age. She had not had a life worth writing home about, but she was still quite attractive. She was 5'1" and always wore three-inch heels that belied her shortness. Having never been married herself and not having had any children of her own, she had taken Chris under her wing since the first day he had come to work in the lab.

Chris smiled and changed the subject. "Would you get me the report on April Crafton and put it on my desk. Then take the rest of the day off. I can get the phone."

"Glad to, and you're the only one who's allowed to call me

Granny."

"You're a sweetheart. Someday I'll have lots of kids and teach them to call you Granny. Okay?"

"Okay, but don't wait too long. That ole clock's ticking fast."

With the autopsy report in hand, Chris walked to his office and closed the door. He sat down at his desk and began to carefully examine the document on April Crafton. His face drained of all emotion. It was exactly as Jacob Hughes had reported, 'cervical fracture sustained upon impact.' He could not believe what he was reading. Dr. Sulcer had seemed to be one of the few honest people who, by some natural gift, always looked washed and sterile, with not an enemy in the world. Had he taken a payoff? And, if so, why? Could it have been related to his wife's expensive illness?

The phone on his desk rang, startling him. "Mr. Tipton wants to see you in his office immediately, if not sooner," said the clerical voice on the phone.

"I'm on my way." He placed the report back in its folder and shoved it under his desk pad.

The State Crime Laboratory was a two-story brick building that consisted of several departments offering services to law enforcement in pathology, biology, toxicology, criminal statistics, drug analysis, latent fingerprint identification, questioned documents examination and firearms-toolmarks identification. Each department had its own director, and Michael Tipton was the executive director over all departments.

The pathology lab was on the first floor. Mr. Tipton's office, as well as the conference room, was on the second floor.

Chris buttoned his lab coat, straightened his tie and rushed down the hall to the elevator. He stepped in and pushed the button for the second floor.

Tipton was waiting impatiently, pacing back and forth. "Good morning, Chris, have a seat."

Chris seated himself in one of the large leather chairs but

Tipton continued to stand. "I'm sure by now you've heard about Dr. Sulcer."

"Yes sir. I'm very sorry."

"Of course. We all are. You're a good man, Chris. Thirty is awfully young to have the job of lab director dumped in your lap, but I'm confident you can handle it. Dr. Sulcer had planned to retire at the end of the year, and you were chosen to take his place anyway. Your appointment to this position has just been moved up a few months. As of now, you are the new pathology director. Of course, there will be a substantial raise in pay."

"Thank you, sir, for your confidence in me. I'd be very pleased to serve as director."

"Do you have anyone in mind to take your place as the assistant director?"

"Yes sir. I have a friend who's interested. Right now he's working at one of the local hospitals."

"Good, get in touch with him and set up an appointment as soon as possible. Anytime will be all right with me."

"Yes, sir, I'll get right on it."

"That'll be all, Chris, and good luck."

"Thank you, Mr. Tipton."

Seconds later, Chris was back in his office. He dialed the number to Hamilton Medical Services. A male voice answered.

"Ashley Denton, please," Chris said.

"Just a moment."

Must be that brute Ashley spoke of, he thought as he waited.

"Ashley Denton here."

"Hi, Carrot Top."

"Chris! What are you calling me here for?"

"I got some bad news this morning, Ash. My boss, Dr. Sulcer, was found dead this morning."

"Oh my god! Foul play?"

"I don't want to talk about it over the phone. Right now, they're calling it a heart attack. But I will say this. I checked the autopsy reports this morning and the information our friend in the hat gave us was correct."

"I see," Ashley said. She tried not to sound alarmed, but she knew Chris was referring to Jacob and the true cause of April's death.

"Anyway," Chris continued in a lighter tone, "Dr. Sulcer left a ton of paper work I'll have to finish. That's another reason I called; I'll be late getting home tonight, so don't wait up for me. If it's not too late, I'll stop by. Okay?"

"Okay, Chris, and I'm sorry about Dr. Sulcer."

"Yeah, it's really sad. Do you have the key to my apartment with you?"

"Yes. Why?"

"Go by the cleaners when you get off and pick up my laundry for me. Do you mind?"

"No. Which cleaners?"

"The one a couple of blocks from our apartments, Dixon Cleaners."

"Okay, I love you, Chris."

"I love you too, babe. See you later."

Soon after Chris's call, almost too soon it seemed, Beth summoned Ashley to her office. As Ashley stepped out into the hall, Louis Hamilton strolled from the elevator. His hair and eyes shared the same dark glow, and he was dressed in a double-breasted navy suit, white shirt and a cranberry floral tie. He was tall, thin, handsome and, in style and attire, left no detail to chance. "Good morning, Ashley, how's everything going?"

"Just fine."

"Good."

Ashley had an uneasy feeling, almost amounting to dread, as she entered Beth's office with Louis Hamilton. "You wanted to see me?" she asked.

"Yes," she said without looking up from her calender. "Have a seat."

Ashley seated herself and Louis Hamilton walked around behind Beth's chair and stood by the window.

Beth looked up and smiled. "Ashley, I have some exciting news. In a few days, we have an important event you'll need to attend with Louis. It'll be held at the Driskill Hotel here in Austin, and you're included on the program." Before she could finish, Louis Hamilton was paged to take a phone call. He left the office abruptly, went to his office and closed the door.

Beth continued, "It's a political fund-raising dinner for the presidential campaign. This is election year, you know. As I was saying, you're included on the program. The state campaign director has heard about your singing, and he'd like for you to sing after the meal and before the speeches begin. Will you do it?"

"Sure."

"Arnold Leitzen, the campaign manager, would like for you to sing 'You'll Never Walk Alone.' Do you know it?"

"Oh, yes, it's one of my favorites."

"Good. There's another thing. We'll go downtown next Thursday and select a dress from The Fashion Shop. This store is very expensive, but they have the best and most beautiful clothes in Texas."

This was the news Ashley had dreaded to hear. She remembered Jacob's warning about the social events the day she and Chris met him at Sugar's. Suddenly she felt perspiration seeping through the skin on her forehead. She had to relax and stay calm. Now was not the time to let her nervousness show. "Sure, that's fine with me," Ashley said. It would have been acceptable with her to dismiss the shopping entirely. She could now afford her own clothes and wasn't especially overjoyed with the idea.

Beth eyed Ashley trying to read her expression. "Also, one night next week, we'll need to go over to the Driskill Hotel, where the dinner will be held, for a rehearsal with the band on your song selection. I'll have to check with the campaign manager and find out which night. Can you go any night?"

"Yes, any night'll be fine."

"Good, I'll get back with you on that."

Ashley stood silently for a moment. "I have an evening gown that would be perfect, if there's not enough time to shop for one."

"We'll see," Beth replied.

"Will you be at the dinner?" Ashley asked.

"Yes, the campaign manager's asked me to be his guest."

"Good. I won't feel so lost if you're there."

"Now, if you'll excuse me, Ashley, I have a phone call to make."

Ashley nodded and left the office. It was noon. She went to the same table in the breakroom and waited for Savannah, but according to one of the other girls, she was home with a summer cold. Ashley was disappointed and decided to call her later in the day.

Beth closed her office door, punched the intercom and called Blade. "Back from your morning assignment?" she asked as she held out her right hand and studied her long red fingernails.

"It's done. The phones and all the rooms in Ashley's apartment and her boyfriend's. We're set."

"Well," she said in a low, almost menacing voice, "I hope you did a better job with the listening devices than you did with the brake job. Ashley's two-day delay didn't accomplish too damn much."

"I did the best I could without killing her. How do you half rig something? Huh? Maybe I should have thrown her down on the sidewalk and beat the hell out of her. That would have laid her up for a week or two."

"Maybe it was too much to ask."

"Well...according to the letter I found in her apartment, she doesn't have to work anyway."

"What letter?"

"From a bank in Mississippi. The girl's wealthy."

"Why didn't you tell me about it before now?"

"I didn't see that it was important."

"You need to let me decide what's important and what's not."

"If you want to get rid of the girl, Beth, why don't you just run her off?"

"That's enough, Blade."

"Excuse me if I don't seem to understand what in God's name is bothering you."

"I'm just a little edgy, that's all and you're right. You did the best you could. I'll be all right in a couple of days."

"Oh hell, I should've known."

At the end of the day, Ashley was the last to leave. She turned off her computer, grabbed her purse and flipped off the light switch. She walked quickly down the hall and waited for the automatic door to open. As she passed the glass cuboid, Blade curled his lips, blew smoke rings in the air, winked and waved goodbye. She managed a faint smile and didn't stop until she had reached her car. She shuddered as she felt her flesh crawl and muttered aloud, "Creep!"

She started the car and looked down at the dash. The fuel indicator hand sat firmly on empty, so she drove to the first available gas station. While the young schoolboy filled her tank, she dug in her purse for the table napkin with Savannah's phone number. She walked to the pay phone on the side of the station and dialed the number.

"Hello."

"Savannah?"

"Yes," she answered without enthusiasm.

"This is Ashley. How are you feeling?"

"I've felt like trash all day but I'm so glad you called. I've been thinking about you. How did things go?"

"It's been hectic today. I started a couple times to call but never got the chance. I missed you. Do you think you'll be able to come to work tomorrow?"

"I should be, but if I can't, I'll call you."

"That'd be great. Take care."

"Thanks for calling."

Ashley drove east with the traffic, her sunroof open, letting the wind blow through her long, red hair. It was after six. People were cursing each other over parking spaces at the shopping mall. Teenage drivers were cruising with their convertible tops down and music blaring loud enough to wake the dead. Suddenly, she spied Dixon Cleaners, parked the Honda, picked up Chris's laundry then blended into the traffic again.

She could hear the phone ringing as she unlocked her apartment door. She threw the clothes and purse on the sofa and picked up the receiver.

"Hello."

"Hi, Carrot Top."

"Hi, Chris."

"Listen, babe, I'm not going to make it in tonight."

"Why?"

"I've still got two more autopsies to do, a teenage boy who's suspected of cocaine overdose and a middle-aged woman from down state who was found dead in a ravine. It seems like everybody wants a path report yesterday."

"How long will this night work have to go on?"

"Probably a couple of weeks until I can get some help. I'll try to get home in the morning for a shower and shave before you go to work."

"I'll be waiting, big boy," she whispered seductively.

Chris pushed up his sleeves and went back to his cadaver. Tired as he was, he somehow was able to whistle while he worked.

CHAPTER SEVEN

Wednesday, 5:30 a.m. An insistent noise woke Ashley. She tried to convince herself she was only dreaming but the sound persisted. She sat up in bed, her eyes wide open. Instinctively, she looked toward the door, and at the same moment, the click of the doorknob came loud and clear. She quickly slid from the bed, crawled to the bathroom and fumbled around the casing for the light switch. The burst of bright light blinded her for a moment, but even with blurry vision, she could see the form of a man standing at the foot of her bed. Her vision cleared quickly, and she became full of mixed emotions -- rage at first, then relief when she realized who it was.

"Christopher Burns!" she cried out hoarsely. "You almost gave me a heart attack!"

"Myocardial infarction, you mean."

"You technical quack, I could kill you."

He chuckled at her as she sat froglike on the floor. He pulled her up against him and held her close. She felt his hands move up her arms, his voice became tender, and his eyes glowed as they looked into hers. The only sounds in the world were his love words and their ragged breathing. Her blue silk gown fell free from her shoulders to the floor as his lips sought hers with hunger and possessiveness. He carried her in his arms and placed her gently on the bed. All thoughts were driven from their minds, and they were at peace with the world.

Ashley showered, dried her long hair and dressed in a green knit dress that clung softly to her curves. She pulled the cover from Chris's handsome face, kissed him goodbye and told him not to wake up.

It was 8:30 a.m. when she placed her code card in the box at the security door. Blade was in his usual position, listening to his tape recorder. She had passed by the cuboid unnoticed. The building was quiet and seemed almost deserted.

She flipped on the light switch in her office, sat her purse down and turned on the computer. She decided to get a cup of coffee while the computer booted up and walked down the hall to the breakroom.

Blade was there getting a cup of coffee also. "Good morning, beautiful," he said provocatively.

"Good morning," she replied in a low voice.

Without warning, he pushed her against the Coke machine, hard enough to drive the breath from her and, with a harsh laugh, pressed his body hard against hers. His mouth was close, almost touching hers. She placed both of her hands on his chest and pushed with all her strength. He laughed as he held her shoulders with his strong hands and attempted to kiss her lips. She could not free herself and knew it would be useless to cry for help.

She was about to cry for help when, just at that moment, Savannah entered the breakroom. Blade relaxed his grip and stepped back with a smug grin.

Ashley stiffened her arms and clenched her fists in anger. Tears filled her eyes until his face became a blur. Fear gave way to anger, and she brought her hand up swiftly with all her strength, slapping him across the face.

With a mocking glint in his eyes, he walked to the door. Suddenly, he turned and said, "Catch you later, beautiful."

Ashley was furious but speechless. Savannah placed her arm gently around Ashley's shoulders. "Are you okay?"

"Thank God you came in when you did. I'd hate to think what might have happened if you hadn't."

"I've never known Blade to get out of line like that. Beth would be real unhappy if she'd walked in and caught his act."

"He's a son of a bitch!" Ashley's voice was tremulous. She smoothed her dress and after a moment asked, "How are you feeling today?"

"Much better, but I'm worried about you now. I wish my office was closer."

"I'll be okay." She smiled and took a deep breath, trying to slow her racing heart.

Together, they left the breakroom; Ashley went to her office, and Savannah disappeared into the elevator.

At 9:00 a.m., Beth's voice came over the intercom system summoning all 20 girls to the ground-floor breakroom. She marched in with two large stacks of accounts followed by the office boy carrying two additional stacks. They placed them on one of the tables, and Beth dismissed the office boy. She stood motionless until everyone was seated.

"Girls," she paused, "I've just received a telephone call from a group of heart surgeons in Houston, and they'll be coming next week to look over the operation. I realize you're stretched to your max, but I must ask you to come in at seven o'clock each morning and work until late at night. It's imperative we get all these accounts entered before the surgeons get here next week."

If someone had dropped a pin, it would have sounded like thunder. Beth was aware that she had lost popularity as she had done so many times before. She shuffled the accounts and dealt them out like a deck of cards, giving each girl equal amounts, except Ashley.

"You'll get overtime pay, of course, and a dinner break, but if we aren't finished by Friday evening, we'll have to work this weekend. Put your current accounts aside for the moment and concentrate on these. I'm sorry, girls. Any questions?"

She waited a moment. No questions. No one would challenge her. "Okay, let's get with it."

Beth left the breakroom, went through the security door and walked swiftly to the cuboid. "Any news from our bugs?"

Blade winked. "Nothing important. The good doctor is quite a stud though."

"What do you mean?" Beth looked at him quizzically.

"Well...he worked all day and most of the night, got home about five this morning, showered and made love to the redhead in her apartment. Twice, no less. Slipped in on her and scared the hell out of her."

"Blade, you're an ass."

"You want to hear the tape? Might learn something new."

"No, but I bet you enjoyed it. You probably closed your eyes and dreamed it was you instead of the stud. The redhead has lied about having a serious relationship. Wonder what else she's lied about?"

"Hard to say, but it's worth keeping an eye on her."

"I'll do the eyeing, Blade, you just stick to the bugs and the tapes, okay? And try not to get too carried away." Beth knew how far she could carry her remarks, but she had seen the look in his eyes the first day Ashley had come to work. She had also seen a spark of tension and sensed Ashley's dislike for him, then she recalled her own distaste when Louis had introduced him as the new chief of security. It was a challenge for Blade, to be obnoxious at first, then take his pleasure taming them down. Certainly the thought crossed her mind that his approach had worked with her.

At four-thirty in the afternoon, Ashley's phone rang. She turned from her computer and rubbed the ends of her fingers. She had pounded the keys so long, it felt as though little needles were sticking in the ends of each one.

"This is Ashley Denton."

"Hey, Carrot Top, how 'bout meeting me at the Magnolia Cafe at 6:00 p.m. I'm not going to work late tonight."

"I can't, Chris."

"Why not?"

"We have to work late here."

"How late is late?"

"Ten or so."

"Well...hell! Tell them to take that job and shove it."

"I wish I could, but I can't do that, Chris, and you know it."

"Okay, then, I'll see you when you get home, whenever."

"I'm sorry, Chris."

She heard the click on the other end of the line. This had been one of those days that had started out bright and sunny but was ending on a sour note. Blade attacked her, her coffee cup had jumped off the desk and broken into a million pieces, she had torn the knee out of her stocking on the breakroom table at noon, spilled half her lunch down the front of her dress, dropped her lipstick in the john and now Chris was irritated about her late hours. She hadn't wanted to wish her life away, but she'd be grateful when this day was over.

She was sitting gloomily at her desk when Savannah came down for dinner. She walked down to the breakroom with her to try and cheer herself up.

"What's wrong, Ashley? Are you sick?"

"No, well...not yet anyway. Chris is upset because I have to work late tonight, and God knows, I didn't dare tell him it'd be every night this week. He already wants me to quit."

"What are you going to do?"

The breakroom was filling up with everyone on their dinner hour, so Savannah motioned for Ashley to follow her to the bathroom. It was deserted. Savannah hit the large button on the automatic hand dryer to distract Blade while they talked.

"I'm not going to quit until I find out what happened to April. I'm in too deep to back out now."

"I'm glad."

"Do you think the vice president knows she was murdered?"

77

"I don't know. I don't have any way to find out."

"I'll be going to my first social event a week from Saturday. It's a political fund-raising dinner at the Driskill Hotel. Who'll be there?"

"In the past, it's always been the bigwigs from Washington. Louis Hamilton and Beth'll be right in the middle of it. You can bet on that."

"Well, one thing's for sure. If the vice president is there and the opportunity presents itself, I intend to ask some questions about April."

"Please be careful, Ashley. If the wrong people hear April's name, you could be in deep trouble and maybe even danger."

"Oh, don't worry, I won't take any chances."

"I wish I could go with you."

"By the way, Savannah, there's something that's bothered me since I started to work here, but I kept forgetting to mention it."

"What is it?"

"I noticed three floors in this building, but the elevator only shows two. What's the deal?"

"Beats me. I've never been up on the third floor. I do know there's a back elevator, but it takes a special code card to open the door."

"How do you know?"

"I saw Beth go out that way one day, so I opened the door from the hall and sneaked a peek."

"Did you see her use the code card?"

"Yes, she keeps it in her purse. I tried my card and it didn't work."

"I wish there was some way we could get our hands on it. I'd like to know what's up there."

"Maybe there is a way we can get it."

"How?"

"If we could catch her out of her office long enough without her purse, we could make one. The card machine's in her office, you know."

"Yes, I watched her make mine the first day I came to work. Do you know how to make a card?"

"I've never done it, but I've seen enough of Beth's handy work to have figured it out. It only takes a second or two." At that break in their conversation, almost as if on cue, the hand dryer shut off. Ashley hit the button and reactivated the dryer. "You know," she said, "if these people are paranoid enough to bug this place, what's stopping them from monitoring our private lives as well? I wonder if our apartments are bugged?"

"I doubt if mine is. There's not much about my life that anyone would care about. Since you're a new employee, they might want to know more about you."

Ashley felt the blood drain from her head. Oh my God, she thought, Chris was there this morning. Maybe that was the reason Blade had come on so strong. He had heard. She would tell Chris as soon as she got home and they would search both apartments. Suddenly she slapped her forehead with the palm of her hand.

"Ashley, are you okay?" Savannah looked worried.

"I forgot about Chris's parents coming this weekend. I have to find out if our apartments are bugged. I've never met his parents, and I'm sure I'll get the third degree."

"How long will they be here?"

"Just Saturday night and Sunday morning."

"Why don't you keep them out late Saturday night and let them ask their questions someplace else."

"Sure, we could do that. Thanks, Savannah."

"Call me anytime," she chuckled. "I'm at your service, but now we'd better get our butts back to work, my friend."

Just then the dryer cut off again, and they had to laugh at its uncanny timing. "See you later, Ashley."

"Ciao."

Ashley walked back to the window of her office and stared

at the emptiness of the grounds beyond the building. For a moment, she thought of giving up, grabbing her purse and running like hell. She thought of the morning's episode with Blade in the breakroom and frowned with contempt. She heard herself whisper, "You creepy son of a bitch," and brought her hand up over her mouth, her eyes searching the room, hoping no one had entered and heard. She closed her eyes, took a deep breath to reduce the tension and went back to her keyboard.

At 10:00 p.m., Beth's voice roared over the intercom. "Let's call it a day, girls."

A rumble of sighs rolled through the building as 20 girls crowded through the last security door. The glass cuboid was locked and the television monitor cast a green glow as it recorded their departure from the deserted building.

Chris was watching television in Ashley's apartment when she arrived home. He gave her a cool glance as she sat her purse down on the table and picked up her mail. The word 'Occupant' on all five envelopes put the final touches on a perfectly lousy day. She slipped out of her shoes and walked without speaking to the bathroom to change clothes. She had to get Chris out of the apartment to talk.

Chris followed and sat on the side of the bathtub, picking up bottles of lotion and bubble bath, reading each label, putting them back in their places, still without speaking. His coolness thawed, and he placed his hand on hers, leaving it there motionless. She shifted her eyes sideways without moving her head and giggled.

He drew a sigh of relief and watched admiringly as she dressed in a lightweight jogging suit.

"Let's go for a walk. I need some fresh air," she said.

He rose and nodded approval. "I think that's a pregnant idea."

They strolled out of the entrance and sat down on the concrete steps in front of the apartment building.

Ashley told him about Blade's approach in the breakroom, about the bug in her office and of her fear that there could be bugs in their apartments.

Chris's face paled and his lips twisted with contempt. "Those dirty bastards! Who in the hell do they think they are? Nobody's gonna invade my privacy and get away with it! If they want war, they'll get war!"

He jumped to his feet. He was so angry, the man slouched on the bench ten feet from him with the open newspaper covering his face, went unnoticed. "Let's go in and check it out."

They got off the elevator and tiptoed to Ashley's apartment first. He slipped the key in the lock and opened the door without making a sound.

For 30 minutes they searched each apartment, finding bugs in the telephones, in floral arrangements, under the tables and under the medicine cabinets in the bathrooms. He turned to Ashley and whispered, "Son of a bitch! There're more bugs here than cockroaches in the housing project."

Suddenly, something he had overlooked interrupted his thoughts. He grabbed Ashley's arm and led her silently out of the apartment and back down to the ground floor. "He's still there."

"What are you talking about, Chris?"

Chris crept over to the bench and snatched the newspaper from the man's face. "Jacob Hughes, what are you doing here?"

Jacob pulled a hand down his face and blinked his eyes. "Chris? I must have dozed off. I thought I'd hang around for awhile since I haven't heard from either of you today. Any news?"

They walked around the side of the building in the darkness of the trees.

"Our apartments have been bugged, Jacob."

"Bugged?"

81

NORTH LOGAN CITY LIBRARY
475 East 2500 North
North Logan, UT 84341
435-755-7169

"Yes, bugged, and another thing."

"What's that, Chris?"

"That damn security guard tried to assault Ashley this morning. If he touches her one more time, Jacob, I'll be forced to blow this whole charade."

"Just calm down, Chris. He'll get his dues. We've got to be patient. We're in this thing too deep to mess up now."

"I want those damn bugs out of our apartments now."

"I don't think that would be very wise, Chris."

"Why the hell not?"

"Someone would know you're on to them and that could force them to do something rash. I think you should leave the bugs where they are for the time being until we can get a handle on this thing."

Chris folded his arms across his chest and thought for a few moments. "I guess you're right. We need to concentrate and work harder for the answers."

"I think we're making good progress. Somebody's worried about something or they wouldn't go to the trouble of bugging your apartments."

"If we just had a hint of what they're looking for, we could set them up."

"That could be dangerous, Chris. Let's just sit tight and not get too anxious. That's when you make mistakes and we can't afford to do that. Okay? Don't do anything until you talk to me. I've been in this business a long time, and sometimes it gets a little hairy."

"Why didn't you tell us Michelle was your daughter?" Ashley asked.

"I thought it best you didn't know, that's all."

"I'm very sorry, Jacob. You're a nice man and I like you. You remind me of my father."

"Thank you, Ashley. I take that as a compliment. When you get married, I'd be honored to be the proud man to give you away."

"I'll keep that in mind."

"Do I detect a hint of wedding bells?"

"You're a damn good detective, Mr. Hughes," Chris said.

Jacob tipped his hat. "I'll be in touch."

Chris and Ashley rode the elevator back to the third floor. He unlocked the door and they stepped inside Ashley's apartment. He stood for a moment scratching his head, then dashed for the television remote control. He flipped on the late movie, a wild Western with Clint Eastwood, and motioned for Ashley to follow.

They tiptoed to the bathroom and closed the door. Chris grabbed a pair of eyebrow tweezers and carefully lifted the listening device from under the medicine cabinet, dropping it gently into a glass jar of bath beads with an airtight lid.

He smiled broadly, turned on the water and adjusted the temperature. They undressed, stepped in and Chris adjusted the shower head to the fast pulsating mode. She dropped her hands to her sides and fastened her eyes on his lips. Large drops of water hung near the end of his eyelashes as he looked down into her shining face. He brushed her wet hair back and pulled her into his arms. "I love you, Ashley." His voice was only a whisper as the words melted away on her lips.

CHAPTER EIGHT

The next two days were hectic as 20 sets of hands pounded the keyboards at Hamilton Medical Services. Finally at 7:00 p.m., Friday, all accounts had been entered. The needle on the electric meter dropped drastically as 20 computers shut down. All of them, including Beth, congregated in the ground-floor breakroom and made a toast with Diet Cokes. They relaxed for a while and chatted.

Beth pecked on the glass-top table with her key ring. "Girls, I'm very proud of you. You've done a splendid job and you'll be handsomely rewarded." She smiled and waved her hands in the air. "Now...let's go home and I'll see all of you Monday morning."

Ashley stopped by the supermarket and bought big, thick steaks and all the trimmings. Since she had moved to her new apartment, the thick steaks she had promised herself had been on hold. She swore tonight would be the night.

When she reached her apartment entrance, she could not wait for the elevator to come from the third floor. She felt light on her feet and raced up the stairs in record time. Where is Christopher Burns? she asked herself. He should have been home by now.

She set down the groceries and went out on the patio to examine the grill that she had not had a chance to use. A loud thump hit the front door. She ran through the living room, peered through the view-hole and opened the door.

Chris was standing there with a sack of Mexican food in one hand and a funny-looking cake in the other. He later admitted that the cake had slipped from his hand and he had crushed it against the car. They laughed heartily.

The patio and bedroom windows of their apartments faced east and were located on the front side of the apartment building. Tenant parking was located on the back side of the building with an entrance close to the stairway and elevator. A drugstore, snack shop and four business offices occupied the bottom floor. Across the street, more of the same apartment buildings, three stories high.

Chris poured charcoal in the grill and lighted the fire. He leaned over the ornamental rail that surrounded the patio and looked down at the street below. He glanced up the street, then quickly looked back. A tall, blond man with bangs had been standing by a late-model blue Cadillac when he had parked his car in the rear. He was still there, now sitting behind the wheel, reading a newspaper. Chris recalled having seen this same car parked across the street from the State Crime Lab. He thought a few moments, then decided he would not alarm Ashley at this point. Maybe it was just a coincidence. However, he would watch the man closely and make a decision later in the evening.

Ashley appeared through the patio door carrying a new portable tape player and tapes by Garth Brooks. She snapped in the tape and turned the music to medium loud before going back inside to discard the now-cold Mexican food and prepare the steaks as per Chris's instructions.

While the steaks cooked, she dressed the table with a new white tablecloth and large blue candles. She opened a bottle of expensive wine and poured each a full glass.

Minutes before the steaks were done, Chris excused himself on the pretense of going to his apartment to change from his business suit to something more comfortable. She smiled and nodded, keeping perfect time to the music while she put the finishing touches on the table and lit the candles.

Chris ran down the steps, two at a time, to the drugstore on the ground floor. He quickly placed a coin in the pay phone near the front entrance and dialed the night number Jacob had given him. A voice answered, "Hello."

"Jacob?" he asked.

"Yes, this is Jacob Hughes. Who is this?"

"Chris Burns. I need a favor."

"What is it, Chris?"

"There's a blue Cadillac sitting across the street from my apartment, and the same driver was outside the lab when I left this afternoon. Would you check it out for me?"

"Okay, Chris, just sit tight. I'll drive around and take a look. Maybe I can get a make on him at police headquarters. Give me an hour and call me back."

Chris raced back up the stairs to his apartment and changed into a pair of shorts and a T-shirt. He sat on the side of the bed to catch his breath and quiet his pounding heart. He glanced at his watch. Nine-fifteen. He would call Jacob back at 10:30 p.m.

By the time he returned to Ashley, the steaks were ready. She asked what took him so long. He smiled and said, "You ask entirely too many questions," then kissed her on the tip of her nose. She returned his smile and dropped the subject.

The steaks, baked potatoes, salads, chilled wine and the funny-looking cake were all perfect. They ate, made comments about his parents, who would be arriving at 4:00 p.m. the next day, and danced as Garth Brooks sang the blues. Finally Ashley could no longer choke the question back.

"Chris?"

"Yes, my love?"

"Why do you keep looking at your watch? Are you taking medicine or something?"

"Yeah."

"Yeah? Yeah what?"

"Well...I'm not taking medicine, so it must be 'or something.'" Chris became silent. He had fully evaluated the situation and felt guilty for withholding information from her. She had leveled with him and she was as deep in this dilemma, or maybe deeper, than he. They danced to the end of the Garth Brooks tape that was playing, then he took her by the hand and led her to the rail.

"See that blond-haired man sitting down there in the blue Cadillac?" he said as he pointed.

"Yes, I've seen him before."

"Where?" Chris looked puzzled.

"I stopped at a gas station close to the Hamilton Building a couple days ago and he was there."

"He was also outside the crime lab when I left work this evening."

"Do you think he's watching us?"

"It's beginning to look that way. I went down to the drugstore and called Jacob. He's checking him out right now."

"So that's what took you so long. Why didn't you tell me earlier?"

"I was afraid I might be wrong and I didn't want to upset you. I'm supposed to call Jacob back at ten-thirty and see what he found out."

At 10:30 p.m., they both went down to the drugstore and Chris placed the call to Jacob. No answer. They went into the Snack Shop and ordered coffee. At eleven, he placed the call again. Still no answer. They began to worry. Chris checked and the blue car was still parked in the same place.

"One thing's for sure," Chris said, "Blondy can't follow both of us at the same time. Do you have your car keys with you?"

"Yes, right here in my purse."

"Good. It takes 20 minutes to drive to the police station and back. You get in your car and leave. If he follows you, then I'll go and see if Jacob is still at police headquarters. Be back here at midnight. Okay?"

"Okay. Be careful, Chris."

"You too, babe."

Ashley went out the back entrance, got into her car and drove around the building past the blue Cadillac. Chris watched from the drugstore and, just as he had thought, the blue car made a U-turn in the street and followed her.

Chris raced through the back and sped down the street in the opposite direction. He circled police headquarters and spotted Jacob's car two blocks north of the station. He drove back to the apartment and waited for Ashley, who arrived minutes later. The blue Cadillac returned and used the same parking space.

Back in the drugstore and 15 minutes later, Chris placed the third call to Jacob, who answered after three rings.

"You had me worried, Jacob. What'd you find out?" Chris asked.

"Not much. The car's a rental, and there's no officer or undercover agent who fits this man's description in any of the departments in Austin. I don't like it, Chris."

"What should we do?"

"Just pretend you don't see him for the time being. He's watching you, so I'm going to be watching him. Take this number down, memorize it, then destroy it. It's the number to my car phone so you won't have to waste time going through my secretary. You got a pencil and some paper?"

"Yeah, right here, shoot."

"Dial one, nine two six, seven eight eight nine. Remember, memorize it and destroy it. It's an unlisted number. Okay?"

"Okay. Be careful, man."

"I'm always careful. You take care of Missy."

"That's a promise. I've decided to stay at her place tonight."

"Good idea. Catch you later."

Ashley lowered herself into the hot tub of water, enriched with bath oils and beads of sweet smelling soap. Suddenly, she felt that the bugs, which only had ears before, were now beginning to sprout eyes. She felt degraded and stripped of her privacy. She closed her eyes and could see the smug grin on Blade's face as he had held her hard against the Coke machine in the breakroom. His hands had looked so big as he pushed her shoulders firmly back. She shuddered and forced her thoughts away.

She slipped under the bed cover, dressed becomingly in a pink shortie, and snuggled close to Chris. "Hold me, Chris," she whispered.

He did, willingly. She felt warm, and he could smell the sweet scent of her soft skin. He kissed her and said, "I love you, Ash." Suddenly, he sat up in bed like a jack in the box. "Oh, hell." She quickly sat up, looking puzzled. He pointed to the floral arrangement on the table close to the bed and silently formed the word, "Bugs."

He jumped out of bed, motioned for Ashley to get up and stripped the bed of its coverlet, blanket and sheets. He carried them out onto the patio, draped the blanket and sheets over the ornamental rail and made a bed on the floor with the coverlet. She followed with two pillows and quietly closed the patio doors.

They laid in each other's arms on the patio floor and gazed at the beautiful sky. The stars were bright and plentiful. The moon seemed to smile approval, and occasionally a lonely cloud would drift by, hiding its face. Ashley's lips were soft and trembled under Chris's. He sensed the fear Ashley always tried desperately to hide under her bold exterior.

"Chris?" she asked.

He opened his eyes. "Yeah, Ash."

"Do you think the patio's bugged too?"

"I hardly think so, my love." He smiled and pulled her close.

"When do you think all of this will end? I'm ready for our lives to get back to normal."

"Me too. Close your eyes and try to get some rest. I'd hate for you to look like a haggard old woman when my parents get here tomorrow."

"Have you told them about our engagement?"

"Sure did."

"And?"

"That's the purpose of this visit. To meet you and see if they approve. And they will, now go to sleep."

"I can't."

"Try anyway. I'm exhausted."

It was almost 5:00 a.m. when Chris awoke. He nudged Ashley and they retrieved their sleeping paraphernalia and went quietly back into the bedroom. It was noon the second time they awoke.

"What do you think I should wear to the airport to meet your folks?"

He pointed to the listening device and smiled. "A string bikini would be nice."

She tried to remain silent but suddenly burst into a loud chuckle. "Good idea."

At 3:00 p.m., they parked at the airport and went inside to await the arrival of Senator and Mrs. Brandon Burns. They were informed at the airline desk that the plane was on time and scheduled to land in 55 minutes.

They ambled down to the coffee shop for a cup of coffee and made plans for the evening. Blondy was across the wide walkway in the bookstore, trying to look as inconspicuous as possible.

As the passengers deplaned and began coming down the ramp, Chris smiled and pointed. "There they are. Mom's wearing the dark blue dress."

Ashley could see a tall, stocky man with brown eyes and hair like Chris's, dressed in a dark gray suit of the newest style, his face relaxed and happy; beside him, a tall, sophisticated blonde with blue eyes that sparkled and wrinkled in the corners when she smiled.

Chris jumped up and waved. They smiled at his childlike manner and waved back.

"Mom! Dad!" he said as they approached and sat their carry-on bags down. "This is Ashley, the beautiful redhead I've been telling you about."

Ashley blushed. Chris chuckled and hugged her close.

"I'm glad to meet you, Senator and Mrs. Burns."

"Please," Mrs. Burns spoke, "call us Laurel and Senator."

"Well, Chris." His father beamed. "She's just as beautiful as you said she was."

Laurel took Ashley by the hand. "I'm so glad to finally meet you. Chris has talked about you so often."

"Come on," Chris said, "I'll drive you to my apartment so you can freshen up before I take you to the place where I met my love."

"I'm sorry, son," the senator said, "I forgot to tell you. We have a room reserved at the Marriott."

"Well...Judas Priest, Dad!" He tried to sound annoyed although he was grateful, since he was now aware their conversations in his apartment would be overheard.

"We're not too old to tango, son. We kinda like our privacy too. It's not very often we get the chance to get away from Washington."

"Okay, Dad, excuse accepted."

"What time will you be picking us up for dinner?" his mother asked.

"Is 7:00 p.m. okay?"

"Seven will be fine."

For Ashley, it was a strange sensation as Chris seated her at the Candlelite. She had never been there as a guest, and this was the first time she'd even been back since she started her job at Hamilton Medical. Her eyes searched the room and found many familiar faces and smiles.

The waitress came and cheerfully left menus and a wine list. She returned shortly, and they all ordered wine while they continued to study the menu.

Ashley ordered fresh crab meat, minced, seasoned with sweet pepper and baked in its shell; a side order of peas and rice with grated coconut; carrot cake with nuts and raisins. This was the chef's specialty and her favorite, she explained. They all agreed it sounded wonderful and placed the same order.

The Candlelite owner, 'Boots,' as he was known, walked to the microphone. "Ladies and gentlemen," he said with a wide smile, "we have one of our all-time favorite singers in the crowd tonight, Miss Ashley Denton. Would you like to hear her sing a song for old times?" The crowd responded with enthusiastic applause.

Ashley looked at Chris and her face reddened.

"Go on, Ash," he pleaded, full of pride.

Ashley stood, straightened her black lace dress and walked slowly through the crowded dining room. It was like old times.

She placed her fingers around the chrome pole of the microphone and began to sing. The Senator and Mrs. Burns sat motionless and were visibly impressed.

"You failed to mention this, son," his father said.

"There are so many wonderful things about Ashley, Dad, I just couldn't remember them all."

"How did you get so lucky, Chris?" his mother asked.

"I don't know, Mom, but I hope my luck never runs out."

Ashley received a standing ovation as she worked her way back to the table to join the others. Chris seated her again, just as the waitress appeared with their orders.

After they had eaten, Senator Burns placed his napkin on

the table and stood. He walked around, held out his hand and asked Ashley to dance. He led her to the dance floor and placed his arm around her slender waist. "When do you and Chris plan to get married?"

"We haven't set a date yet, sir."

"Well...I'm ready for Chris to settle down and have us some grandbabies. How do you feel about having a family?"

"I want lots of babies," she replied.

"Good girl," he said and pulled her close.

The appraisals and judgments were unanimous. She instantly felt warmth and love for Chris's parents, and they obviously adored and were very impressed with her.

While his father and Ashley danced, Chris excused himself from the table and stepped outside into the shadows. The blue Cadillac was parked down the street, but Blondy had been replaced by a black-haired man. Chris stared for a long moment, studying the man's profile. He had an uneasy feeling he had seen him somewhere before.

Chris went back inside, joined his mother and waited for the dance to end. His father seated Ashley, then himself.

"Where do you work, Ashley?" the senator asked.

"Hamilton Medical Services," she answered and gave a brief history.

"Dad," Chris interrupted, "let's go back to the hotel. There's something I need to discuss with you."

"Oh!" His father grinned. "Are you about to become a father?"

"Someday but not right now," he answered and wrinkled his forehead. "It's far more serious than that. Can we go?"

They all crowded onto the bed in room 626 at the Marriott. Chris began his story and related the events of the past two weeks.

The senator took a long breath and let it out slowly. "Son, I'm afraid you two are possibly getting into something heavy and dangerous. FBI Director Frank Russom is a good friend of mine. I'll discuss this with him the minute we get back to Washington. In the meantime, don't let your guards down."

"You can't call me at home, Dad. Our phones and apartments are bugged."

"The hell you say!"

"Brandon! Watch your language." Laurel frowned.

The senator ignored her orders. "How in the hell am I supposed to get in touch with you? Is there a bug in your phone at work too?"

"I don't know, but I can't take any chances. I'll call you from a pay phone tomorrow night."

"It's hard for me to believe the vice president could be so careless. He should never have gotten involved in something like this to start with. If he has, he should take full responsibility. Another thing, there's a host of people in the party who wanted the president to choose another running mate. All the opposition needs is an excuse, but what's more important, if this girl...what's her name?"

"April Crafton," Chris answered.

"If the young lady's death is exposed and linked in any way to the vice president, the election would be over for the party. It would be a disaster in many ways."

Laurel slid off the bed, kicked off her shoes and began to pace the floor. "Why don't you two pack up and go back to Washington with us tomorrow?"

"Mom, that sounds wonderful, but you can't run from crime and corruption. There's no place to go but home. Anyway, D.C. is the crime capital of the world."

"You're right. Maybe we should move back to Texas sooner than we'd planned."

"What do you mean?" Chris directed the question to his father.

"I don't plan to run again when this term is up."

"Are you serious, Dad?"

The senator reached for his handkerchief, silk and initialed, and mopped his forehead. "Dead serious. I want to come back to Austin, resume my law practice and, hopefully, spoil some grandbabies."

Laurel ordered expensive champagne and four glasses from room service. When it arrived, the senator filled all the glasses, made a toast to their return to Texas and the prospect of pattering little feet.

CHAPTER NINE

The flight attendant had just removed the last of the passenger trays as the Delta 727 soared smoothly over the darkening Appalachians toward Washington, D.C. They had left Austin on flight 819, departing at five-ten in the evening. With a 53-minute layover in Dallas, they were scheduled to arrive at Washington National at 8:35 p.m. On take-off from Dallas, the forecast had called for good weather conditions.

Laurel Burns fastened her seatbelt and retrieved a novel from her purse. She read a couple of pages, then snapped the book shut and placed it down beside her in the seat.

"What's the matter, Mama?" the senator asked.

"I'm worried about Chris and Ashley."

"So am I." He frowned. "I'm going to call Frank Russom from the airport and see if he'll have coffee someplace with us."

"Good," she said, "the sooner the better. I just pray it's nothing serious."

The senator studied his wife's beauty as she closed her eyes and rested her head against the back of the seat, rubbing a locket between her fingers. She was a former Miss Texas and Miss America. Even at age 54, she still possessed her beauty and charm.

As a young lawyer, he had met her at one of her functions as Miss America in Austin. They had fallen deeply in love and married shortly after her reign. She was 22 and he was 30. Two years later their only child, Christopher, was born. Laurel had done well raising their son, mostly alone.

She stirred in her seat and placed her head on the senator's shoulder. He could smell the sweet fragrance of her blond hair, that she kept cut short to emphasize the graceful lines of her neck and shoulders. She had bloomed in her maturity. 'A damn beautiful woman,' he told himself. Watching her doze filled him with quiet, peaceful pride.

Unlike Laurel, who had been raised in wealth, the senator had worked hard to overcome his early years in poverty. As a child, he was terrified of his father, who suffered from alcoholism, and was ignored by his mother, who clearly favored his younger sister. Now the most important thing in his life was his family and he wished it were larger.

He had toiled night and day to work his way through law school and establish a reputable practice. He remained in his practice until Chris graduated from high school. Then he ran for the United States Senate and upset a 20-year congressional veteran, despite all the experts' predictions to the contrary.

The captain maneuvered the 727, turning onto the final approach and lining up with the runway. It was a perfectly executed landing, and Laurel released a long pent-up sigh as she felt the wheels touch the ground. Flying was not one of her favorite pastimes, and she was always grateful to feel contact with the earth again.

All 148 passengers deplaned right on schedule. Senator and Mrs. Burns retrieved their baggage from the overhead compartment, hurried down the ramp to the nearest phones and placed the call.

Ellen Russom answered, "Hello."

"Ellen, Brandon Burns here. Is Frank in?"

"Yes, just a moment. I'll get him for you, Brandon."

FBI Director Frank Russom was a solemn-faced man with

intelligent, brown eyes. He was in his late fifties, and his hair was beginning to gray at the temples. He was tall and had a noticeably precise manner.

"Brandon, how are you? Did you have a nice trip to Texas?"

"Sure did. We had a nice visit with our son and met his lovely fiancée, and that's why I'm calling, Frank. There's something rather important I need to talk to you about. Could you meet Laurel and me somewhere for a cup of coffee?"

"Is it that urgent, Brandon?"

"Yes, Frank, I feel it is."

"Sure, how about the Rendezvous...say, 30 minutes?"

"We're at the airport now, but we can meet you there."

"Would you mind if Ellen came along?"

"Not at all. Thanks Frank."

"You bet."

It was late July and the sun was setting, turning the sky crimson red and throwing bright rays across the tall buildings as the Senator and Mrs. Burns drove to the Rendezvous.

They were seated at one of the last tables in the crowded restaurant when the Director and Mrs. Russom arrived. "What's on your mind, senator?" Director Russom asked as he seated his wife and then himself.

"What do you know about Hamilton Medical Services in Austin?"

"Nothing. Never heard of it. Why?"

"Have you heard the names, Blade Henderson or Beth Wagner?"

"No, can't say that I have."

The senator went through the story Chris and Ashley had told him, step by methodical step.

The director sagged in his chair, pursed his lips and stared in surprise. "This is the first I've heard. I wish I could tell you the two fellows tailing your son and his fiancée are mine, but they're not."

"What can we do?"

The director leaned forward and propped his elbows on the table. "I'll talk to the CIA director first thing in the morning. I'll also send one of my agents to Austin tomorrow and see what I can find out. I'll get back to you as soon as I have something."

The senator nodded and suppressed a smile. Frank Russom rose to his feet and placed a hand on the senator's shoulder. "Try not to worry. We'll get to the bottom of this, you have my word."

"That's all I need to hear. Thank you, Frank."

"You're certainly welcome. Besides...I owe you several."

CIA Director Lionel Nesbitt was sitting in his office when Frank Russom arrived at 8:00 a.m., Monday. His heavily muscled thighs poured over the sides of his chair, threatening to crack the frame. He looked like a heavyweight champion, with large arms that could carry an average-sized man without a strain or could snap bones and crack heads as though they were toothpicks. His head was large, as were his green eyes, and his face was puffed like a wad of dough that had too much yeast. His brown hair was thin on top and combed straight back, revealing a receding hairline.

His office was plush; a leather sofa, two brass-studded chairs, three-dimensional pictures of various D.C. scenes, thick carpet of gray and teal, and drapes that matched with highlights of berry red.

Director Russom passed the secretary without speaking, knocked on Lionel Nesbitt's door and entered without waiting. Lionel Nesbitt looked over the top of his reading glasses without raising his head. "Well...come on in, Frank. What brings you out here so early? I know it's not a social call."

"You're right, Lionel." It was obvious there was no love lost between the two directors. "You want to tell me about Hamilton Medical Services?"

"Tell you what, Frank?"

"What's going on?"

"What makes you think there's something going on?"

"You have two men in Austin, don't you?"

"Who told you that?"

"I have my sources too, Lionel. Now...do you want to tell me or do I have to go see the president?"

Director Russom thought that over the course of his lifetime he had heard every word ever used in the vocabulary of profanities, but he had missed a few.

"Leave the president out of this, Frank."

"Ah, then there is something going on."

Nesbitt tossed his pen on the desk and folded his arms.

"Start talking, Lionel. I don't have all day."

"Calm down, Frank. It's no big deal. Have a seat and settle down." He opened the bottom drawer of his desk and retrieved a folder, three inches thick. "What do you know so far?"

"Senator Brandon Burns's son, Dr. Christopher Burns, and his fiancée are being followed night and day. The young lady's predecessor and possibly another young woman supposedly died under mysterious circumstances while working for the organization. Am I right?"

"You're right."

"Were they murdered?"

"Don't know that yet."

"When will you know?"

"Soon. Here's what I have on a man named Blade Henderson. He's an ex-cop from Dallas. Kicked off the force there for sexual harassment. In the past two years, he's made four trips to a third-world country that's hostile toward the United States, which brings this case under my jurisdiction."

"What do you suspect him of?"

"I'm not sure yet, but I have to make it my business to know how he can waltz in and out of the country without any problems."

"Who is he connected with there?"

"I'm not sure, yet."

"Is Beth Wagner or Louis Hamilton involved?"

"The director of the State Pathology Lab, Dr. Steve Sulcer, took a $100,000 pay-off for falsifying the autopsy report on one of the Hamilton employees. We don't know for sure if Wagner and Hamilton are involved or not. They're slick, and so far we haven't been able to prove anything. If these trips and his connections pan out not to be any kind of threat to national security, the case will be turned over to the local authorities."

"What else?"

"That's about it, Frank."

"Come on, Lionel. That's a pretty thick folder you're holding for such a short speech. Are you going to level with me or will I have to walk all over you to get the truth?"

"You just don't ever stop hounding, do you Frank?"

"We've been slinging mud in each other's eyes for a long time, Lionel. I can tell when you're holding out on me."

He leaned back in his chair, and with his cold eyes, shot a few daggers at the director. "I'm pretty certain that the vice president was involved with the last dead girl. A young man I've known for years and one of the vice president's Secret Service men, came to see me for advice. He was worried sick." Nesbitt opened his large hands wide and tapped his fingertips together. "He told me on several occasions, Mr. Ramsey had slipped out of their hotel suite and was gone for several hours. After he discovered this was going on, he told me he had followed the vice president to the Hamilton Building where he met this April Crafton."

"Oh hell."

"I tried to convince the vice president to bow out before it became an embarrassment, but he laughed in my face and told me to stick to national security."

"I can't believe Ramsey is so damn stupid. Where is his brain?"

"I'm afraid right now, it's below his belt. I'm told he's having a lot of problems at home. I've managed to keep this under wraps so far, but I don't know how much longer I can keep it up. Now I have to add you to the list of counselors."

"I don't plan to hold a press conference. What else?"

"Against our better judgment, the president refused to choose another running mate. Of course, if any of this should leak out, he's politically dead. I can't let that happen. He's a good man and a damn good president."

"Well, Lionel, it looks like the news might be on the verge of getting to the president. What do you plan to do now?"

"I don't have many choices, do I?"

"How do you plan to handle this if the press gets a sniff?"

He smiled. "I plan to commit suicide."

Russom chuckled. "It would probably be time. You'll let me know if something else comes up, won't you, Lionel?"

"Yeah, Frank. I wish now I had sent my young Secret Service friend to you instead of getting involved myself."

"Don't do me any favors, Nesbitt." He stood and chuckled. "You're way out in the quicksand and I'm all out of rope."

"Show yourself out, Frank."

Frank Russom spent the rest of the morning pacing his office. He walked out a dozen times and down the sidewalk in the blazing sun. He thought about phoning Senator Burns, but he realized this was serious, far more serious than he had anticipated. He had a strong feeling that Lionel Nesbitt knew more than what he was telling. There were too many unanswered questions. He had to make a decision. He had to tell the senator something. He got up from his desk and went to the window where he watched the Monday morning traffic for a while, checked his watch, then snatched up the receiver and buzzed his secretary. "Where's Tony Camper?" he asked.

"He's taking a few days off, sir," she replied.

"Find him and tell him I want to see him now."

"Yes, sir."

She located Tony Camper and he drove at breakneck speed to the FBI Building. The director was still pacing when Tony burst through the office door.

"What took you so damn long, Camper?"

"Slow-moving traffic, sir."

Director Russom stopped pacing and rubbed the back of his neck while Tony stood quietly. "Sit down. You won't be able to handle this standing up." Director Russom sat heavily in his chair and began to spit out the details of the sordid story he'd been told.

Tony sat in shock. His first reaction was a frown but, as the director continued, his face became expressionless.

After a long silence, the director said, "I want you on the next flight to Austin. I want a report as soon as you can get me one. If you need more help down there, just give me a call."

"I understand, sir."

Camper, a former college football linebacker, was 6'4" and powerfully built. The gray flecks in his closely cropped dark hair gave him the appearance of an older man. He would tip the scales at 250 pounds, but he carried his weight well and, at first glance, appeared slim.

Tony left the office, and the director sat thumping his pen loudly on his desk. With an IQ of 170 and graduating from the FBI Academy in the top five of his class, Tony Camper was his choice of agents to investigate this potentially explosive situation and make his own assessment of Lionel Nesbitt's allegations, since the CIA director was not above a coverup.

Russom buzzed his secretary again. "Get me Senator Brandon Burns on the phone."

"Yes, sir."

Moments later, she heard his voice. "Senator Burns here."

"Director Russom is holding for you, sir."

"Thank you," he said, pecking the top of his desk with his fingertips as he waited.

"Senator Burns?"

"Yeah, Frank. Have you come up with something on the Austin affair?"

"Let's go for lunch. There's a nice little cafe down the street a few blocks. I'll pick you up in 15 minutes."

"Fine, I'll be waiting for you."

Senator Burns seated himself in the car and glanced questioningly at the director, who by now was calm and very much in control of himself.

"It doesn't look good, Brandon. I have a man on his way to Austin as we speak. There's not much I can tell you right now, but I suspect it's much bigger than either of us first thought. I'll try to keep you informed as soon as I get a report back from my man. I'll give you the details at the cafe."

CHAPTER TEN

CIA Director Nesbitt sat alone in his office, hearing the door close and the click of his secretary's heels as she left for lunch. He rose from his chair, walked to the window and for a long moment, stared into space. He made mental notes outlining plans but rejected most all of them. He realized more and more people were being drawn into this scenario and this disturbed him.

He opened the Hamilton files and sat down at his desk. He read and reread, looking for something he might have missed. The reports were detailed and accurate. He reconsidered his first plan; it wasn't foolproof, but such plans seldom are. There was always the random possibility of the unexpected and the unimagined, but it was the only logical, workable solution.

He reached for a pen and his legal pad. He began to plan it out carefully in his methodical way. Finally he was convinced his basic method of approach was sound.

He dialed the number to the Oval Office, breathing more rapidly as he listened to the phone ring each time. There was no answer. He let it ring several more times. His face became contorted with fury, and he found himself cursing under his breath.

He slammed the phone back in its cradle, wondering how many of his waking hours were spent on the telephone, waiting for a call or trying to complete one, especially to the

White House.

At 1:30 p.m., Director Nesbitt walked into the Oval Office unannounced. It was deserted. He planted himself in one of the armchairs, glanced around the room, then stared down at the briefcase balanced precisely on his knees. He would wait.

President John Graves entered from the upstairs living quarters. He looked tired. He had just returned from a seven-day tour of Russia and his pinstriped navy suit hung loosely from his tall frame, indicating a recent weight loss.

His top aide, George Bivens, followed a few steps behind. He stopped abruptly and glared at Director Nesbitt sitting in front of the president's desk. He looked shocked. "Do you have an appointment, Mr. Director?" he asked.

"Well...as a matter-of-fact, I do." The director rose slowly, gripped the aide by the right arm and almost lifted him off his feet. "Now if you'll excuse us," he said harshly.

Bivens quickly searched his calender. "I don't see your name, director."

"That's your problem, George. Obviously, you failed to write it down."

"I don't think so, director." Bivens looked at him with distaste, recognizing his brute strength and becoming obviously angered by his bullying. The president nodded, and Bivens stalked from the Oval Office.

"Lionel..." President Graves started, then stopped.

"I'm sorry, Mr. President, but this is my fourth attempt to see you in the past two months. It's obvious Bivens has some kind of ax to grind, and he doesn't make any attempt to cooperate with me."

"Don't be too hard on him, Lionel. He spends more time trying to protect me than he spends coping with the problems in front of him. Anyway, what's on your mind?"

"I have some reports I need to discuss with you, Mr. President."

"Well...let's see what you have."

106

The confidential reports on Beth Wagner, Blade Henderson, the two dead girls and the vice president constituted a stack of almost 400 pages of reports and photos all organized into five manila folders.

The director opened his briefcase and spread the mass of material on the desk. The president began to examine the reports and photos in astonishment, releasing long, agonizing moans.

"God have mercy. If this gets out, the press will crucify me, Lionel."

"Yes, Mr. President. It would be a political disaster."

The president slumped in his chair with his eyes glued to the top of the desk. He sat motionless in total shock.

The director paced, pounding his fist into an open hand, feeling helpless and outraged.

Bivens had regained his composure and broke the silence with a tray of hot coffee. He handed the director a cup and sat one on the desk for the president. He sensed the tension and slipped from the office, hardly noticed.

By four in the afternoon, Nesbitt and President Graves had read and discussed every report and stared several times at each of the photos, especially those of the two dead girls.

The president rose to his feet and stood silently for a few moments, pondering his options. What would he say or what would he do if these files became public knowledge?

"Well...Lionel." He paused and shrugged. "I should have listened to my staff and advisors and picked another running mate. I've been a fool and it's too late to turn back. Ramsey's already on the ticket and has given his acceptance speech. He's an ambitious man and has plans to be the next president. I might as well clean out my desk and forget about the election."

The director looked at him admiringly. "Don't do anything for the moment. I may have a solution, Mr. President."

The president nodded, not looking at him, and made an impatient wave of his hand. "Do what you have to do to straighten this mess out, Lionel."

"It's as good as done, sir."

The director replaced the reports and photos back in their folders and in his briefcase. He left the president standing with his back to the door, staring out of the window in silence.

Director Nesbitt went back to his office and placed all the files in a secret safe. He picked up the phone and fingered the numbers to Vice President Drew Ramsey's living quarters.

"Ramsey residence," a female voice answered.

"Yes, this is Director Nesbitt. Would you put Mr. Ramsey on the line please."

"Just a moment, director."

Nesbitt tapped his fingertips on top of his desk while he waited for several moments to pass.

"Yes, director," Ramsey answered.

"I need to talk to you, sir."

"I'm listening."

"I'm afraid I can't discuss this matter over the phone. I can be at your home in 30 minutes. Are you alone?"

"Yes, but I'm getting ready to go to Texas. Can it wait until I get back?"

"No sir. I'm afraid not."

"All right, but I don't have much time."

"Thank you, sir."

As he was approaching the Naval Observatory on Massachusetts Avenue, Director Nesbitt tried desperately to arrange his thoughts and his proposed argument. For a moment, he contemplated letting the press expose the vice president, but he dreaded the penalty which he knew the president and Ramsey's two young sons would face in the future. He tried to smile but was unsuccessful.

He knocked and standing outside the vice president's door,

he felt the tension which had been building higher and higher in his body. His shoulders hunched forward as he heard the lock turn from the inside and the door slowly opened.

"Come in, director."

"Thank you, sir. I'll get right to the point."

"Please do, I'm in a hurry."

"Mr. Ramsey, I'm asking you one last time to resign and step aside."

"Why are you so hell bent on getting me out of the election? Is this some personal vendetta with you, Nesbitt?" With a handsome, boyish face, his acts of innocence were always superb.

"No sir, it isn't, and I believe you know what I am referring to."

"What are you talking about?"

"The Austin affair. Does that refresh your memory?"

"Not at all. I don't have the slightest idea what you're talking about, and I'd appreciate it if you would drop the damn subject and get off my ass."

Avoiding his eyes, Director Nesbitt looked outside the window, biting his bottom lip for a few moments. His first impulse was to be angry, his second to be frightened. "It would be best for all concerned if you would resign and get out of politics before it's too late. Take your wife and boys and move away from here."

Ramsey looked at him with undeniable hatred. "I have no intentions of doing any such thing. Now, if you don't mind, director, I still have some packing to do."

Nesbitt closed his eyes and dropped his head. "I'll see myself out, sir."

The trip across the Potomac and back to the CIA office became a blur. He retrieved another file from the back and sat down at his desk. He opened the folder and began to study the contents.

Benjamin Sarrelli -- one of the first professional criminals he had investigated as new CIA director. Benjamin's parents had been killed in an auto accident when he was 14. He had been placed in numerous foster homes but had always felt rejected and a misfit. He finally claimed the streets as his home and quickly learned every criminal technique in the book. He could scale two stories as though he were a tree frog with suction feet, operate tumblers of a safe faster than the owner, and pick a pocket faster than the naked eye could catch. Even though he had only finished the tenth grade, this handsome boy, with sad innocent eyes, had a very high IQ. He had never been caught in a crime nor had he ever been fingerprinted, and he intended to keep it that way. He lived in a business world all of his own and was accepted, respected and recognized by the Mafia.

Director Nesbitt closed the file and placed it back in his secret safe. He picked up an old hat and a pair of sunglasses he kept in the top drawer of a regular file cabinet, along with a brown plaid suit coat with noticeable age. He notified his driver that he was returning to D.C. but would not require his services.

Thirty minutes later, he left his car at a parking garage in D.C., caught a cab to the subway, then a bus to North Capitol Street. From there, he walked six blocks to the Sarrelli Building in the northwest section of D.C. It was not a safe place to walk alone, but he took his chances. The streets were hectic with after-work traffic, and the sidewalks were crowded with loud-voiced pedestrians, most of them young, wearing the latest kinky fashions and haircuts of the day.

As he approached the Sarrelli Building, two men were replacing one of the shattered panes in the row of windows that ran the length of the bottom floor, occupied by several offices, a beauty shop and a bakery. He stopped for a moment and looked around at the surroundings, shops of all kinds, hotels, business offices and all were open as usual.

The street girls, some young and beautiful and some not so young and painted like clowns, were beginning to come out and take their usual places on the corners and against the walls. Young men and old hovered in circles buying and selling drugs. He cast a final glance over his shoulder, entered the Sarrelli Building and walked down the short hall to the elevator. He pushed the button, and while he waited, glanced up and noticed the monitor at the end of the hall pointing to the elevator. Benjamin Sarrelli was still his same cool, cautious self.

In the 15 years he had been CIA director, they had had only one business deal. Mr. Sarrelli was a professional and alive with a clean record to show for it.

At that moment, the elevator door opened. The director stepped inside and leaned against the wall as it lifted him to the second floor, the top floor of the building. When the door opened again, he stepped out on the white plush carpet and looked around at the assembled bodyguards.

Benjamin Sarrelli nodded his head and the three men disappeared into an adjoining room. He smiled and shook hands with the director. "Mr. Nesbitt, it's been a long time."

"It sure has, Benjamin."

Benjamin lived in this six-room suite; two large living room windows faced east, the bedroom windows faced south and the kitchen and bathrooms faced north. The decor had not changed much since the director's last visit six years ago; still it was very modernly furnished and very plush. There was an elaborate bar in the corner with a wall of mirrors, a built-in stereo system, a computer and a television monitor on the adjoining wall.

Benjamin was seated at the long glass-top table placed at the back of the sofa. He rang the bell on the table and the chef, a large black man, appeared. "Fix two dinners, John, we have a guest."

"Yes, sir," he replied and disappeared into the kitchen.

The director pulled off his coat and hat and tossed them on the floor beside the sofa. He rolled up his cuffs and seated himself at the table next to Benjamin.

There was a noticeable difference in Benjamin since their last meeting. His weight gain of ten pounds or more made his average height appear shorter. His dark, curly hair had been sprinkled with gray flecks, and his eyelids seemed to droop over his large black eyes. He looked tired and much older than 55.

At that moment, the chef placed the plates on the table. The director greeted him and accepted the steaming hot lamb, potato salad, hot rolls and black coffee.

The director ate for a few moments and placed his fork on the side of his plate. "Benjamin, your choice of chefs is superb."

"Yeah." He beamed. "John's a certified public accountant."

"Is that right?"

"Uh-huh. He was working in an office in San Francisco when I met him, a brilliant man. I called him up one day and offered him a position in my business. And you know what he told me? He said 'Mr. Ben, I'll come to work for you, but don't stick me in an office with a bunch of damn books and a computer.' I said, 'Well John, what do you want to do?' And he said, 'My specialty is in the kitchen and that's where I wanna be.' I've never been sorry and neither has he. He's as happy as a damn pig in the sunshine. And speaking of pigs," he said picking up the bulge that was hanging over his belt and smiled at the director, "just look at this. I'm killing myself."

"I can understand that. This is without a doubt some of the best food I've ever eaten."

"John's not only my chef, he's one of the best friends I've ever had." Benjamin chuckled again. "I'll bet he's got more money in the bank than I have."

The two men made a few comments about the weather, and

during the conversation about the upcoming election, the director found the opportunity to discuss the purpose of his visit.

Benjamin Sarrelli sat silently as the director laid out his plan in precise detail. He rose from the table, went to the bar and poured two glasses of wine.

The director stood and faced Benjamin. "One million," Nesbitt said firmly.

"You have a deal. Five hundred thousand now, and the rest after the job is finished. Fair enough?"

"Fair enough."

"Make all the arrangements and wait for my call."

"Consider it done, director."

It was dark when the director stepped from the Sarrelli Building and out onto the sidewalk. All the shops had chain gates locked across the doors and a dim light burning within. The cars on the streets were dark and empty. The streets were almost deserted except for a few neglected ladies of the night still standing under the street lights on the corners, still hopeful.

He would take the same careful and thoughtful route back to his office. It was almost a 30-minute ride on the bus back to the subway, which was crowded, hot and smelled like the city dump. He pulled his hat low on his forehead and sat slumped in the seat next to an elderly lady, who continuously muttered to herself, clacked her false teeth and blessed everybody's heart.

He stepped off the subway and went directly to the men's room. It, too, was crowded, but he was able to get to the basin. He moistened two paper towels under the tap and went into the pay toilet. When he had locked the door, he used the wet towels to mop the nervous perspiration from his face. He had a sudden and uncontrollable urge to vomit, and did. He washed his mouth, stuck the wet towels in his pocket and

113

opened the toilet door, looking pale and smiling faintly.

In the mirror over the basin, he caught the eye of an elderly, shabbily dressed man staring at him.

"Cheap wine?" the old man asked.

"No, potato salad." He patted the old man on the back and left the hot, smelly room.

He caught a cab back to the parking garage, paid the driver, got in his car and went home. Home to safety and seclusion.

CHAPTER ELEVEN

Jeri Lynn entered the pathology lab with all the cardboard boxes she could carry. "I need some help," she muttered.

Chris looked up from the stack of paper work that had piled up in one day. "Help with what, Granny?"

Her voice stuck in her throat. "I have to clear out 20 years of memories Dr. Sulcer left behind."

Chris scratched his chest and stretched. "Sure, I'll give you a hand."

One wall of Dr. Sulcer's office was dominated by pictures of his daughter, a registered nurse, and his son, a naval officer. There were three frames of inked prints formed by the little hands of his three grandchildren, who took the office apart each time they came for a visit.

Within the hour, they had removed and boxed all his personal belongings. "What are you going to do with this stuff?" Chris asked.

"Dr. Sulcer's daughter will be here to pick it up tomorrow."

Chris parked his car and walked down the street to the Pizza Hut for lunch. It was after one o'clock and most of the crowd had cleared. He sat in the far back to catch his breath and read the morning paper. He ordered and the pizza was served in five minutes, as guaranteed. He finished the pizza and the paper at the same time.

A tall man, dressed pleasantly in pleated khakis and an opened-collar blue oxford, approached his table. He unfolded a newspaper and flashed a badge. "FBI Special Agent, Tony Camper. May I sit down?"

"Certainly. What can I do for you?"

Agent Camper seated himself, pulled up his pant leg slightly and crossed his knees. "You are Dr. Christopher Burns, aren't you?"

"Yes, I've been expecting you."

"As you know, I'm here on special assignment as a favor to your father."

Chris looked at him curiously for a moment, then sat back in his seat and began to drum his heavy fingers on the tabletop. "You don't sound too pleased about being here."

Tony smiled. "I always enjoy coming to Texas. Austin's a beautiful city and quite a contrast to D.C."

"Don't take offense, but I hope you won't be here long."

"Point well taken. Director Russom personally briefed me on the situation before I left Washington. What can you tell me about Hamilton Medical Services?"

"An inordinate number of their female employees are dying mysteriously. Ashley Denton had better not be next." Chris picked up a toothpick and speared the pizza crumbs left on his plate. He looked up, arched an eyebrow and asked. "Are we in any kind of danger?"

"You might be. Here's my card. If you need me, call."

"Just like that? You waltz in here, tell me I could be in danger, hand me a card and leave without telling me why?"

"There's not much to tell you now, except be careful."

"Careful of what or whom?"

"I should have some answers for you in a couple of days."

"So, in the meantime, I just roll over and play dead?"

Agent Camper smiled and made a friendly gesture. "Have a nice day and don't lose my card."

THE AUSTIN AFFAIR

The afternoon mail brought a large brown envelope from Austin State Bank addressed to Dr. Christopher Burns. Instructions had been left with the bank president to mail the letter in case of Dr. Steve Sulcer's death or disappearance.

Chris ripped open the envelope and began to read. His hands trembled as he held the letter.

Dear Chris,

When you read this letter, I'll probably be dead. I am an honest man who has become an unwilling pawn in a very serious game. Person or persons unknown to me, by threatening me with the deaths of my family, forced me to falsify my autopsy report on April Crafton. I falsely listed the cause of her death as cervical fracture sustained upon impact, but as you and I know, she actually died from the massive overdose of barbiturates we found in her system. I was also instructed to omit the fact that she was three months pregnant at the time of her death.

Chris, I pray for your sake that the Crafton report will be the end to this dreadful nightmare, but in the event you are approached in the future, I strongly urge you to follow instructions. These people are ruthless and will stop at nothing to achieve their goal. Their threats to my family convinced me that this was, without a doubt, a very powerful force. Not knowing who ultimatley wielded this power, I was terrified to seek aid from any branch of law enforcement.

I apologize for the awkward position I have placed you in, but I cannot bear the thought of taking this heavy burden to my grave.

God bless you and yours,
Steve Sulcer, M.D.

Chris leaned back in his chair and closed his eyes. He was devastated. He suddenly felt as though someone had lowered him into a vat of ice-cold water. He shivered and fought waves of nausea.

Jeri Lynn burst through the door and Chris jumped as though he had been shot. "Telephone," she said. "I buzzed you three times on the intercom. Where were you?"

"I'm sorry, I didn't hear you. Who is it?"

"Your new assistant, Dr. Stubblefield."

"Good. Thanks."

"Are you feeling okay today? You look pale."

"I'm okay."

Jeri Lynn shrugged her shoulders and left the office. Chris folded the letter, placed it back in the envelope and slid it under his desk pad. He paused and took a deep breath to calm his nerves. His hand trembled as he picked up the phone and answered.

"Lance, how are you?"

"Fine. Listen, Chris. I'm just calling to confirm the time we start tomorrow. It's 7:00 a.m. right?"

"That's right, Lance. Be here at seven in the morning. It will be nice to have someone to ease the workload. I've been under pressure from all sides lately."

"Well, I'm excited about working with you, Chris. See you in the morning."

"Thanks, my friend."

Chris placed the receiver back and sat for a long time pondering. He was beginning to get a glimpse of the picture that was forming from the bits and pieces he had gathered and, up until now, had been puzzled about.

He punched the phone for an outside line and dialed the number.

"Hamilton Medical Services," a young male voice answered.

"Ashley Denton, please."

"One moment, sir."

Chris waited, tapping the top of his desk with his pen.

The young voice came back, "She's not here, sir."

"This is Dr. Burns. Do you know where she went?"

"No, sir, I'm sorry. Could I take a message?"

"No message, thank you."

Chris began to pace back and forth, like a caged animal. His tall, lean frame radiated confusion and concern. He reached into his shirt pocket for Agent Camper's card and dialed the number.

"Good afternoon, Federal Bureau of Investigation."

"This is Dr. Chris Burns. Is Agent Camper in?"

"No, sir. May I have him return your call?"

"Yes, please. Tell him it's urgent."

"Does he have your number, Dr. Burns?"

"Yes, he knows where I work."

"I'll give him the message, sir."

"Thank you."

Chris went into Jeri Lynn's office and poured himself a cup of fresh coffee. She noticed the uneasy expression on his face.

"Christopher Burns, what's your problem? Is Ashley late?" she asked.

Hesitating for a moment and looking over his shoulder to be sure they were alone, he threw up his hands in despair. He could hold it in no longer. "Granny, there's something I have to tell you, and it's going to knock your socks off."

"What is it, Chris?"

He dropped wearily into the chair next to hers and began to relate the whole story.

She sat motionless against the back of her chair, her eyes fixed on her untouched coffee and struggled to control her emotions. "I understand now and I know why he died. Who are these people, Chris?"

"I don't know, Granny. That's what's so frustrating. We don't know who's behind all of this or whom to watch for."

"What are you going to do?"

"I don't know, Granny. I just don't know."

Chris walked slowly down the hall to the men's room. He heard the door open, and when he looked around, Agent Camper stood near the first basin. "I got your message, Dr. Burns. How can I help you?" he asked.

"I have something you need to read," he said as he pumped the lever on the soap dispenser.

"What's that?"

Chris stared through the mirror. "A letter from Dr. Steve Sulcer."

"What's it about?"

Chris vigorously cranked two paper towels from the holder on the wall. "One of the girls you were telling me about."

"Where's the letter?"

He popped his hands dry and disposed of the paper towel. "In my office."

Well...let's go take a look at it."

Chris and the agent left the restroom and walked with long strides back to the office. Chris handed him the letter and he began to read, slowly shaking his head from time to time. There was a long moment of silence after he had finished reading and his eyes stayed focused on the letter. He released a long sigh, then placed it back into the envelope. "I'll have to keep this letter, Dr. Burns."

"I know that, Agent Camper. I don't mind telling you, I'm frightened."

"You have a right to be."

"Who or what is this 'powerful force' Dr. Sulcer spoke of?"

"That's what I'm here to find out."

"When will you know? I feel like time is running out."

"Just sit tight and don't panic. We'll get to the bottom of this."

"I just feel like it needs to be soon."

"Well of course you do, but we can't afford to rush this thing, Dr. Burns. I know how you feel. We have to cover all angles and not take any chances."

"Do you think Blade Henderson's involved in any of this?"

"I don't think so. Henderson is just an amateur who was kicked off the police force in Dallas for sexual harassment. I don't think he's dangerous at all. It goes much higher. That's why time and expertise are so critical. Just try to be patient and let me do my job."

"Okay, but I hope you realize that Ashley's life, and mine too probably, are in the palm of your hands."

"Of course I realize that. I've been in this business a long time, Dr. Burns. Trust me. Maybe Dr. Sulcer is dead because he didn't know whom to trust. You were very wise in going to your father with the information you had."

"Someone has bugged our apartments, and Ashley and I are both being followed."

"Dr. Burns, you're the son of a United States Senator. That alone could pose certain threats. Now, you've accidentally stumbled on to something. Don't ever underestimate the danger you could be in, but try to live as normally as possible."

Chris relaxed his white-knuckled grip on the chair arm, popped a handful of tissue from the box on his desk and mopped the perspiration from his face.

Chris swallowed. "That's going to be hard, but we'll try."

"That's all I need to hear. I'll be in close contact and you know where you can reach me."

Agent Camper walked out of the pathology lab, checked the parking lot and watched the passing traffic for a long moment.

Minutes later he burst into the FBI's Austin field office, stopped and leaned over the counter. The desk clerk looked up from his typing with a blank expression. "You need something, sir?"

"Yes. Who's your electronics expert here?"

"Agent Dean Morgan."

"Find him and tell him to get here immediately."

"Yes, sir."

Thursday, 2:30 p.m. Beth and Ashley entered The Fashion Shop on Fourth Street and were greeted by the owner, Randall Maddox. He was a short, scrawny man with a fringe of gray hair that encircled his bald spot on top. His neck and face were red and covered with tiny broken blood vessels, indicating a chronic, excessive intake of alcohol.

"Beth, my dear, come in, come in." He gave her a slow smile. "This must be the young lady you phoned me about."

"Yes, this is Ashley Denton," she said with a sigh. "We need to look at something suitable for a political dinner."

Randall Maddox didn't answer at once, he was too busy looking.

Beth snapped her fingers close to his face.

He blinked and smiled. "Right this way, ladies."

Their feet sank into the plush carpet as they made their way to the back of the showroom.

"We have a new line of gowns that just arrived." He gave another drooling smile.

They walked slowly down the long rack of evening gowns, and Beth made several selections, all in the most exact taste.

"We'll try these," she said.

Randall Maddox was only half-listening. He was standing with a smug grin on his bony face and his eyes fixed on Ashley.

Ashley smiled and tried to ignore his stare. There aren't enough buses in Texas to transport all the creeps out of Austin, she thought.

"The dressing room's this way," he said and led Ashley across the room. He opened the door and hung the gowns on a rack.

Ashley entered the dressing room, removed her dress and folded it across the bench. The first four gowns she modeled did not appeal to Beth, so Randall handed two more through the door.

"Randall." Beth pointed. "Do you have that black gown on

the mannequin in my size?"

"Yes, dear, of course I do. I had you in mind when I bought it."

"I'll take it. You know to charge these to Hamilton, don't you?"

"Naturally."

While Ashley was still in the dressing room, Beth handed Randall a white envelope containing ten $100 bills.

"What's this for?" He looked puzzled.

Beth handed him a second envelope. "You get the first envelope for sewing this into the gown I select for Ashley."

He opened the envelope and smiled. "If you say so, dear."

As Ashley stepped into the last, mint green, one-shouldered gown and buttoned the one button on the left shoulder, Beth entered the dressing room and said, "That's perfect. It's absolutely breathtaking."

Beth handed the gown to Randall, who disappeared into the alterations room. He gave his seamstress the second envelope with verbal instructions. She placed the green gown on the table and made a small slit under the large rhinestone button that fastened on the left shoulder, slid the roaming wireless bug in, then made long stitches with green thread to close the slit and hold the device in place. She put the dress back on the hanger and covered it with a long plastic bag.

He stepped from the alterations room. Moments later he returned and handed the seamstress yet another envelope that had not come from Beth. "Put this in Beth Wagner's gown," he said.

She followed the same procedure with the black gown Beth had selected. Randall waited and, as soon as the dresses were finished, returned to the showroom. He handed the dresses to Beth and Ashley, then walked with them to the shop exit.

As soon as they were out of sight, Randall hurried into his office, closed the door and dialed the phone.

A gruff voice answered, "Yeah?"

"Stefano, Maddox here. Let me talk to Sal."

"Just a minute, Maddox."

Stefano placed the phone on the table by the sofa. "It's Randall Maddox for you, sir."

"Yeah, what is it, Randall?"

"Wagner was just here."

"Has the seed been planted?"

"Yes, sir, just as you instructed."

"Good."

"But Wagner may be up to something herself."

"How's that?"

"She paid me $1,000 to put another seed in the new redhead's dress. I think you may have problems."

"I do the thinking, Maddox."

"I'm sorry, sir, but I'm worried."

"I also do the worrying. You just keep your mouth shut and do what I tell you, understand?"

"Yes, sir."

Stefano took the phone and placed it back in its cradle.

"He's too much of a risk, Stefano. If someone gets wise to the bug on the girl and puts pressure on him, I'm afraid he'd sing like a bird. He's too nervous, and I don't trust him. Take care of him."

"Yes, sir."

"Did that shipment of goods go out today?"

"Yes, sir. It left for Austin early this morning."

"When will it get there?"

"Saturday afternoon, sir."

"Call our man in Austin and have him pick it up Monday. Tell him to hold it until he hears otherwise."

"Yes, sir."

It was a 20-minute drive back to the Hamilton Building. The temperature in the white Corvette, which had been parked in the sun, was unbearable. Beth patted her face with a tissue and, with the touch of a button, lowered the windows until the air conditioner had cooled the car. She and Ashley rode in silence until they entered the expressway.

"Are you pleased with the gown?" Beth asked.

"Yes, it's lovely, and so is yours."

"Are you nervous?"

"Not much. I'll be okay once I get there."

"Tell me about Chris."

"What would you like to know?"

"Are you two planning to get married?"

Ashley stared straight ahead, but the words on the tip of her tongue remained unspoken. Instead, she replied, "Possibly, someday."

"You know it's against our policy."

"I don't understand your policy."

"Don't worry about it. We'll work out something. You're a very good employee, and we'd hate to lose you."

"I like my job. I'd like to go back to school and get a degree. You have a degree, don't you, Beth?"

"Yes, in computer science. I got mine the hard way."

"What do you mean?"

"It's not worth discussing."

Again, they rode in silence. Ashley waited for her to say something else, ask more questions, but instead Beth patted the fine line of perspiration over her upper lip and stared quietly at the highway. It was 4:25 p.m. when they arrived back at the Hamilton Building and parked the white Corvette.

"There's no point in going back inside, Ashley. I'm going home. You can too if you like. I'll see you in the morning."

Ashley placed the gown in the back seat of her car and pulled out of the drive into the traffic.

When she arrived at the apartment, Chris was sitting outside on the concrete bench. "Where were you all afternoon?" he asked with relief as she sat down beside him.

125

"Beth took me downtown to get a gown for Saturday night. Why?"

"I was just worried about you, that's all. I called and the office boy didn't know where you went. Where was the security guard?"

"I don't know. Are you okay, Chris?"

"I love you, Ashley."

"What kind of answer is that?"

He wrapped his arm around her shoulder and pulled her close. "Let's go in and freshen up. I'm starved."

CHAPTER TWELVE

At seven that evening, Chris and Ashley drove to Wylie's Bar and Grill on Sixth Street for dinner. They parked on the asphalt lot and walked around the corner of the building to the front entrance. It was one of those hot, sultry nights in early August, and the air felt like it had come out of a teakettle.

Chris stopped at the door and looked around. He had not seen the Cadillac that day. Maybe the hounds had been called off, or maybe they were more careful about being seen.

The maitre d' seated them, and while they discussed the menu, he closed the folding doors of the private dining room located to the right of the main seating area. Smoke drifted from the overstuffed room as friends and co-workers boisterously cheered and clicked expensive stemware to one of Austin's most prominent lawyers.

Chris eyed the folding doors, frowned and, releasing a loud sigh, waved to the maitre d' who came immediately and asked, "How may I help you, sir?"

"Do you have another table with a little more privacy?" he asked in an angry tone.

"I believe we do, sir. Just a moment and I'll check for you."

Ashley leaned over the table and asked, "Chris, what on earth's bothering you? I've never seen you get so upset over a little noise. What's going on?"

"I'm sorry, Ashley. I'm just a little on edge."

The maitre d' returned and escorted them to a table near the

127

back of the large dining room. "I'm sorry for the inconvenience, sir. Just a little victory dinner for Mr. Sloan. He won a tough trial today, and they tend to get a little loud sometimes. I hope this table meets with your approval."

"Yes, this is fine, thank you. We're ready to order now."

"Yes, sir."

A waiter came, took both orders and left. Ashley reached across the table and placed her hand on his arm. "Why are you acting so strangely, Chris? You questioned me about where I was this afternoon and never finished the conversation. Tell me what's going on. You're scaring me."

He propped an elbow on the table with a forefinger encircling his mouth. "I got a letter from Dr. Sulcer today."

"You got a letter from Dr. Sulcer? He's dead."

"He wrote it before he died."

"I don't understand, Chris."

Chris took several deep breaths to calm his quivering voice. "In the letter, he confessed that he'd been forced to falsify the autopsy report on April Crafton."

"How could someone force him to do that?"

"By threatening his family."

"Oh God, the poor man!"

"He had planned to retire in October, but Jeri Lynn told me he got a phone call the day before he died that really seemed to upset him. Then he told her he wouldn't be retiring until the end of the year. I wonder if there was something about that phone call that made him change his mind?"

Two waiters returned, popped open their small folding tables next to the unoccupied chairs and gracefully lowered the large trays of food from their shoulders. With swiftness and ease, they removed the silver domes and placed the meal neatly on the table. They refilled the water glasses, snapped their tables together and marched back to the kitchen.

Ashley folded her fingers around the stem of the glass. "There's more to this, isn't there, Chris?"

"Yeah. I'm afraid so, Ash. Dr. Sulcer advised me to do the same thing if someone should approach me in the future. That's why I'm so upset."

"Who are these people?"

"That's what's so frightening. No one seems to know. A special FBI agent followed me to the Pizza Hut today at lunch and told me that you and I could be in danger."

"Did he say why?"

"No."

"What do we do in the meantime?"

"Try to live as normally as possible."

Ashley pushed her salad aside and placed her napkin beside her unfinished plate. "How can we live, 'as normally as possible,' looking over our shoulders every minute of the day, and how can we sleep at night knowing that every time we sneeze, someone, somewhere, probably smiles and says, bless you?"

"I don't know, Ash. I don't seem to have the right answers. I'm sure FBI agents will be following us now, so maybe the unknown force will recognize them and back off. That's about the only hope I have right now."

"Chris, how in the hell did we get ourselves in such a mess?"

The maitre d' appeared and handed Chris a message, bowed and vanished. Chris opened the note and read aloud. "Call me as soon as possible. Camper."

"Who's Camper?" Ashley asked.

"The FBI agent I was telling you about. Wait here, I'll see what he wants. Be right back, Ash."

Chris worked his way through the Wednesday-night regulars and went through the lobby to the pay phones. He removed a coin from his pocket, dropped it in a phone and dialed.

After two rings, a pleasant voice answered, "Federal Bureau of Investigation."

"This is Dr. Burns. I'm returning Agent Camper's call."

"Yes, sir, one moment, please."

His call was placed on hold, and Chris propped his elbow against the wall, rubbing the back of his neck as he waited.

"Dr. Burns?" Camper asked.

"Yes, I got a message to call you. Is anything wrong?"

"No, I was wondering if you knew some place we could meet?"

For a moment, Chris's mind went blank, then he had an idea. "Yes, Hogan Funeral Home. Right now I can't remember the address."

"I'll find it. Can you meet me there in 30 minutes?"

"Yes. Come to the back door."

"Is Miss Denton with you?"

"Yes, she is. Why?"

"Bring her with you. I need to talk to both of you."

"Okay. We'll see you in 30 minutes."

"Be careful, Dr. Burns. Make sure you're not followed."

"I'll do my best."

Uncle Charlie Hogan had married Senator Burns's younger sister, Evelyn. They had bought an old funeral home 20 years ago and renovated it into one of the nicest in the state. Chris spent most of his childhood vacations with his two cousins, Chip, his own age, and Max, a year younger, running through the parlors and playing hide-and-seek in the coffins. He smiled as he remembered the old fly swatter Uncle Charlie kept hanging by the office door to swat their behinds if they misbehaved.

Helping Uncle Charlie in the funeral home was where he decided to become a pathologist, and those were some of the happiest days of his life. He found himself longing for yesterday and wishing he could once again slip into one of those satin-lined coffins and hide until all of the ghosts and goblins had disappeared. For a fleeting moment, he wondered how soon it would be before he would actually be placed in one and returned to the earth. He shivered and forced those thoughts from his mind.

He walked around to the entrance of the dining room and, after a few seconds, caught Ashley's attention. He motioned, she picked up her purse and joined him at the cashier's desk.

Twenty minutes later, they parked in the rear of the funeral home. Ashley slid across the seat to Chris's side, and he reached for her hand. They looked across the parking lot and casually walked to the entrance. Chris checked his watch for the hundredth time, fingered the knot of his tie and knocked lightly. Uncle Charlie opened the door and smiled broadly. "Well, Chris and Ashley, what are you two doing here?"

They stepped inside the long hall without speaking. Uncle Charlie pushed the door shut and looked at Chris, noticing the tense muscles of his face and the anxiety in his eyes. "What's going on, son?"

"I wish I knew, Uncle Charlie."

"What do you mean?"

"It's a long story, and right now, none of it makes much sense."

"I have plenty of time, so why don't you start at the beginning and maybe I can help you."

Chris relaxed his shoulders and slowly recounted his story as Uncle Charlie stood speechless. When he had finished, he lifted both hands and shrugged. "That's about all I can tell you right now, Uncle Charlie."

"Good Lord, Chris, I had no idea. What are you going to do?"

"I'm meeting an FBI agent, and he should be here any minute. I hope you don't mind."

"Well, of course not. If there's any way at all I can help you, son, just let me know."

"Just being able to talk to someone helps a lot, Uncle Charlie."

"I wish I had some answers for you, Chris."

A soft knock was heard, and Chris glanced nervously at the back door. Uncle Charlie held his hand on the door knob and looked at Chris. "Just stay put. I'll get it."

A few seconds later, Uncle Charlie led Agent Camper into the office. "I'll be in the lounge if you need me."

"Thanks, Uncle Charlie." Chris nodded.

"Agent Tony Camper, this is my fiancée, Ashley Denton."

"Pleased to meet you, Miss Denton."

"Likewise, I'm sure."

"Were you followed?" Camper asked.

"No," Chris answered quickly. "I made sure of it."

"Good." He paused for a second and rubbed his forehead. "Miss Denton, Chris told me this afternoon about the listening devices in your apartments. How did you find out they were there?"

"A girlfriend at work told me our offices were bugged and probably my apartment."

"Did she say why?"

"Not exactly, but we assumed for security purposes. All the files in the Hamilton Building are confidential."

"I see. I can understand the tight security at the office, but bugging your apartments doesn't make sense...unless something else is going on. I noticed the building has three stories. How many offices are there?"

"Twenty-three, counting the security guard's office at the front entrance."

Camper bit on his bottom lip in thought. "Could you give me a description of the floor plan inside the building? For instance, how many offices are there on the first, second and third floors?"

"There are ten offices on the first floor and twelve on the second. I've never been on the third floor, so I don't know what's up there."

"Is it off limits or something?"

"I don't know. I don't ever see any of the other girls go up there, but there is another elevator just for that floor and it takes a special code card. My friend, who's worked for Hamilton four years, told me that."

"Has she ever been up there?"

"No."

"If she's never been up there, how does she know about the special code card?"

"She opened the door at the end of the hall one day and saw Beth Wagner use a card to get on the elevator. Later, my friend tried one of the cards we use and it didn't work."

Camper wiped the sweat from his forehead and blotted his hand on the side of his pants. "Miss Denton, I'm going to ask you a question and I'll understand if you say no."

Ashley looked at him solemnly. "What's that, Agent Camper?"

"Do you think you could place a listening device in Miss Wagner's office without being seen?"

Ashley thought for a long moment before answering. "I believe I could."

"It will involve some risk, but would you be willing to do it?"

"Do you think it would help us get to the bottom of all this?"

"I believe it might."

"Then I'll do it."

"Oh, by the way, Miss Denton," Agent Camper added, "it would certainly be helpful if you could somehow get us a copy of that special code card. I need to know what's on that third floor."

Thursday, 8:30 a.m. Ashley entered the Hamilton Building, pausing a moment as she passed the cubicle, and placed her card in the last security door.

She switched on the light in her office and sat her purse

under the phone table. She turned on her computer and walked down the hall to the restroom where she stared at her reflection in the mirror above the basin, hoping the uneasy feeling in the pit of her stomach would soon calm itself. Her common sense told her there was little else to do but accept the situation, because, like it or not, she had a job to do and she was going to give it her best.

Ashley opened the restroom door and stepped out into the hall just in time to see Beth enter the elevator and the doors close behind her. Now was her chance, she thought.

She walked briskly down the deserted hall, through the security door to Beth's office, opened the door and slipped inside. She found herself perspiring profusely as she hurriedly reached into her pocket and retrieved the device Agent Camper had given her. The artificial flower arrangement on Beth's desk was exactly where she had seen it before. Quickly, she positioned the bug inconspicuously among the flowers. Now, she thought, if only she could find Beth's purse, she could probably find the card to the third floor elevator, and, if all went well, make a copy.

She walked behind the desk and quickly pushed the chair aside. In vain, she searched frantically through the three drawers on the left. The purse was not there. Her heart pounded.

She turned to the drawers on the right and thought, it has to be here somewhere. She knelt down and pulled the bottom drawer open. There it was.

She stared at the contents, and her hands trembled as she attempted to locate the card. A noise in the hall startled her, and she automatically raised a hand to her mouth. She strained to hear more, but silence returned and she felt her panic disappear.

She hurriedly searched and, seeing the wallet, pulled it from the purse, snapped it open and found a card. "Oh, God, is this the right one?" she whispered to herself. Then she remembered, Beth was on the second floor. This had to be the right card.

Suddenly she was aware of the rumble of the security door as it opened. She listened carefully, then heard another familiar sound -- the clicking of Beth's heels against the tiled floor. She thought, "Oh no, she's coming back to the office." How would she be able to explain what she was doing there?

Breathlessly, her eyes searched the room for a way out. She was gripped with fear as she suddenly realized she was trapped.

Moments before the office door opened, Ashley stepped inside the darkness of Beth's bathroom, pulling the door shut behind her. She could hear the shuffling of feet as she stood quietly in the corner. There was silence for a moment, then there was the sound of the bathroom door opening. Ashley held her breath as she watched a slender hand slide along the wall in search of the light switch. At that moment, she heard a man's voice in the office.

"Beth?" Louis Hamilton asked.

The slender hand slid from the light switch and pulled the door shut again.

"Yes, Louis. What can I do for you?"

"Do you have the sheets for this month's business yet?"

"Not yet. I was just about to print them out. Do you want to wait?"

"Sure," he replied.

After an eternity, the soft clicking of the computer keys and the noisy printer ceased. Beth ripped off the printout and handed it to Louis. "Thank you," he said. "Do you have a minute?"

"Sure, what else do you need?"

"Come down to my office, there's a couple of things I need to go over with you."

Beth grabbed a pencil and her steno pad, closed her office door and followed Louis down the hall.

Ashley slid weakly to the floor and braced her head on her knees, breathing deeply and slowly. Her nerves tingling, she placed her head against the door and strained her ears for any unusual sound. Hearing nothing more, she stood and slowly opened the door. She walked quickly to the code machine and placed a blank in the card slot. With a trembling tracing finger, she followed the instructions, punching in the code numbers as she read. She tapped the enter key. The machine rumbled and made loud screeching noises, then ejected the unchanged card onto the floor.

For a moment, anger swept through her as she picked up the blank and placed it back into the slot. What had gone wrong? She punched in the code a second time and looked down. There, below the enter bar, was a triangle-shaped key marked, 'press to emboss.' She closed her eyes and pressed. It worked. She picked up the new card and put it in her dress pocket. She returned Beth's card to the purse and closed the desk drawer.

She slowly opened the door and looked down the hall. It was deserted. Staring straight ahead, she hurried through the security door and back to her office. After several long breaths, she sat down in front of her computer, propped her elbows on the desk and held her face in her hands. "Thank you, God," she whispered.

Beth settled herself comfortably in Louis Hamilton's office, and he closed the door. "Is everything all set for the political dinner Saturday night?" he asked as he pulled his chair from the desk and seated himself.

"Yes. Ashley will be rehearsing tonight, and I'll be putting the final touches on the tables."

"Good. When will the vice president arrive?"

"Only a few hours before his speech."

"Good. Will his wife be joining him?"

"No, she's too involved in her D.C. socials."

"That's too bad. She needs to be by his side at these functions. It's very important. It's bad business when the little woman always stays at home."

"Well," she sighed, "it's her loss."

"What do you mean by that?"

"Nothing...just thinking out loud."

He nodded, put his reading glasses on and opened a folder on his desk.

"There's one more item I wanted to discuss with you, Beth."

"What's that, Louis?"

"Are we all set for the heart surgeons next week?"

"Yes, everything's been entered in the computers."

"Good." He lifted the folder from his desk.

"Is all the bookkeeping up-to-date?"

"Yes."

"Bank accounts?"

"Yes. What's with all the questions, Louis? Are you expecting to die or something?"

"No, the truth of the matter is, the surgeons will be here next week to look over the business to buy, not join, and they'll be bringing in their own auditors to go over the books."

Beth's eyes bugged out on a stem, and she strongly resembled an albino bumblebee. "Louis, have you lost you're ever-loving mind?"

"No, I've never been more serious in my life."

"What are you going to do?"

"Retire. I've bought a place down on St. Thomas. I plan to spend the rest of my days basking in the sun."

"What about the rest of us?"

"There'll be no change as far as employee status goes. That'll be in the agreement."

He closed the folder and removed his glasses. "I have to go to a meeting at the country club in a few minutes. I'll be back sometime this afternoon."

He came around his desk, leaned over and kissed her on the

cheek. He left his office, and shortly afterward, she heard the security door click behind him.

She sat there for a moment longer, completely stunned, then bolted down the hall and slammed the door to her office. She paced back and forth and mumbled, "Blade, you picked a helluva day for a dental appointment."

Thursday, 8:00 p.m. Chris and Ashley sat in the dimly lighted ballroom of the Driskill Hotel waiting for the band to tune their instruments for rehearsal.

"Chris, I wish I didn't have to do this. I'm nervous and I suspect everyone who smiles at me."

"I know, Ash, but we've got to go on living and not let this get to us. I feel like it'll be over soon."

"I sure hope you're right."

"Where's your boss?" he asked, to change the subject.

"Mr. Hamilton?"

"No, Beth Wagner."

Ashley pointed. "Up there. She's in charge of the table arrangements for the dinner."

"She's nice looking."

"Yeah."

Chris leaned back in his seat, made himself comfortable and the band director motioned to Ashley. She walked to the front and began her part of the rehearsal.

Beth joined Chris in the back of the room. "So, you're Dr. Burns?"

"Yes, and you must be Beth Wagner."

She turned her head toward Ashley. "She certainly has a beautiful voice."

"She does, doesn't she," he answered.

After a few moments of deliberate silence, Chris excused himself and walked down the hall to the men's room. As he bent over the basin to wash his hands, Camper entered, looked in the mirror and asked, "Is there anyone else in here?"

"No."

"Was Miss Denton able to do what I asked?"

"Yes."

"Good, maybe now we can come up with some answers."

"I sure hope so."

CHAPTER THIRTEEN

Friday, 7:00 a.m. Agents Camper and Morgan parked the green surveillance van on the service road that ran parallel between the highway and the back of the Hamilton Building. They took their places in the back, flipped on the recorders and adjusted the receivers.

Morgan leaned back in his seat and popped the top of a Diet Coke. "Think you'll find anything here, Camper?"

"It's a little early to tell, but I have to start somewhere."

Morgan scratched his bushy head. "It's hard to believe something shady could be going on at Hamilton Medical. They're such a large, well-known company."

Camper frowned. "Sometimes we get the hell shocked out of us where we least expect it," he said, as he leaned back and folded his arms across his chest.

"Is this your first trip to Texas, Camper?"

"No, I've been here several times to visit an old college buddy."

"What part of Texas?"

"Dallas. My buddy went into the cattle business. Artificial insemination, he called it."

"Well...when we wrap up this case, you should take a few days and pay him a visit."

"I'd love to see him, but he's not in Texas anymore."

"What happened to the cattle business?"

"He lost his ass. I haven't kept track of him since then."

Morgan chuckled. "Well...that artificial business ain't all it's cracked up to be."

Suddenly Camper pulled himself upright and centered his eyes on the receivers. He planted his feet apart and braced his elbows on the narrow shelf that supported the equipment.

Morgan, sucking loudly on a peppermint stick, sprang up with his back straight and began adjusting the knobs. "What was that loud noise?"

Camper waved a hand in the air for silence.

Eight o'clock. Beth stormed through the front entrance of the Hamilton Building, barking orders to Blade, who had just unlocked his cubicle and made himself comfortable with a cup of fresh coffee.

"Come to my office, Blade," she said with a vigorous motion of her arm.

He picked up his cup of coffee and followed her into the office. She slammed her purse on the desk and seated herself firmly in her chair.

"What's wrong, love?"

"We've got problems, Blade."

"What are you talking about?"

"Louis Hamilton is selling out and the group that's buying will be here next week with their own auditors."

"Can't you fix the books so they won't find anything?"

"No, there's not enough time. I was planning to do that at the end of this month."

"What the hell are we going to do?"

"We'll have to leave a lot sooner than we'd planned."

"How much money do we have?"

"Not nearly as much as I'd hoped to have."

"Don't worry, Beth. If that's not enough, I have something in my apartment that would be worth a few million."

"What the hell are you talking about, Blade?"

"Videos."

"What kind of videos?"

With a smug grin he replied, "Mostly of the Vondonitti family."

"What do you mean, mostly?"

"I taped all our drug deals with the Vondonittis, and I didn't let you loan my apartment to the vice president and your friend April just because I'm a nice guy."

"Are you telling me you had the nerve to videotape April Crafton and Drew Ramsey in your apartment? And right under the nose of the Secret Service? Don't you know you wouldn't live to see the sun set if certain people found out about this?"

"I'll take my chances. Besides, you're the only person who has a code card to my apartment, so how will anybody find out?"

"Those videos will probably turn out to be a mistake, Blade."

"Relax, love. Sometimes you have to gamble a little to make a lot. Have you made all the bank transfers yet?"

"Yes, or I should say, all I'll be able to make now. Do you have a buyer for the yacht?"

"That can be arranged with a simple phone call."

"Then do it."

At the usual time and the usual place, Jacob Hughes pulled around to the same drive-through speaker and heard the same cheerful voice say, "Thank you for choosing McDonald's. May I take your order, please?" This had been his routine every morning for the past five years; a sausage and biscuit and a cup of black coffee. Not eating too fast or driving too slow, he was always parking the car at his office as the last bite was swallowed.

Lena Chadwick, his devoted secretary for the past five years, jammed the brush of her red fingernail polish back into the bottle and secured the lid as he entered the office. "New color?" he asked.

She blushed and set the bottle aside.

"Get me the file on April Crafton, if you can spare the time."

He reached for the stack of mail that Lena had picked up at the post office on her way to work, thumbed through it and placed it back on the desk. Nothing important, just a couple of bills to be paid and a letter with Ed McMahon's picture on the front.

Lena opened the file cabinet with one hand and flipped the folders until she reached April Crafton's file. She stuck the other elbow between the folders, pulled up one behind April's name and closed the file drawer, all without smudging one wet fingernail.

She handed him April's folder and he thanked her. He had marveled many times during the past five years at her speed and accuracy using only one hand.

He sat down at his desk and opened the folder. His file differed somewhat from the reports he had turned in to the Hamilton group. He had known what they expected and all his reports had met their specifications. For instance, he had not reported the existence of April's brother or her mother, both living and well. He had never felt that relatives were relevant to the company.

April's brother owned the Lake Travis Resort, just 13 miles west of Austin. He couldn't remember the last time he had been to Lake Travis. He closed the file and left the office.

Jacob drove slowly and admired the resort communities and homes of the wealthy that lined the banks of Lake Travis, wondering how many anglers, in search of largemouth and striped bass, spent their vacations there each year. He remembered that Lake Travis was one of seven lakes that stairstepped 150 miles down the Colorado River to Austin.

Bud Joe Crafton was a true bona fide Texan. Bud Joe chewed tobacco and loved the Dallas Cowboys.

143

Bud Joe liked women, fried chicken and Ross Perot. Bud Joe hated snakes and spiders. Bud Joe's resort was Bud Joe's life. He had bought Lake Travis Resort with the insurance money left by his deceased father six years earlier. He had seen the ad in the *Austin Chronicle*, seeking a buyer for the so-called popular resort, and after a serious discussion with his mother, he persuaded her to accompany him to make inquiries and inspect the possibilities.

Unlike his mother, he could see potential and a sound investment in the dilapidated cabins and long row of boat docks. After a short meeting with the elderly owners, he felt something approaching shame at his rock-bottom offer, not dreaming they would consider such a ridiculous price, but to his surprise, they accepted. Despite his mother's frequent comments about possibly losing his father's hard-earned money, Bud Joe closed the deal and within a month had started renovation of the ten run-down cabins.

After a few minutes of pleasurable driving, Jacob passed a sign that read, "LAKE TRAVIS RESORT, ONE MILE AHEAD, BUD JOE CRAFTON, OWNER." He slowed his car to a crawl as he entered the last curve and could see the resort office straight ahead. All the cabins looked the same, attractive and warm. This haven of solitude was a far cry from the big city, he thought, and two weeks here would be a nice gift of appreciation for a couple of kids he had grown very fond of. Pleased with his impulsive idea, he pulled under the office canopy, turned off the motor and went inside.

Bud Joe was just a 'good ole boy.' He wore blue jeans, a plaid cowboy shirt and boots. He was 35, tall and lean, still single and comfortable with that arrangement. With his strong facial features, deep tan and a mane of dark, wind-blown hair, he carried a strong likeness to one of the rugged mountain climbers in a major beer ad. He lived with his mother in a six-room apartment built onto the back of the resort office.

Jacob removed his hat and sunglasses. "Bud Joe?" he asked.

"Yeah, that's me."

"I'm Jacob Hughes."

"Yeah, I remember you. You came to April's funeral. I never forget a name or a face."

"I've heard that."

"What brangs you out here, fishin'?"

"No."

"Then what?" He squinted his black eyes. "Runnin' from the law?"

Jacob smiled and wiped his forehead. "Wrong again. I have a couple of friends getting married, and I wanted to give them a nice wedding present."

"This resort ain't fer sale."

"Don't want to buy the resort, Bud Joe, just a couple of weeks out here in the peace and quiet. Both of my friends like to fish."

Bud Joe laughed heartily. "You thank them newlyweds is gonna take the time to fish?"

"How much for two weeks?"

"Two hundred and fifty dollars."

"That's fine," Jacob muttered and handed him cash.

"What's the name?"

"Just put it on the books in my name. Okay?"

"Anything you say, Mr. Hughes. When will they be coming?"

"I'm not sure, just keep the date open. Can you promise complete privacy?"

"Sure can, Mr. Hughes, nobody'll ever know they're here."

Jacob handed him a crisp $100 bill. "That's just for you. Take care of my friends. Okay?"

"You bet, Mr. Hughes, and I thank ye."

"Thank you, Bud Joe. By the way, how's your mother

doing?"

"She ain't. Since April died, she ain't been worth killing."

"That's too bad, Bud Joe. Tell her I asked about her."

"I'll do that. You have a nice one, Mr. Hughes."

Jacob walked out to the end of the resort driveway and took several deep breaths. The soft breeze was cool and smelled clean. He had forgotten that air used to be invisible.

He sauntered down to the edge of the lake and propped his right foot on a large rock. He tossed a pebble into the water and watched his reflection disappear into the ripples. April and his own daughter weighed heavily on his mind. Suddenly, the painful memories of his wife's death, ten years ago last month, flooded his mind. After her death, he and Michelle had been especially close. He felt alone and tears welled up in his eyes.

He tossed another pebble into the water and turned to go back to his car when a large yacht docked at a pier about 300 yards away caught his eye. He pulled off his sunglasses and strained to read the name printed in gold on the side, "THE ELIZABETH." That name suddenly struck a raw nerve.

He quickly walked back and stepped inside the resort office.

Bud Joe sprang up from his lazy sprawl. "Forget something, Mr. Hughes?"

Jacob ignored the question. "Who owns that big yacht down the way, Bud Joe?"

"Oh...some rich dame from the city. Why?"

"Do you know her name?"

"Sure do, Mr. Hughes. I never forget a name or a face. She was at Sissy's funeral too. Her name's Beth Wagner. Sharp looking, but she's way outta my league."

"Has she been in here?"

"Yeah, she came in here and asked me to keep an eye out for her fancy tug."

"What'd you tell her?"

"Told her I already had enough to do."

"Have you seen anybody else down there?"

"Yeah, some big dude. Looks kinda like a football player."

"Did you find out his name?"

"Naw, he ain't been down here to the office. He was down there last night, carried a few boxes on the boat, then left."

"Has anybody else been here asking questions?"

"Yeah, now that you mention it, there's been two other fellers."

"Do you remember what they looked like?"

"Yeah...well, one of 'em had a badge. Said his name was Tony Camper, a big-shot Fed."

"What'd he want?"

"He asked me a bunch of questions about my sister. He didn't say anything about the boat."

"What kind of questions?"

"Oh...had she ever been in trouble before and had she ever took any dope. That made me real mad and he could tell. I told that sum-bitch to get the hell outa my face, so he left."

"Who else's been here?"

"The other feller didn't leave a name. He was tall, had blond hair and combed it down in front, like a girl's. I got bad vibes from him and I acted dumb. He didn't hang 'round long either."

Jacob patted Bud Joe on the shoulder. "You're a damn good man, Bud Joe, don't you ever change."

When Jacob got back to the office, Lena handed him two telephone messages. One was from Chris and the other from Louis Hamilton. "Get Chris back on the line and tell him I'm on my way over to the lab. I need to talk to him, but not over the phone."

"Yes, sir," she answered.

Jacob parked in one of the visitors parking spaces and entered the State Crime Lab on the ground floor. He opened the door marked Pathology Lab and stepped in on the green tile floor, noticing that some of the tiles were chipped on the corners. It felt like the North Pole and smelled of strong chemicals. He walked a few steps down the hall and stopped at the first office on the right.

Jeri Lynn sat typing with her back to the door when he knocked. She whirled around and flashed a slight smile. "Could I help you?"

"Yes, I'm Jacob Hughes and I believe Dr. Burns is expecting me."

"Yes, sir, he is. Right this way."

She slid out of her chair, wiggled around the desk in her three-inch heels and motioned for Jacob to follow. Down the hall another ten steps, she knocked twice on the door. "Mr. Hughes is here."

"Good, show him in."

She smiled and swayed back down the hall.

Jacob opened the door and went in. "Chris, how are you?"

"Fine." Chris scratched the top of his head with his pen. "Listen, Jacob, I've been thinking. Maybe we should get in touch with Louis Hamilton and have a talk with him, maybe even tell him about the letter from Dr. Sulcer. What do you think?"

"You really think it's possible he may not know what's going on at his office? It would be tragic if he doesn't and we sit on this. Remember, I've worked for Louis Hamilton, and this just isn't his style."

Jeri Lynn appeared in the doorway. "Excuse me, Mr. Hughes, there's a Lena Chadwick on the phone. She says it's urgent."

"Thanks."

Chris handed him the receiver. "What is it, Lena?"

"Mr. Louis Hamilton called back and says he needs to see

you right away. He says it's urgent."

"Do you still have him on the line?"

"Yes, he's holding on line one."

Jacob muffled the receiver and spoke to Chris. "Louis Hamilton wants to talk. What do you think? Should we consider this a good omen and ask him to meet with us?"

Chris nodded.

"Good. Lena, tell him to come over to the State Crime Lab and ask for Dr. Burns. He's located on the ground floor in the pathology lab."

Twenty minutes later, Louis Hamilton entered Jeri Lynn's office. "I believe Dr. Burns is expecting me."

She stopped typing and turned around. "You must be Mr. Hamilton."

"Call me Louis."

She rose and started around the end of her desk. One of her heels caught on a chipped tile for the tenth time and she stumbled. He caught her in his arms and could feel the flutter of her heart pounding against his chest as he held her close. He loosened his grip, she regained her balance and stood. Their eyes held for a long moment, then she smiled. "I'm Jeri Lynn."

He smiled back. "Are you all right?"

"Yes, I think so," she said as she straightened her form-fitting dress. "Dr. Burns's office is the first door on the right."

"Thank you, Jeri Lynn." He walked smoothly and rapidly down the hall and knocked.

Jacob opened the door, made introductions and Chris offered Louis a seat.

Chris excused himself and walked back to Jeri Lynn's office. He brewed a pot of fresh coffee, giving ample time for Louis to discuss his urgent business with Jacob. He poured three cups, went back to his office and distributed the hot liquid.

He set down his coffee and seated himself.

Louis nervously sipped his coffee as Chris verbalized Dr. Sulcer's letter. Slowly the blood drained from his face and his deep tan all but vanished. "My God, I had no idea," he swore in a perfectly audible whisper. "I've been such a damn fool."

For the next 30 minutes, Chris and Jacob went over the details they had gathered and told him of their suspicions.

"It should come as no shock to you that since you're one of the wealthiest men in Texas, there could even be a motive for your murder here somewhere," Jacob warned. "What kind of business arrangements do you have with Beth Wagner, if you don't mind my asking?"

"She gets ten percent of net profits at the end of each year as long as I live. At my death, she would have the option to buy, and if she chooses not to buy, she would only get five percent of the net profits and the remaining 95 percent would be divided equally among my three nephews."

"What happens if you sell your business to the group of Houston surgeons?" Jacob asked frowning.

Louis took a sip of coffee. "The contract with Beth would be null and void."

"Louis, do you realize what kind of position this puts you in?" Jacob asked.

"I've never really stopped to think about it. Selling out was one of those spur of the moment things. I suddenly realized I was just plain burned out and needed to find a good woman, get married and live a little before I get too old."

Chris eyed Louis intently. "Maybe you should reconsider selling out right now."

"I'll certainly take your advice and give this some more thought."

Jacob crushed his Styrofoam cup and tossed it in the waste can. "Chris and I thought this was important for you to know."

"I certainly appreciate your concern." He stood and walked

toward the door, placing his hand on the knob. "Oh, Jacob, I almost forgot. I was supposed to escort Ashley to the political dinner Saturday night, but I have an urgent matter in St. Thomas that requires my immediate attention. In fact, I'm flying down there today. Would you mind making other arrangements for me?"

"Not at all, I'll take care of it. Have a nice trip. It's good that you'll be out of harm's way. The next few days are going to be crucial."

Louis stopped in Jeri Lynn's office and cleared his throat. She looked up from her typing and smiled.

"I'll be gone for a few days, but when I get back, would you have dinner with me?" he asked.

"I'd love to, Mr. Hamilton."

"Call me Louis." He gave her a dreamy smile. "I didn't see a ring on your hand."

"That's right, No ring, no man."

"Good, I'd like to know you better." He glanced at his watch. "I have a plane to catch, but I'll see you as soon as I get back."

She watched him leave the office and ran to the window. She stood with her face pressed against the glass until he was lost in the traffic.

God! What a prize, she thought. Handsome, debonair and one of the richest men in Texas. And...he wanted to know her better. That did it. Her mind was very clear now, and Luther had disappeared for the last time. When she got home, she would put his ass in the street, once and for all!

151

CHAPTER FOURTEEN

At age 16, Benjamin Sarrelli knew he had the ability to forge and counterfeit. He had studied counterfeit money and forging in various museums, money exhibits and libraries. He had concentrated on the mistakes of the amateurs, incorrect paper and inks, vowing that he would never be sloppy or unprofessional.

By age 25, he had accumulated over one million dollars in exchange for his bogus $100 bills. He had become a perfectionist, and studied carefully by the banks, his counterfeit bills had been declared authentic.

He had bought property and invested heavily in the stock market. Through these honest dealings, he succeeded in earning over two million dollars a year. His business began to expand, and he needed associates, men he could trust. Those he selected to become his confidants had backgrounds similar to his own, and each had a specific talent.

At twelve noon, Dr. Mel Vincent walked into the Riverside Country Club, one of Washington's most elite. The maitre d' greeted him with a grin. "Mr. Sarrelli is waiting for you in the private dining room, sir."

Dr. Vincent had a pleasant smile, and at the age of 48, his thick, black hair, without any signs of graying, and his tall, well-proportioned physique gave him the appearance of a much younger man. There are those men who can catch every eye in a room with their presence, and Mel Vincent was one of them. He had an undeniable look of rich breeding.

"Mel, how are you?" Benjamin stood and shook his hand. "Have a seat." He motioned for the waiter.

Lunch consisted of salads with hot rolls, coffee and chocolate cake, Benjamin's favorite. They ate at a small table near the double glass doors that led out to the swimming pool.

After the meal, Benjamin took a large piece of cake on his fork and shoved it between his teeth. As he chewed and talked at the same time, cake spilled from the corner of his mouth. He took his ring finger, pushed it back and wiped his mouth and fingers on the napkin.

"What's on your mind, Benjamin?"

"I need a favor."

"How can I refuse? You kept me out of prison."

"That was a long time ago and you were set up."

"What's the favor you need?"

"There's not much to it. No risk involved. No danger."

"What, then?"

Benjamin outlined the specific details of his plan in a matter of minutes.

"How do I fit in all of this?" the doctor asked.

"I want you to go over to the Veterans Hospital in Baltimore and find me such a man as I described. You'll pick him up when the time comes and take him to the designated area. I'll prepare all the necessary identification cards and papers for him. Have him wear an Air Force colonel's uniform when you pick him up. "Here's the ID card you'll need to get in the hospital and the other papers I told you about. As of now, you are Dr. Jeff Trenton. Make it sound good and bring me a full report."

Dr. Mel Vincent drove to the Veterans Hospital in Baltimore, Maryland. The secretary slid the glass window open, and he flashed his credentials. She glanced down at the ID card, turned pale and looked up with a forced smile. "Just a moment, Dr. Trenton." She snatched the phone out of the cradle, turned her back to the window and muttered something short and low.

Seconds later, a tall, slender man with gray hair introduced himself as the administrator. He looked like a retired Army colonel. "What a surprise, Dr. Trenton. We weren't expecting anyone from the Joint Commission back so soon. Is there a problem?" His voice was loud and deep and he spoke like an Army colonel.

"No problem, we're just full of surprises."

"What can I do for you?"

"I just want to check some of your medical records and maybe talk to a few of the patients. This is something new since the hospitals have been getting so much publicity in the media."

"Well...that we have, Dr. Trenton. Follow me and I'll take you to Medical Records first."

"Thank you, sir."

"Nice weather we've been having," the administrator commented on the way to the elevator.

"A little too hot for me," Mel replied.

The elevator door opened and the two men stepped inside. They stood in silence until it stopped on the sixth floor.

"Mrs. Watkins, this is Dr. Trenton. He's here to review some of our records and talk to some of the patients. Make sure he gets what he needs."

Mrs. Watkins was in her late fifties, round and plump and didn't really seem to mind. She was jolly, with laughing eyes, and Mel wondered if she was laughing at him or herself or just the whole damn world. She wore her light brown hair in a short mannish cut and looked as if she had run under the neighbor's clothesline and stretched her neck out of proportion to the rest of her body. Her pink silk blouse was just a little too snug, each button pushed to the limit, and he smiled, thinking he could have stuck three fingers through the gaps.

She led him to a small adjoining room with a table pushed back against the wall, two chairs and a copy and fax machine. To the left, another door opened into a large room with aisles and aisles of medical records.

"I want to review the records from the oncology wing."

She led him down three aisles and pointed. "That would be in these two aisles, doctor."

"Thank you."

"Would that be all, sir?"

He nodded, smiled as she walked back toward her office and wondered how her birdlike legs carried so much weight without snapping.

He pulled several records and walked back to the small room. He spread the charts out on the table and pulled his legal pad and a Flair pen from his briefcase.

Mrs. Watkins stuck her head around the door frame. "Coffee, sir?"

"That would be nice." He smiled.

"How would you like it?"

"Black."

She returned in a few moments with a cup of steaming coffee and added. "You can just leave the charts out if you like, Dr. Trenton. I'll be happy to put them back in the bins when you're finished."

"Thank you, Mrs. Watkins, you're very kind."

Mel took off his suit coat and hung it over the back of the folding chair. He raised slightly from his chair, slid the ashtray closer and lit a cigarette.

After two hours of browsing through records and several cigarettes, he had not come up with anyone who met Benjamin's specifications. He put his Flair and legal pad back in his briefcase, snapped it shut and went back to Mrs. Watkin's office. She was sitting in front of the typewriter,

155

picking lint from the front of her black knit skirt. "Mrs. Watkins?"

"Yes, Dr. Trenton."

"I'd like to see your inpatient charts."

She led him down the hall to the nurses' station and made introductions. He went over all the inpatient charts and after 30 minutes, spoke to the head nurse. "I'd like to speak to the patients in rooms 615, 620 and 626, if you don't mind."

"Yes, sir." She smiled broadly.

She hustled around the nurses' station, and he followed her to the first room.

Mel pulled a chair up close to the bed and began to ask questions. After a few short minutes into a one-sided conversation, he got the distinct impression that this was not the man for the job. It was the same disappointment with the second patient.

He stopped outside the door of the third patient and noticed a tall, frail man lying half covered on the hospital bed, staring up at the ceiling; a Vietnam veteran, helicopter pilot and, according to his military history, an expert in demolition. This could be his man, he thought.

Mel knocked lightly on the partially opened door, and the veteran shifted his eyes in that direction. "Mr. Forester? May I come in?"

"Sure," he said and adjusted his pillow.

"I'm Dr. Jeff Trenton. I'd like to talk to you for a few minutes, if you wouldn't mind."

"What kind of doctor are you? I thought I'd already seen every doctor in Maryland."

"I'm not on staff here, and my visit doesn't concern your condition."

" Well...you'd be wasting your time if it did."

"I've studied your record and understand that your chemotherapy hasn't helped you any."

"That's right. It's just a matter of time. If it wasn't for my family, I'd end it today."

"I'd like to talk to you about your family."

"What about my family?"

"How long do you have?"

"They say three months, at the most."

"How will your family be, financially I'm speaking, after you're gone?"

"That's my biggest worry now, Dr....what did you say your name was?"

"It's not important. Go ahead, you were saying?"

"Oh yeah, my wife and three kids are my biggest concern. I don't sleep at night worrying about money. We can hardly make ends meet right now. My wife works as a waitress and has to be away from the kids a lot. I hate that. They'll need her more than ever after I'm gone." He paused a moment. "Why do you ask?"

"I have a job for you that would help out. It's not a big job, but it pays well."

"What kind of job could I do in my condition?"

"You'd be surprised."

"How much money are we talking about here?"

"Three hundred thousand, and it wouldn't require a lot of work or strength. Would you be interested?"

The veteran's mouth fell open, and he made a choking sound deep in his throat. "Well, hell yeah, I'm interested, but what's the catch? There's gotta be a catch with that much money involved."

"No catch, just simple and clean...and no questions asked."

"Where's the hidden camera?"

"What camera?"

"You must be from *20/20* or *Prime Time Live* or one of them other programs looking for a story. I don't feel like talking any more."

"You sound bitter."

"Hell yeah, I'm bitter. I could tell you some things you'd

find impossible to believe. I might not be dying of cancer if they hadn't sent me to 'Nam."

Dr. Vincent glanced down at the frail veteran. Leaving a wife and three helpless children behind with no visible means of support, of course he was bitter. He knew he had found his man.

"All the more reason to hear me out, Mr. Forester."

"I don't think I want to hear anything else you have to say."

"What do you have to lose?"

"I don't have a life to lose, that's for sure."

"Just give me three minutes, and if you're still not interested, I'll leave and no hard feelings."

The veteran shrugged and focused his eyes on the ceiling.

After a few seconds, he looked at the doctor. "What the hell, three minutes and no more."

"Do you know anything about remote-controlled explosive devices?"

"Yeah, we used 'em in 'Nam all the time."

Dr. Vincent then explained the plan in detail. The veteran frowned. "It's that simple?" he asked.

"That simple," Dr. Vincent replied.

"Don't jive me, man."

"Why would I want to do that?"

"You work for the government, don't you?"

"No."

"When will this job need to be done?"

"Soon. I'll let you know when."

"It'd sure as hell take a load off my mind."

"There's just one stipulation."

"I knew there was a catch. I knew it! I knew it!"

"No! No! Mr. Forester. Listen to me."

"I'm listening."

"The only stipulation is this. No one, and I repeat, no one, is to know about this. Do you understand?"

"It's clear as mud."

"Then I'll make it crystal clear. Do not discuss this conversation with anyone. Not even your wife. No one. When will you be leaving the hospital?"

"Tomorrow. I get the last of my chemotherapy today."

"Good. You'll be contacted by phone about the exact time when I'll pick you up. Any questions?"

"Just one. How'll my wife be able to explain all of this money after I'm gone."

"That's already worked out. Five days after your funeral, my employer has prepared, and will send by me, an insurance policy showing her as beneficiary. She'll sign the necessary documents in exchange for the policy."

"How do I know I can trust you?"

"I'll be right back."

Dr. Vincent returned minutes later and pulled a brown envelope from his briefcase. "Here's a copy of the insurance policy back-dated five years. When you go home from the hospital, show this to your wife and tell her to put it where she can find it. The money's already in the bank, drawing interest. Here's $5,000 in cash. You'll need to pick up an Air Force colonel's uniform and the other supplies you'll need." Dr. Vincent paused. "Can I safely say we have a deal?"

"Yes, sir."

"Any more questions?"

"No, sir, I think we've covered everything."

"Good, you won't regret this, Mr. Forester. Your family will be well taken care of."

The veteran pulled the sheets over his chest and closed his eyes. For the first time in a long time, he smiled.

Dr. Vincent went back to the little room, opened his brief-case and wrote the name and address of Donald Forester, final diagnosis, terminal carcinoma of the lung. He placed his Flair in a side pocket and snapped it shut again. He removed his brown suit coat from the back of the chair, slid his arms in and shook it up over his broad shoulders. With both palms of his hands, he pushed his hair straight back, picked up his brief-case and walked to the front of Mrs. Watkins's desk. "I'll be on my way now, Mrs. Watkins," he said.

"Finished so soon, Dr. Trenton?" she asked.

"All finished for now. You have a nice day."

"Thank you and the same to you."

He waved over his shoulder and whistled on the way to the elevator.

CHAPTER FIFTEEN

Friday, 10:30 p.m. The alarm system for The Fashion Shop sounded at police headquarters. The desk sergeant picked up the phone and routinely dialed the number of the dress shop. There was no answer. He immediatley dispatched two officers to that location.

According to the numbers printed in white letters on the glass panels lining each side of the door, The Fashion Shop was open on Friday and Saturday evenings until 10:00 p.m. The arriving officers found the doors to be securely locked, even though the lights in the showroom were shining brightly. After their investigation, one of the officers radioed headquarters that they had found no evidence of a crime and requested the alarm system be reset.

Saturday, 2:00 a.m. Emily Maddox placed a frantic telephone call to police headquarters. "This is Mrs. Randall Maddox. I'm afraid something's happened to my husband."
"Why do you think that, Mrs. Maddox?"
"He's never this late getting home from work, especially on Friday night. I've called the shop several times, and he doesn't answer the phone. I'm afraid something's happened to him."
"Where does your husband work, Mrs. Maddox?"
"We own The Fashion Shop on Fourth Street."
"Do you have a key?"

"Yes, sir, I do."

"I'll send a patrol car around there. Why don't you bring your key and meet them there so they can check it out for you. Okay?"

"Thank you very much, officer, I'll be there in 20 minutes."

"Yes, ma'am."

Emily Maddox parked behind the patrol car in front of the dress shop. Two officers greeted her and she handed the key to one of them. He unlocked the door, returned the key and instructed her to remain outside the building.

The officers entered and began to survey the large showroom. "Mr. Maddox?" one of them called. No answer. They walked cautiously through the aisles until they reached the back of the store. So far, nothing seemed out of order except for the bright lights in the showroom.

Officer Beatty pointed. "Williams, you check the storeroom over there and I'll check the office."

At first glance, Officer Beatty noticed nothing unusual, but as he stepped further into the room, he made a grisly discovery. "Williams, get in here."

Within minutes the street was blocked off. Squad cars, an ambulance, a laboratory van and two unmarked cars soon were on the scene.

The victim lay sprawled face down behind his desk, his head lying in a pool of blood. His hands were tightly bound behind his back.

Homicide Captain Michael Warner walked glumly into the office. He turned to Officer Beatty and asked, "Who's the victim?"

"Randall Maddox, sir. He owned the shop."

"Any evidence of forced entry?" Captain Warner asked.

"No, sir."

"Any evidence of robbery?"

"Apparently not. The safe is locked, and he had $1,200 in his wallet and a diamond ring on his hand."

The captain knelt down and examined the body. The victim's short hair on the side of his head was filled with blood, which had begun to clot around the wound at the base of the skull. Captain Warner stood, shook his head in disgust and stepped back to make room for the police photographer to take pictures.

Warner stood quietly for a moment stroking his chin. "What goes around comes around. He's been under suspicion of drug dealing for a long time, but we've never been able to get anything on him. This looks like a typical gangland execution. If he was dealing drugs, I guess he's through now. I wonder what he did to upset his suppliers?"

One of the officers chalked an outline on the floor around the body. Two EMTs entered the office with a stretcher and a plastic body bag.

Emily Maddox, who was waiting outside, had become hysterical when the EMTs rolled the body to the ambulance and was being comforted by one of the plain-clothes officers. The ambulance drove slowly down the street past the barricade.

Captain Warner approached and spoke to one of the officers. "Williams, take Mrs. Maddox home and find out who she wants to notify."

"Yes, sir." Officer Williams took Mrs. Maddox by the arm and placed her in the patrol car, then motioned. "Beatty, follow me in Mrs. Maddox's car."

Captain Warner turned to Officer Beatty and said, "Even though it's bad guy against bad guy, I never get used to these damn gangland killings."

Saturday, 5:30 a.m. Chris rolled over and turned off the new alarm clock that had awakened him with soft music instead of the loud, nerve-racking, persistent bell possessed by its predecessor. He opened one eye and remembered that he had the day off. The political benefit was scheduled for that evening, and he would be escorting Ashley in Louis Hamilton's absence. He was pleased.

He raised up, and with a fist, pounded the feathers in his lumpy pillow before pulling the covers over his head to block out the street light from the window. Again, he closed his eyes and hoped to enjoy several more hours of sleep.

Dr. Stubblefield had settled into the routine at the lab without difficulty, and they had caught up with most of the work load that had backed up since Dr. Sulcer's death. He had agreed to take emergency call for the weekend to give Chris badly needed time off. The past week had been one of sleepless nights and headaches at the office, confusion and a hundred different new things to deal with. He needed rest.

Suddenly Chris's eyes popped wide open, and the idea of sleep became something in the past. He threw the covers back and crawled wearily out of bed. He stretched as he walked through the silent apartment to the kitchen, where he plugged in a pot of coffee. After he had dressed in a pair of white shorts, T-shirt and tennis shoes and while the coffee perked, he jogged down the three flights of steps to the all-night drug store for the morning paper.

He rode the elevator back upstairs to his apartment, where he spread the newspaper on the table and devoted himself to the sports page. His favorite baseball team, the Houston Astros, was still on top in their division. After three cups of coffee, he read the rest of the paper. The headline screamed: "FASHION GURU MURDERED!" Chris immediately shaved, showered and dressed for work as usual.

When Chris walked into the pathology lab, Dr. Stubblefield looked up in surprise. "What are you doing here? You're supposed to be catching some shut-eye."

"I know, but old habits are hard to break. What you got going this morning?"

"I've got an autopsy on a gangland killing last night."

"Yeah, Randall Maddox. I read about it in the morning paper. That's why I came in. Ashley was just in his shop a couple of days ago. The police think he was mixed up in drugs."

At that moment, the door to the pathology lab opened and Commissioner David Thornston stepped in. He was a stocky man of 60 with streaks of gray in his brown hair and a reddish beard that wrapped around his cheeks like a Halloween mask. He seated himself on a tall lab stool with his legs outstretched, crossed at the ankles and folded his arms across his chest. "Good morning, Dr. Burns."

"Good morning, Commissioner Thornston. This is Dr. Lance Stubblefield. He'll be working with me in the lab."

The commissioner stood and extended his hand. "I'm certainly glad to meet you, Dr. Stubblefield. When did you start working here?"

"Just started this week."

"You'll probably get your fill of seeing me pop in the door. I'm almost a permanent fixture around here." He grinned at Chris. "By the way, do you two have anything on that corpse they brought in here early this morning?"

"Just that the guy apparently died of a single gunshot to the base of the skull," Dr. Stubblefield answered.

"Yeah, execution style. It was a professional job, and I'm sure this one will be placed among the unsolved. These kind of crimes usually are."

"Why do you say that?"

"We've dusted the entire office and made a double check on everything, and it's clean as a whistle. One of the employees had left her purse, which I thought might give us a lead, but that didn't pan out. I don't expect you'll find anything we'll be able to use on the body either." The commissioner drew in a deep breath. "When will you have a report ready?"

"Monday morning, at the latest."

He nodded. "Give me a call, would you?"

"As soon as it's ready, commissioner."

Chris was entering his office when Agent Camper opened the door to the pathology lab and said, "Could I talk to you a minute, Dr. Burns?"

"Sure, come on in."

Agent Camper followed him into the office and closed the door. "I need to talk to you about some videotapes."

"What kind of videotapes?"

"I'm not sure, yet."

Chris, seated at his desk, leaned forward. "I don't understand what you're talking about."

Camper spoke carefully, "I learned yesterday morning that Blade Henderson lives on the top floor of the Hamilton Building. We got that from a taped conversation he had with Beth Wagner. On that tape, he also spoke about videotapes he has hidden up there. Those videotapes supposedly involve powerful people, and I need your help to get them."

"What could I do to help?"

"I've been ordered to hand-deliver the tape we made of the conversation between Henderson and Wagner to Director Russom in Washington. We don't have any agents in Austin who are familiar with this case, and my plane leaves in 45 minutes. Understand, Dr. Burns, this is not the usual routine, but I was wondering, since you already know most of the facts, if you'd be willing to help me find those videos."

"How much danger will there be?"

"Minimal, if you'll follow my plan."

"Okay. I'll do what I can."

"I'm only going to be able to go over this a couple of times."

Agent Camper quickly went over the details of the plan he had carefully constructed. Chris agreed to abort the attempt if, at any point, any part of the plan became a threat. Camper stood and extended his hand. "Dr. Burns, I can't tell you how much I appreciate your cooperation."

He smiled. "Wait until I hand you the videos before you thank me."

"By the way, I saw the report on your accident today."

"What about it?"

"Someone did a pretty sloppy job on your brakes."

"That's what I've been told."

"I'm glad neither of you got hurt."

"So am I."

"I also saw the report on the break-in at Miss Denton's apartment."

"Did they come up with anything?"

"Nothing. A clean job."

"Somehow that doesn't surprise me."

"Well, doctor, I'd better hurry if I'm going to catch my flight. I'll see you in a couple of days. Be careful and good hunting."

Camper left the office and Chris quickly changed from his casual wear into a pair of surgical scrubs and began to help Lance with the autopsy. At 4:00 p.m. they were finished, except for the report that would be typed on Monday by Jeri Lynn. Chris left the lab and drove east with the traffic, feeling as though the eyes of Texas truly were upon him, from every direction.

On Friday and Saturday nights, a five-block stretch of downtown Austin's Sixth Street resembles Bourbon Street in New Orleans at Mardi Gras time. Cars are allowed on Sixth, but the steady stream of pedestrians keeps the traffic moving at a snail's pace. Numerous clubs offer happy hour at 7:00 p.m. and live music all night.

At 5:00 p.m. the Paradise Cafe on Sixth was quiet except for a few early arrivals. Chris entered and carefully picked a table in the corner and waited. When a waitress came to his table, he explained that he would be joined shortly by two friends and asked her to return when they arrived. She nodded and went about her chores getting ready for the seven o'clock rush.

Jacob and Savannah arrived and joined Chris at his table. When the waitress returned, all three ordered coffee.

"What's happened, Chris? Is Ashley okay?" Savannah asked.

"Ashley's fine. She's at the beauty parlor getting her hair curled for the dinner tonight."

"Thank goodness. She called me this morning to tell me that the vice president would be there, and she was going to try to talk to him about April. I'm worried, Chris. I'm afraid the wrong person could hear her."

"I don't think Ashley would do anything foolish."

The waitress returned with the coffee, placed the cups on the table and left.

Jacob asked, "What did you want to see us about, Chris?"
"Agent Camper approached me today and asked a favor. He was called back to Washington and I need your help."

Savannah said, "Whatever we can do, we'll do. Right, Jacob?"

"Sure, Chris, you know we'll be glad to help."

"Good. Camper outlined a plan for us to follow and we shouldn't have any problems."

Jacob took a sip of coffee. "What's the plan?"

"Here's what we have to do." Chris went over the outline, spelling out in detail each job to be done.

Savannah and Jacob left, drove to the record shop, picked up the supplies Chris asked for and each hurried home to wait.

As Chris parked his car at the apartment, he noticed that Ashley's yellow Honda, all washed and shined, was parked four spaces away. What a classy set of wheels, he thought as he stepped out of the mud-splattered blue and white rental.

He hurried through the back entrance, caught the elevator to the third floor and jogged down to Ashley's apartment. He knocked on the door. No answer. He dug in his pocket for his keys, let himself in and walked eagerly to the bedroom.

Ashley was putting the final touches to her makeup when he appeared. She examined the hair, piled high on top, the sides sloped toward the back in a sexy twist, very stunning. Well worth the 40 bucks and two hours torture in the chair, she thought. She looked up startled as Chris entered.

"We need to talk." He silently formed the words with his lips.

Ashley nodded and began to dress.

They walked out into the hall and Chris slowly went over the instructions for her to follow.

"I'm sorry I can't be there, but Jacob will be with you. I'll see you at the Broken Spoke at ten tonight. Okay?"

"I hope you know what you're doing."

"Believe me, Ash, I do too. And take some extra clothes with you. I don't want you wearing that damn sexy dress at the Broken Spoke."

CHAPTER SIXTEEN

Jacob left his home a few minutes before the designated time.

He estimated, at normal speed and Saturday night traffic, it would take him at least 40 minutes to reach Ashley's apartment, pick her up and get back to the Driskill Hotel. The dial on the dashboard clock read 6:10 p.m. when he entered the Ben White Boulevard.

He turned on his signal light and exited onto the curving street next to the Best Western South. Traffic had backed up close to the intersection. Jacob pulled to a stop and could see three policemen making their way down the long line of motorists. He turned off the radio and sat slumped in the seat.

Finally, one of the officers approached the car. "Could I see your driver's license, please?" he asked.

"What's the trouble, officer?" Jacob asked as he handed his license to the patrolman.

"No trouble, just a routine license check."

The officer scanned the driver's license and walked to the rear of the car for a moment, then came back to Jacob's window.

"Here's your license, sir."

"Thank you, officer. How long do you think it'll be before I can get through here?"

"I can't say for sure, but it takes time to check every car. I'm sorry for any inconvenience. Hope you're not in too big of a hurry," he said and walked back to the next vehicle.

Jacob muttered to himself, "Hurry? Hell yes, I'm in a hurry. I don't have time to sit here all night." He glanced at the clock on the dashboard again, 6:25 p.m. There wasn't enough time to pick up Ashley. He reached for his car phone and dialed.

Ashley answered, "Hello."

"Ashley, this is Jacob. I'm stuck in a road block, and there's not enough time for me to pick you up. I'm sure by now all the parking places at the Driskill are filled, so how about meeting me at the Triple Cinema parking lot, at Highland Mall?

"Sure, no problem."

"Fine, I'll be there as soon as I can."

Ashley pulled the Honda out of the parking lot and drove past the front of the apartment building. As she passed, a car pulled away from the curb across the street and headed in the opposite direction. She glanced in her rearview mirror in time to see it make a U-turn behind her. She nervously watched through her mirror as the car followed for several blocks. As she approached the red signal light at the next intersection, the car pulled alongside. It was an old rusty Vega, moving as slowly as she was. The young male driver, as well as his male cohort in the passenger seat, had long shaggy hair. Each had a stubby cigarette clenched between his teeth. Ashley felt their stares and glanced around at the car. Both boys smiled and raised their eyebrows in a seductive manner as they waited. She quickly turned her head back in the direction of the signal light. When it changed to green, the boys waved and whistled as the Vega sped away.

As Ashley parked her yellow Honda on the large parking lot of the Triple Cinema Theater, she noticed the two boys who had passed her in the rusty Vega. They had also parked on the lot and were heading for the ticket window. She turned off the motor and reached for her purse and brown bag of extra clothes as she waited for Jacob. Ashley felt completely out of place in a theater parking lot dressed in an evening gown.

The two shaggy-haired boys bought tickets and went inside the theater. They stood against the plate-glass window, watching, talking and pointing to the yellow Honda. They were still planted against the window when Jacob arrived and Ashley seated herself in his car.

Jacob's car pulled to a stop at the Sixth Street entrance of the Driskill Hotel and Ashley stepped out. She entered the building and waited just inside the glass doors for him to park the car.

As Jacob drove down Seventh Street, Blade Henderson's Bronco caught his eye. He smiled, turned the corner and drove slowly down Brazos in front of the hotel. The blue Cadillac was parked directly across from the front entrance and Blondy was leaning over the steering wheel, staring straight ahead. Halfway down the block, Agent Morgan sat in his car watching the blue Cadillac. The entire block surrounding the Driskill Hotel seemed to be alive with eyes and ears. Jacob smiled again as he took a final look through his rear-view mirror. He turned the corner, drove slowly down the side street and back into the hotel parking garage. After circling several times, he noticed a sports car backing out of a parking space. He waited until the car was out of sight, then parked his car in the empty space. Moments later, he joined Ashley inside the hall leading to the hotel lobby.

They walked into the magnificent massive lobby that occupied most of the ground floor. Jacob placed a hand under Ashley's elbow as they worked their way through the crowd and up the grand stairway that led to the ballroom. They paused outside the ladies' powder room, and she stepped inside to leave her brown bag of extra clothes.

Ashley stopped abruptly in the wide entrance, and her eyes swept across the beautiful ballroom. The five large chandeliers, hanging low from the tall ceiling, cast a warm glow on the satin tablecloths and fresh floral arrangements that had been carefully placed on each long row of tables. She smiled as she stood in awe, admiring the long shimmering evening gowns, dark tuxedos, white ruffled shirts and black bow ties.

She whispered, "Damn, Jacob, look at all these people. Are we in the right place?"

"I'm afraid we are, Missy. Are you ready for this?" he asked smiling.

Ashley released a long sigh. "I guess I'm as ready as I'll ever be." She placed a hand around Jacob's arm, and they began mingling with the crowd, smiling, nodding and exchanging pleasantries, slowly edging their way toward the head table as Beth had instructed on the night of rehearsal.

As they approached, Beth began working her way in their direction. She reached for Ashley's hand. "Thank heavens you're here. I was beginning to worry."

Blade was standing nearby and extended his hand. "Jacob, how are you?" He nodded and smiled at Ashley.

"Fine," Jacob answered. "Quite a crowd here tonight."

"To say the least. Beth and I came an hour early just to get a parking space."

"Well, we weren't so lucky," Jacob frowned, "I got caught in a license check, of all times, and had to call Ashley to meet me at the Triple Cinema parking lot. I had no idea there'd be such a crowd."

Beth smiled and glanced around the room. "This is the largest turnout we've ever had." She stopped smiling and looked in the direction of two men standing together near the entrance to the Maximilian Room. "Excuse us gentlemen, there's someone I want Ashley to meet."

Ashley followed closely behind Beth, looking around the room as they approached the two men.

Beth placed a hand on Ashley's arm and pulled her close to the tall, dark-haired man. "Ashley Denton, this is Vice President Drew Ramsey." The vice president, grinning in his seductive way, took her hand in his and said softly, "I'm so glad to meet you Ashley. I couldn't help but notice your beautiful red hair when you entered the room."

"I'm honored, sir. Thank you"

The back of her neck and head tingled, and her arms and legs felt an electric surge she wasn't prepared for. She felt herself go numb as his eyes swept across her face and stopped, looking deeply into her eyes. For a fleeting moment, she thought of April and how entranced she must have felt to be recognized by such a powerful and handsome man. She swallowed quickly and said, "I'm looking forward to your speech tonight, Mr. Vice President."

Beth turned to the other man. "Ashley, this is Arnold Leitzen, local campaign manager for the party and a very dear friend of mine."

"Nice to meet you, Mr. Leitzen."

Arnold Leitzen smiled. "Likewise, my dear. You're as stunning as Beth told me you were."

The vice president joined Ashley and Beth at the head table with Jacob and Blade. The men stood and seated the ladies as Arnold walked to the podium, picked up the microphone and began speaking.

"Ladies and gentlemen, let me have your attention, please." He paused a moment. "Please take your seats, the meal is ready to be served. It pleases me to see all of you here tonight, and I hope you'll enjoy your meal as well as the program we've prepared for you."

After the crowd had seated themselves, an army of waiters rolled their food carts down the aisles and began placing each meal on the table, filling water glasses and coffee cups. Minutes later, they had finished and vanished to prepare desserts.

Blade glanced down at the moderately proportioned meal, leaned over and whispered to Beth, "Is this all we get for a thousand bucks?"

"For goodness sake, Blade," she whispered back. "Stop acting like a spoiled brat. This is a political fund-raiser, not a pig-out. Besides, Hamilton Medical is paying for it, so relax and enjoy yourself. If you're still hungry when it's over, stop by McDonald's."

Blade thought a moment, but it wasn't from a careful thought process that his next words came. "I knew it would be a mistake to come to this stupid event. As soon as you get around these social snobs, you turn into an unbearable bitch."

Beth answered carefully with a cold expression, "Well Blade, you can leave anytime you want to."

"Maybe I will," he said and shifted in his chair.

Chris parked his car at the Blue Ridge Apartment Building on Decker Lane and rode the elevator to the second floor. He hurriedly walked down the long hall to apartment six and knocked on the door.

Savannah opened the door and slid a suitcase out into the hall. She grabbed her purse, locked the door behind her and followed Chris back down to his car.

"Is everything okay so far?" she asked.

"I think so, at least everyone's in place."

"There's something I forgot to mention at the Paradise."

"What's that?"

"The security monitors are turned on at the front entrance after hours."

"Oh hell, what'll we do about that?"

"I can go through the front and let you in the back door. Blade won't think anything about that when he looks at the film. Someone's always forgetting something and coming back to the office."

"Let's just hope he doesn't come back for something himself."

Savannah shivered, "Perish the thought."

After 20 minutes of fighting the heavy Saturday night traffic, Chris parked on the west side of the Hamilton Building. Savannah stepped out and ran around the building to the front entrance, hurried through both security doors and down the hall to open the back door for Chris. He stepped inside with the suitcase and Savannah's purse. She grabbed the purse and ran back down the hall, through the security doors, making sure the purse was in plain view as she slipped the key in the front door lock. She dashed back around the building and, as Chris held the back door open, stepped breathlessly inside.

Chris picked up the suitcase and they walked the short distance to the elevator. Savannah crossed her fingers and held her breath as she inserted the new card into the code box. Instantly she heard the click and the door opened. She grinned at Chris as they stepped inside and punched the up button.

They stepped out of the elevator onto the plush carpet, and Chris shook his head from side to side slowly. "Damn, what a perfect setup for a rendezvous. Away from the noise of the city, hidden from the highway by the trees, this is perfect. So this is what April and the vice president called home. I would've never guessed."

"It's so beautiful and fancy, it just doesn't look like Blade. He's the rustic type."

The spacious bedroom was also lavishly furnished with a king-sized bed, a large walk-in closet and beige drapes, sprinkled with threads of burgundy that matched the living room.

Chris smiled. "Savannah, if you can tear yourself away from the beauty, we need to find those tapes. Check the closets in the kitchen and living room, I'll take the bath and bedroom."

She began to search the closets, which were badly cluttered, and smiled to herself, thinking that this was the only eyesore in this small paradise, but Blade was Blade and neatness was not one of his virtues.

After the last closet was searched, she joined Chris in the bedroom. "There weren't any tapes in those closets. Have you found anything yet?"

"Not yet. Wait...those two green boxes on the top shelf. Let's see what's in them."

He lifted the boxes to the floor, knelt down and opened the lids. He looked up and smiled, "Here they are. This is what we've been looking for, kid."

She looked down at the tapes packed neatly inside. With her mouth wide open, she glanced up and noticed two folding doors at the end of the walk-in closet.

"What's behind those doors, Chris?"

"I don't know, I didn't get that far."

She walked to the end of the closet and pulled the doors open. "Holy Moses!"

"What?" Chris asked.

"Look at all of this stuff."

"What is it?"

"There's loads of large Ziploc bags, trash bags, casting material, heat-seal tape and all kinds of brown tape. What would Blade do with all this stuff?"

"That's material used to repackage multi-kilos of cocaine for distribution."

"How do you know?"

"I work for the crime lab, remember?"

"Look at this, Chris. It's a video camera and it's pointed right at the bed."

"You shouldn't be shocked, Savannah."

"Well...I am. Why would anyone want to make that kind of movie or tape personal conversations?"

"Knowledge is power...if you know enough about the right people."

"What could they get with such trash, except maybe killed."

"If they can stay alive, anything they ask for."

Suddenly, Savannah stood upright and froze.

177

"Listen! What was that noise, Chris?"

"I don't know. You stay put and I'll check it out." He placed a forefinger across his lips and tiptoed out of the room.

Savannah stood like a statue as she heard another noise. "Oh my God, it's the elevator!"

A few seconds later, Chris came back into the bedroom. She looked at him in shock. "What was it, Chris? I heard the elevator moving."

"The first noise was the air conditioner coming on, and I sent the elevator back down to the first floor. If Blade should come back, I'd rather confront him up here rather than get off the elevator in his face."

"You had me worried for a few minutes."

"Let's get busy. We've got a lot of work to do."

"I'm ready, if my heart'll just stop pounding."

Chris began to lift the tapes out of the box, handing them to Savannah. "Okay, what we'll need to do is take the labels off the originals and put them on the blanks, then we'll put the blanks back in the green boxes and on the shelf where we found them."

"Are you going to label the originals?"

"No, that's not our problem. All we'll concern ourselves with is getting them out of this building and to the FBI."

"Okay, that suits me just fine. The sooner we can get out of here, the better I'll like it."

By eight-thirty that evening, the air in the Driskill ballroom, that earlier had smelled of fresh flowers, now consisted of as many parts of cigar, cigarette and pipe smoke as oxygen.

After the army of waiters had cleared the tables, Ashley stood behind the podium, waiting for her cue from the band director. With a moist hand, she held the microphone and began to sing, her soft voice echoing above the sound of muffled voices. As she was nearing the end of her number, she noticed Blade from the corner of her eye as he stood and abruptly left the room. She placed the microphone back on its stand, bowed and seated herself next to Jacob. "What happened to Blade?" she whispered.

"I don't know. He's been acting a little out of sorts all night. I hope he didn't decide to go home."

At that moment, Arnold Leitzen introduced the main speaker, "Ladies and Gentlemen, the Vice President of the United States."

Ashley scarcely heard any of the vice president's words throughout his 15-minute speech. Questions raced through her mind. Where had Blade gone? What would he do if he returned to his apartment and found Chris and Savannah there?

Her thoughts were interrupted when the crowd applauded the vice president's speech. He held a hand in the air and waved, then seated himself to the right of the podium.

Arnold Leitzen stepped to the podium and adjusted the microphone. "Thank you, Vice President Ramsey, We feel very honored to have you here tonight and look forward to another four years with this administration." Arnold smiled as the guests applauded enthusiastically. He continued, "Now...ladies and gentlemen, the band will be here as long as you like, so the dance floor is yours to enjoy. Thank you for coming tonight and God bless you all."

Beth noticed the worried look on Ashley's face. She slid into the seat next to her and asked, "What's wrong, Ashley? Are you ill?"

"I was just thinking about my spreadsheets."

"You shouldn't be thinking about work tonight. Relax and enjoy yourself. It's not every day you get a chance to rub elbows with the vice president. Loosen up."

"I'm trying, but I can't get them off my mind."

"Tell me what was wrong and maybe I can put your mind at ease."

"I couldn't get them to balance with my credits when I closed out yesterday afternoon."

"How much were you off?"

"A lot and I couldn't figure out why."

"Well...don't worry about it. I'll help you get it straightened out on Monday. Just put it out of your mind tonight and enjoy yourself. Okay?"

"I'll try," she smiled weakly. "By the way, what happened to Blade?"

"He just stepped out for a few minutes, he'll be right back. Why?"

Just then, Ashley felt a light tap on her shoulder and turned in her seat.

"May I have this dance?" the vice president asked.

She blushed and stood. This was her chance. She'd ask questions, and hopefully find some answers.

As the band played softly, he gently pulled her to the crowded dance floor. His arms went around her and held her tight as he led her into a slow dance. She felt his heart pound and the hardness of his masculine body pressing against hers as he moved to the rhythm of the music. Her muscles began to relax, and she settled into the comfort of his strong arms.

He placed his mouth close to her ear, and she could feel his warm breath as he whispered, "You're the most beautiful woman I've ever seen. Why haven't I seen you at any of these functions before?"

She tried to speak. Nothing. She swallowed hard and cleared her throat. "I'm not a native of Austin and this is my first political function. I'm originally from Gulfport, Mississippi."

"Now that you mention it, you do fit the description of one of those beautiful Southern belles."

"I'm very flattered."

"Please, call me Drew, I feel like I've known you for a long time. I'd like to meet you somewhere after the dance. Would that be possible?"

"I have someone waiting for me."

"I wish you'd reconsider. We'd make a good pair, and your friend wouldn't have to know."

"Maybe he wouldn't, but I would."

"You're too hard on yourself."

"I don't think so."

She closed her eyes and thought to herself. What nerve! Was this the line that had eventually cost April her life?

"You work for Louis Hamilton, don't you?"

"Yes. I took April Crafton's place. Did you know her?"

"No, I don't believe I did."

"I was under the impression you did," she added.

"Where'd you get that idea?"

She studied his face as she spoke. "She used to come to all of these functions with Mr. Hamilton."

The muscles in the vice president's face tightened and he stared at the floor. She knew she had struck a nerve, a raw nerve. They danced in silence, and when the music stopped, he led her back to the table and seated her next to Jacob. She leaned over and whispered, "Let's go, Jacob."

"Okay, I'll bring the car around while you change clothes."

She stood, picked up her purse and stopped by Beth's chair. "I'm going to the powder room to freshen up a bit."

"Okay, dear."

Ashley's knees were weak as she nervously walked around the edge of the dance floor, through the ballroom entrance and down the hall to the crowded powder room. She stepped inside and retrieved the brown bag she had placed behind a large chair earlier that evening. She then stood in the long line waiting for one of the stalls where she would change her clothes.

Blade returned to the ballroom and seated himself next to Beth. "Well, love. The redhead isn't interested in the vice president. As a matter-of-fact, she turned down his offer."

"She did?"

"Uh-huh. He asked her out after the dance tonight and she flatly refused. You won't have anything to hold over her head if she finds out about her spreadsheets."

"I don't think that's anything to worry about. I can program her computer to handle the losses. No problem."

"Think again. This girl's got something up her sleeve besides her elbow."

"What the hell are you talking about, Blade?"

"She asked Ramsey if he knew April."

"What'd he say?"

"He denied it, but I don't think she bought it."

"That nosey little bitch. I wonder who she's really working for? You're gonna have to take care of her, Blade, and don't screw up. To hell with Hamilton, we're outta here."

After waiting almost an hour, Ashley finally entered an empty stall where she quickly shed the green evening gown and slid into a pair of black slacks and a white Western blouse. She stuffed the gown into the brown bag and paused a moment at the door. She stepped quietly into the hall and crept past the ballroom, down the grand stairway and through the lobby to the side entrance.

Jacob drove around to the doorway and Ashley quickly slipped into the front seat, tossing the brown bag into the back.

"What took you so long?" he asked.

"The powder room was packed. I just now got my clothes changed."

The parking lot at the Triple Cinema was deserted except for the yellow Honda, a van, two small cars and the rusty Vega. As they approached, Jacob saw two figures emerge from behind the Vega and walk to the Honda.

He slowed the car.

"What's wrong, Jacob?"

"Those two shaggy-haired boys. I think they're trying to steal your car. Hell! They *are* trying to steal your car." He pulled to the edge of the parking lot, turned off his motor and lights and picked up his phone to call the police. At that moment, one of the boys slid a long instrument down the outside of the glass on the driver's side of Ashley's car. He was laughing impishly as he opened the door.

The explosion lit up the sky like an enormous display of fireworks on the Fourth of July. The two teenage boys were hurled into the air then fell silently to the black asphalt parking lot.

Jacob pitched the phone to Ashley. "Call 911," he shouted as he scrambled from his car and ran toward the two boys. He pulled them to a safe distance from the burning car.

The first squad car arrived. The screaming siren and flashing lights brought people from all directions. In a few minutes, more than 100 people had gathered.

The second squad car arrived, and two officers jumped from the vehicle and began to move the crowd back to make way for the ambulance and fire truck. They were all there within minutes, but to Ashley it seemed like an eternity as she sat huddled in Jacob's car hugging her ankles.

The medics began to work with the injured boys and, after taking a few minutes to stabilize each one, loaded them into the ambulance and drove away with the sirens screaming.

One of the officers approached Jacob. "Was that your car?"

"No, sir. It belongs to the young lady seated in my car over there." He pointed in the direction of his parked car.

"What was it doing parked here?"

"She was late getting to the political fund-raiser at the Driskill Hotel tonight and had to park here."

"Do you know the boys?"

"No, sir. I've never seen them before."

"I need to speak with the owner of the car."

"Can it wait, officer? She's pretty shook up."

"No sir, I'm afraid not. I have to make a complete report tonight."

The officer walked to Jacob's car and began to question Ashley. He stood writing for a moment, then spoke: "You can go now. I think I've pretty well covered everything."

"Are the boys hurt badly?" Ashley asked.

"It's hard to say right now, ma'am. They were still alive when the ambulance left. Maybe they'll get lucky."

Chris and Savannah waited at the Broken Spoke on Lamar Street as planned. Chris had begun to worry. "Something must have happened," he said as he rubbed his temples. "They should've been here an hour ago."

"Maybe the traffic was slow. It's horrible this time of night. Let's give them a few more minutes, and if they aren't here, we'll go look for them."

A dark-haired waitress approached their table. "Are you Dr. Chris Burns?" she asked.

"Yes, I'm Dr. Burns."

"You have a phone call."

She led him toward the kitchen area and pointed to the phone. "Thank you," he said. She nodded and left.

"Dr. Burns here."

"Chris, this is Jacob. We've had a little problem."

"What's happened?"

"I don't have time to explain right now. I want you to get in your car, and when I drive by, follow me."

"Okay, we'll be waiting." Chris slammed the phone down, motioned to Savannah, and they weaved their way through the crowded parking lot of the Broken Spoke.

CHAPTER SEVENTEEN

When Jacob passed the Broken Spoke, Chris pulled abruptly onto Lamar Street close behind. After traveling two blocks, Jacob turned on his right signal light and, satisfied that they were not being followed, turned onto a side street to avoid the heavy traffic. With a white-knuckled grip on the steering wheel and a cigar clenched firmly between his teeth, he sped through the green light at the last crowded intersection. Ashley sat crouched in the front seat, looking back at Chris and Savannah who followed two car lengths behind.

Savannah sat braced, gripping the edges of the seat, looking over her shoulder as the lights of Austin faded into darkness. From the dim lights of the dashboard, she could see the tense muscles of Chris's face as he held the car around the deep curves in the road. Once, around a winding curve, the right wheels left the pavement and she could hear the steady pounding of gravel beneath the car. She felt any moment they would skid from the road and roll down into the dense ravine. Chris lightly tapped the brakes and, with a firm hand, quickly maneuvered the car back upon the highway without losing any speed.

After what seemed to be an eternity, Jacob turned the car onto the graveled driveway of Lake Travis Resort. Light from the office window fell on half of his face, leaving the other half in darkness as he walked back to Chris's car. "I'll just be a minute," he said.

Bud Joe's mother was sitting in the resort office watching television and enjoying a piece of custard pie with a glass of milk when Jacob stepped inside. She slowly pulled herself to her feet, blotting her lips with a paper napkin. "Can I help you, sir?" she asked, her dark eyes sparkling as she smiled.

"You must be Bud Joe's mother," Jacob said.

"I sure am. Martha Crafton's the name, but everybody calls me Marty. What can I do for you?"

"Where's Bud Joe?"

"He took a load of folks to Austin tonight to see Sixth Street. It's about the only place in town where you can enjoy music and dancing without gettin' your head bashed in."

"When do you expect him back?"

"Aw...'bout an hour or so. Is there something I could do for you?"

Jacob removed the cigar stump from his mouth. "Mrs. Crafton...."

"Call me Marty." She cast a warm smile and patted the back of his hand that was resting on the registry.

"Marty...I already have a cabin rented, and I'd like to pick up the key. The name's Jacob Hughes."

She opened the registry and ran her finger down the list. "Yes, sir, right here, Mr. Hughes. Would cabin one be okay? It has a nice view of the lake."

"Cabin one would be perfect."

She stepped back to the large board on the wall, removed the key and handed it to Jacob. "Enjoy yourself, Mr. Hughes, and if you need anything else, just let me know."

"Thank you, Marty."

Chris cast a questioning look as Jacob stepped from the office, got back into his car and drove down the driveway to cabin one. Chris followed.

When they stopped, Ashley threw her door open, ran to Chris and flung herself into his arms.

186

"Oh, Chris, it was awful!" she sobbed. "You won't believe what happened."

He brushed her hair back and studied her tear-stained face. "Come on inside, babe, and tell me all about it."

Jacob went through the screen porch, unlocked the door and clicked on the living room light. They all entered and stood in a huddle in the middle of the first room.

"What happened?" Chris asked, looking at Jacob. "Why were you two so late getting to the Broken Spoke?"

"I was running late before the dinner, so I asked Ashley to meet me at the Triple Cinema parking lot because I knew there wouldn't be any place to park at the Driskill."

"And?"

"After the dinner, I was taking her back to her car when I noticed two boys trying to steal it. When they got the door unlocked and opened it, the car blew up."

"I'll be damned!" Chris swore as a red flush came over his face. "Thank God you weren't hurt or killed. I feel like this is all my fault."

"No, Chris," Jacob frowned. "I don't think you had anything to do with the car explosion. Let's all sit down and try to make some sense of this and come up with some reasonable answers."

Ashley sat on the sofa between Chris and Savannah, resting her head on his shoulder.

Jacob was the last to seat himself in a large recliner across the room. He brushed his mustache with a forefinger for a moment. "First," he spoke thoughtfully, "we need to retrace every step after we arrived at the hotel. Do you feel like going over this with me, Ashley?"

"Yeah, I'm okay now."

"I want the names of every person you had a conversation with at the dinner."

"Let's see...I talked with you, Beth and the vice president."

"No one else?"

187

"No."

"Okay, we'll start with Beth. Try to remember everything that was said. What'd you talk about?"

"The only important thing I can remember talking about was my spreadsheets at work."

"What about your spreadsheets?"

"I found a shortage Friday afternoon that I can't explain."

"Were you alone with Beth when you discussed it?"

"Yes, Blade had stepped out for a few minutes."

"What about your conversation with the vice president?"

"I'm almost too embarrassed to talk about it."

"What did he say, Ashley? It's very important."

"He asked me to meet him after the dance."

Chris's eyes narrowed and he spoke through clenched teeth, "That dirty bastard!"

Ashley patted his arm. "Calm down, Chris. I don't think he'll bother me anymore. Besides, that's not important."

"You might be surprised," Jacob said and pulled his hand slowly down his face. "Somebody had to hear something they didn't like."

Suddenly Jacob's expression changed. He sprang to his feet and bolted through the doorway. Moments later, he returned with the brown bag and emptied the contents on the recliner. He picked up the gown and slowly worked his fingers around the edge of the neckline and under the button on the left shoulder. There it was, someone's ears, just as he had suspected. He held his hand in the air and made a circle with his thumb and forefinger. He placed the evening gown back into the bag, opened the front door and sat it just outside the doorway, just in case.

"Where did you buy that dress, Ashley?"

"At The Fashion Shop. Beth took me there Wednesday afternoon."

"Hmmm...somebody at the dress shop planted a bug in your evening gown on Wednesday afternoon, and the owner of the

188

shop was found dead yesterday morning, shot gangland style. That's very interesting."

"Yeah, I know, I did an autopsy on him. What do you make of this, Jacob?" Chris asked.

"Well...we're looking at two possibilities here. Someone could be watching the vice president, or Beth and Blade could be worried about Ashley discovering something she wasn't supposed to."

"Make that three possibilities, Jacob."

"What are you talking about, Chris?"

"Savannah found all kinds of repackaging material for cocaine distribution in Blade's apartment tonight. And I mean big-time repackaging."

"That probably means he's dealing with somebody big, like the Mafia, and that complicates matters even more."

"What should we do, Jacob?"

"First, I think you and Ashley should stay out here until I can come up with some answers. I'll go over to the resort office and tell Bud Joe what's going on. He needs to know so he can keep an eye on you in case you need something. Savannah can follow me back to town and leave your car parked at the rental agency. I'll bring Bud Joe back here after I've told him everything and introduce him to you. I'm sure he'll help in any way he can. Be right back."

"Whatever you say, Jacob."

Jacob walked down to the office and rang the lighted doorbell. He waited several moments and rang again. He saw the office light flicker as Bud Joe opened the wooden door and looked through the ornamental design of the security door.

"What brings you out here this time of night, Mr. Hughes?" he asked as he motioned Jacob inside.

"There's something I need to talk to you about, Bud Joe."

He turned and flashed a warm smile. "Well...okay."

Twodor, the junk-yard dog that slept behind the counter to

guard the office at night, charged around the corner and Jacob froze in his tracks.

"Lie down, Twodor. Ain't nobody goin' to bother you." He smiled at Jacob. "His bark's worse than his bite."

"He could've fooled me," Jacob said.

"Now, what did you want to talk to me about, Mr. Hughes?"

As briefly as he could, Jacob went over the night's events. Painfully, he confirmed the fact that April's death was not accidental. He saw Bud Joe looking at him with a strange expression and could almost read the thoughts that were going through his mind. They stepped back outside for fear of waking Bud Joe's mother.

From time to time, Bud Joe's mouth opened and closed, but nothing came out. He wanted to cry and pound his fists against the outside wall of the resort office. He vowed to himself that the person who had killed his sister would somehow be brought to justice. Finally he spoke, his voice quivered and a tear rolled down his cheek. "This is going to kill mama when she finds out."

Jacob looked up at the starry sky trying to formulate in his mind the words he needed to say. "I'm afraid she'll have to be told, Bud Joe. There's just no way to avoid it. You know it would hurt her more if this should come from someone else."

"I know you're right, Mr. Hughes. Would you do me a favor and tell her?"

Jacob nodded. "Of course I will, but it's late and your mama's already in bed, so let's just wait until in the morning."

"Okay, Mr. Hughes. Why don't you come out for breakfast?"

"That'll be fine. Oh, there's one more thing, Bud Joe. Would you come over to cabin one with me? I want you to meet Chris and Ashley. They may need your help."

"Sure, Mr. Hughes."

The two men walked back to the cabin, shoulder to shoulder, each one feeling the pain of the other.

Jacob glanced at Bud Joe, seeing the tears roll down his face, just as the unexpected overflow from his own eyelids dripped from his chin. They walked in silence until they reached the screen porch. Slowly, sadly, Bud Joe looked at Jacob and shook his head. "Does the pain ever go away when you lose somebody you love, Mr. Hughes?" Jacob looked him straight in the eyes, feeling old and fatherly, and placed his hand on Bud Joe's shoulder. "Time has a way of helping you deal with it, Bud Joe, but it never completely goes away."

They stepped inside cabin one and closed the door. Savannah stood up and walked toward Bud Joe just as his eyes focused. His face lit up like that of a child on Christmas morning. He grinned broadly, grabbed her around the waist, lifted all 160 pounds off the floor and swung her around several times. As her feet touched the floor again, he suddenly felt a need to improve his appearance. With both hands, he smoothed his hair back and tucked his shirttail back into his jeans. "Savannah, what are you doing here?" he asked with a broad smile.

"I'm here with Ashley. She's a friend of mine."

"Bud Joe, this is Ashley Denton and Dr. Chris Burns," Jacob announced.

"Glad to meet you both," Bud Joe smiled and extended his large hand.

"I'm very sorry about your sister, Bud Joe. I wish we could have met under different circumstances," Chris said.

"Thank you, Dr. Burns."

"Please...call me Chris."

Jacob seated himself in the recliner and began to outline his thoughts of the night, to which they all listened attentively. Bud Joe shifted in his seat and interrupted. "Why is it taking so long for the FBI to arrest these jokers?"

"It's very complicated, Bud Joe. They need more proof, and one arrest could screw up the whole works."

"How much more proof do they need?"

"Arresting Blade Henderson right now would be a mistake. We know that he has repackaging material in his apartment, but we have to know first whom he's dealing with. It would be pointless to bring him in without knowing who his accomplices are." Jacob looked at his watch and stood. "Well, my friends, it's one o'clock and there's little else to be accomplished tonight." He looked at Savannah and, nodding his head in a slight bow, said, "If you're ready, Savannah, we'll go back to town and try to get some rest."

They stood and silently filed through the door. Chris removed the suitcase from the trunk of the rental, looked at Jacob solemnly and said, "I hope these tapes are as valuable as you and Agent Camper think they are." He waved good-bye and went back into the cabin.

Before she left, Savannah accepted Bud Joe's invitation to join them for breakfast. He was elated and waved good-bye as she pulled onto the pavement behind Jacob.

Bud Joe stood in the darkness as the lights of the two cars disappeared around the curves in the road. The day's steam and humidity had disappeared, leaving a cool breeze that floated in from the lake. The crickets were in perfect pitch and the friendly waves splashed against the rocks along the water's edge. He whispered, "Good night, Savannah. I'll see you in the morning." He shoved his hands deep in his pockets and walked slowly back to the office.

Ashley pulled a hairbrush from her purse and seated herself at the vanity in the small bedroom. Her spirits were even more depressed as she looked at her reflection in the mirror. The styling mousse and hair spray had lost their grip, releasing thick clumps of hair that dangled in different directions. There were dark circles under her swollen eyes, and the strain of the last twelve hours had obviously taken its toll.

She spotted Chris in the mirror, standing in the doorway

behind her. "How do you feel, hon? he asked.

"Somebody just bombed my car, I can't go home and we're running for our lives. I feel just peachy."

He came up behind her, putting his hands on her shoulders. "I'm sorry, Ash. This is all my fault."

"Don't be ridiculous, Chris, nobody twisted my arm. I walked right into this mess with both of my eyes wide open. If anybody's to blame, it's me."

"Come on now. Don't be too hard on yourself."

"I just never dreamed that half of the people from here to Washington, D.C., would wind up involved in the vice president's affair. He's nothing but slime, the lowest of slime."

He bent and kissed her on the cheek, running his hands up and down her arms. "Come on. Let's go to bed and try to forget about him for now. We'll both be able to think better in the morning." He brought her to her feet and led her to the bed. Totally exhausted, she snuggled in his arms and began to breathe in a steady rhythm.

At 7:00 a.m. the alarm sounded. Jacob reached over with a groping hand, shut it off and rolled back on his side. After a few moments, he raised up on one elbow and glanced at the clock. Slowly, he stood up, using the bed to steady himself, and made his way to the bathroom.

He quickly showered and shaved, then drove to police headquarters. "Is Detective Barron in?" he asked the desk clerk.

"Yes, sir," he answered without looking up. "He's in his office."

Jacob knocked lightly on Detective Hank Barron's door, hesitated a moment, then stepped inside the small cluttered office. "Been here all night, Hank?" he asked and stuck his cigar back into his mouth.

"Close to it. I'm still working on the car bombing that happened on the Triple Cinema parking lot last night."

"What have you come up with?"

"Not a whole helluva lot. It was a simple plastic explosive, amateurish, but that doesn't mean it was. I've seen professionals use this type of explosive to throw the investigation. Why do you ask?"

"No good reason."

"Come on, Hughes. The car owner was employed by Hamilton Medical Services, and I know you do a lot of work for them. What's going on over there, huh?"

"I wish I knew, Hank. By the way, what've you found out about the owner of The Fashion Shop?"

"Don't tell me you're poking your nose around in that case too."

"No, I'm just a curious bystander." Jacob smiled around his cigar.

"Well...I'm making some progress."

"Care to elaborate on that?"

"Not at all. The assistant manager called me yesterday and asked me to come over to the shop and take a look at some new merchandise that had just arrived from Chicago."

"What's so strange about that?"

"There were five large boxes of expensive clothes and packed right in the middle of each box were bags of the white stuff worth megabucks. Get my drift?"

"Man! Who would've dreamed that little bastard was mixed up in drugs? And why bring it in from Chicago? The logical thing would be to get it from across the border."

"Exactly. Logical is the key word. He knew what we'd be thinking. I got a copy of his phone bill and found out he'd called Chicago a couple of days before he was killed. Captain Warner and I believe these people were probably his suppliers, but so far we haven't been able to prove anything."

"Who'd he call?"

"Some guy by the name of Vondonitti."

"Did you say Vondonitti?"

"Yeah, why?"

"When you mentioned Chicago, I should've known. The Feds have been trying to get something on the Vondonittis for years."

"How do you know?"

"I'm a private investigator, remember?"

"Well, Hughes, since you know so damn much, maybe I should put a tail on you."

"Got any idea who was repackaging the stuff for the guy at the dress shop?"

"No, but we'll find out. It's just a matter of time."

"You really think so?"

"I'm sure of it. They always screw up."

"Thanks for everything, Hank. See you around."

"Our doors are open 24 hours a day."

CHAPTER EIGHTEEN

Ashley awoke the next morning with the sun winking through the tall oak tree outside the window. She drowsily watched a bushy-tailed squirrel scamper up one branch, stop and perch on its hind legs. She stared out of the window at the cloudless sky. It was quiet and peaceful, no traffic or noise, just the chirping of birds.

Suddenly, she came back to harsh reality. She looked at the clock--7:30 a.m. The little sleep she had managed had been restless and troubled. She had awakened repeatedly with visions of the car exploding and the two boys being hurled into the air. Her exhausted mind groped with unanswered questions. Why had she been a specific target? Who had hired someone to plant a bomb in her car, assuming they had been hired? Was Blade Henderson somehow responsible? Finally, she abandoned all attempts to make any sense of the situation.

She rolled over and realized she was in bed alone. She rubbed her forehead weakly, then shifted herself to the edge of the bed. She placed her feet on the floor and walked wearily to the bathroom. She stared at herself in the mirror above the sink and muttered, "What a helluva night." She bent over, adjusted the knobs and waited as the water filled the large bathtub. She dropped her clothes to the floor, stepped into the cloud of steam and slid slowly down with her arms raised above her head. She heard footsteps in the hall near the bathroom. "Who is it?" she asked.

"Just me," Chris answered as he opened the door, looking equally tired. "Hurry up, babe, Marty has breakfast fixed for us. Here are the things you asked Savannah to bring."

"Thanks, I'll be there in a minute."

He set the overnight bag on the vanity and closed the door.

Chris and Ashley joined the rest of the group back in the apartment behind the resort office.

"Marty, this is Ashley Denton," Savannah said as they entered the snug kitchen.

"I'm so glad to meet you, Ashley. Have a seat, breakfast is almost ready," she said in a friendly tone.

"Thank you, Marty."

After everyone had finished eating, Marty, with the help of the two girls, began clearing the table. As soon as the unwashed dishes had been stacked near the sink, Jacob rose and took Marty by the hand. "Sit down, Marty, there's something I have to tell you."

Marty sank into a chair. "You look so serious, Mr. Hughes. What's wrong?"

"It's about your daughter."

"April?"

Jacob had to choke back his own tears as he searched desperately for the right words. This was a new role for him and one that he didn't like. He paused and took a deep breath. "She wasn't killed in the car wreck, Marty...she was murdered."

The color drained from her face and she stared at Jacob. "Murdered? Are you sure?"

"Yes, ma'am."

She stood and turned away in a daze. She didn't want to believe what she was hearing. After a long, thoughtful pause, she asked, "But why? Why would anyone want to kill my April?"

Jacob put his hand tenderly on her shoulder. "We don't know for sure, Marty."

She looked at Bud Joe and began to cry uncontrollably.

He rose and went to his mother, trying to muffle his own painful sobs as he held her in his arms.

After a few moments, they became quiet, and she looked up at him. "Did you know about this, Bud Joe?"

Wearily he nodded. "Not till last night, Mama."

Troubled, Jacob left the apartment and walked toward the lake's edge. He understood only too well. He walked further along the sandy bank, kicking rocks into the edge of the water. The morning breeze blew gently in his face, drying his tears. He could not contain himself any longer. He sat down on a large rock, feeling like a whipped child, letting his tears flow freely. Suddenly, he became aware of a rustling noise in the leaves behind him and turned to see Marty making her way down the winding path toward him.

"Mind if I join you, Mr. Hughes?" she asked as she approached.

"Not at all, Marty."

She joined him on the large rock and they sat silently, overlooking the peaceful lake, listening to the waves splash against the deserted bank.

Jacob released a long sigh and resisted an impulse to swear. He stood and kicked something that rang with a hollow sound. He turned and planted a foot on the rock. "You know, Marty, sometimes I feel like the light at the end of the tunnel's a fast moving train and there's no place to go."

"I know, Mr. Hughes, so do I."

Chris rose from the breakfast table and began to pace. "I think I'll call and see if Agent Camper has made it back from Washington."

"You can use the phone in the office, Chris," Bud Joe

offered, his emotions now under control.

"I don't think that's a good idea. I don't want to take a chance on the call being traced."

"Okay, then. There's a pay phone just outside the office door to the right."

"If I can arrange it, would you mind going into town and picking up Agent Camper?

"Be glad to, Chris," Bud Joe said.

Chris walked out of the office and located the pay phone. He nervously shoved a coin into the slot, waited for the dial tone, then dialed.

"Federal Bureau of Investigation," a pleasant female voice answered.

"This is Dr. Chris Burns. Has Agent Camper returned from Washington yet?"

"Yes he has, just one moment."

Chris shifted from one foot to the other as he waited.

Camper answered, "Dr. Burns, I've been trying to reach you since I got back. Where are you?"

"I can't tell you that, Agent Camper. Someone blew up Ashley's car last night and we had to run for our lives."

"I heard about it. Agent Morgan filled me in on the details as soon as I got back to the office. I'm sorry."

"Anyway, the tapes are safe. But if we'd known we would be in such danger, I don't think we would've gotten involved in helping you get them."

"How can you be sure the bombing was connected to the tapes?" Camper asked.

"What else could it be?"

"There are several possibilities. We need to talk."

Agent Camper agreed to meet Bud Joe on the corner near the YMCA. He put on a loose-hanging sport coat and stuffed his revolver into his holster. He put on a brown straw hat and pulled the brim low on his forehead.

He walked out of the FBI office and hailed a cab. For 20 minutes they drove through the crowded streets to the YMCA. He asked the driver to drive slowly. The taxi rolled past the YMCA Building and pulled into a parking lot on the side.

He paid the driver and stepped from the cab. He ran his hand over his side and touched the butt of his gun. He looked in both directions, then walked around a car and crossed the street to the corner.

Bud Joe drove his dusty 1980 Ford pickup, with the mud-grip tires, slowly down the alley several blocks from the YMCA. He narrowly missed scraping against garbage cans stacked in back of the houses. Dogs as big as ponies charged against the fences, snarling, barking and revealing long, jagged teeth that could rip off a leg. He shuddered as he watched them hook their claws into the chain links trying to climb over. He cursed them, turned left and pulled to a stop at the corner. Bud Joe rolled down the window and asked the tall man standing on the corner, "Need a ride?"

The tall man pushed his hat back and nodded.

"Get in," Bud Joe said.

Agent Camper slid in the front seat and fastened his seat belt without speaking.

Bud Joe gave him a long look out of the corner of his eye. He remembered the questions the agent had asked about his sister. Thoughts of the visit brought back strong feelings. He clenched his jaws and his eyes blazed.

Agent Camper finally spoke, "I'm sorry about the other day when I questioned you about your sister." He had sensed that this must be the reason for the dead silence.

"Uh-huh," Bud Joe grunted and said nothing more. There was silence for a few minutes, interrupted only by the clearing of throats.

"There's one thing for sure," Bud Joe finally said through

his clenched teeth, "if you ever find whoever killed her, you'd better lock him away out of my reach." He gripped the steering wheel and stared grimly at the road.

The silence resumed. Agent Camper looked at Bud Joe with sadness in his face. It was the 'I know how you feel' look, and Bud Joe's warning was understood. Camper believed that this man was capable of uncontrollable violence if pushed too far.

Ashley borrowed a long-sleeved shirt and straw hat from Marty to protect her fair skin from the burning sun. Marty insisted that she take an old fishing hat of Bud Joe's for Chris. They walked down to the boat docks and sat side by side on the short pier. The waves rolled in along the edge of the sand. Three young men walked close to the water's edge. Between their bare chests and feet, each wore light colored shorts. They soon disappeared around the slight bend of the lake.

Chris put his arm around Ashley's shoulders. "Have I told you how much I love you, today?"

"No, you're slipping, Dr. Burns."

"Well, I do, Carrot Top," he said and kissed her on the neck.

She smiled and rubbed the back of her hand across his unshaven face. "I love you too, Chris. What's going to happen to us? Do you think we'll ever get out of this mess?"

He nodded and pulled her head close to his shoulder and stroked her hair. "We will. Somehow, we will."

Moments later, they heard the rumbling of Bud Joe's pickup and watched as it pulled to a stop beside the resort office.

Agent Camper stepped out on the white gravel and adjusted his hat. "Thank you, Bud Joe."

"Yes, sir." He pointed toward the row of boat slips. "They're waiting for ye down on the dock."

The agent walked through the loose dirt and leaves toward Chris and Ashley.

Chris cranked the outboard motor and backed out of the slip. The flat-bottomed boat skimmed across the calm water, outrunning the noisy roar of the engine.

Agent Camper removed his straw hat to save it from the wind and pulled his sunshades from his jacket pocket. After they had gone four or five miles, Chris stopped the motor and let the boat drift.

Agent Camper sat in the front seat, the creases in his navy blue slacks sharp as a razor blade. With the palms of his hands, he tried to smooth his hair back in place to put his hat back on.

"Are you all right, Miss Denton?"

Ashley nodded, sitting slumped in the middle seat.

Chris didn't bat an eye. "We have the videos and tapes."

"Where?" Camper asked.

Chris hesitated before answering, "In a safe place."

"Well, I'm here to pick them up."

"Not so fast, Agent Camper."

"What do you mean, Dr. Burns?"

"There's something we want."

"How much?"

"How much, what?"

"How much money will it take for you to hand them over to us?"

Chris laughed with his mouth open, and the gold in his teeth glittered in the bright sunlight. "Money? Is that all you government people know?"

Camper looked surprised. "Then what do you want?"

"We could care less about money."

"What then?"

"There're two things we want. Number one, we want the vice president to resign."

"Pardon me?" Camper blinked.

Chris shot him a look hot enough to boil water. "You heard me. A lovely young girl has been murdered, and I can't bear

202

the thoughts of a cover-up."

"What makes you think there'd be a cover-up?"

"That's the way it works, right?"

"I'm afraid I can't argue that point, but neither can I make any promises."

Chris glared at Camper. "Somebody will."

"What's the second thing you want?"

"We want a guarantee of our safety. We don't want to leave the country or spend the rest of our lives looking over our shoulders. We want to stay right here in Austin and pick up where we left off."

"I can guarantee that, but the other...I don't know. What has the vice president done?"

"Your innocence act doesn't fool us for a minute, Agent Camper, so just cut the crap, okay?"

"How do you know so much about the vice president?"

"From the tapes and videos."

"How many do you have?"

"Twenty-five or 30."

"How many have you seen?"

Chris rubbed his hands together. "Enough. I borrowed a VCR and a tape player from Bud Joe last night. I'm convinced now that the vice president put out a contract on April Crafton."

"Why would he do that?"

"Because on one of the videos, she told him that she was pregnant and demanded that he get a divorce and marry her."

"How do I know you're telling the truth?"

Chris pulled the borrowed tape player from under the boat seat. He handed it to Ashley and she turned it on.

"Here's a sample of one of their phone conversations."

Instantly, Agent Camper recognized the vice president's husky voice and his sun-reddened face began to turn pale. He pulled his hat down over his eyes and lifted a hand in the air. "Turn it off, I've heard enough."

"Well...what do you say, Agent Camper?"

"Money I could promise, but you know the system as well as I do. It's who you are and what you have that counts. I'll call the director as soon as I get back to the office."

Chris licked his dry lips. "I certainly hope you have some influence."

"Or what?" Camper asked quickly.

"I'll do the same thing April Crafton promised the vice president she would do if he didn't meet her terms."

"And what was that, doctor?"

"The V.P. will see his name and face on every supermarket tabloid in the country."

"Is that your idea of justice?"

"That's my idea if justice fails."

"You've placed a tough order, you know," Camper said.

"Well...what'll it be?"

Camper pulled a cigarette from his shirt pocket and tapped it on the side of the boat. "I said I'd try, that's all I can say." He put the cigarette in his mouth and lit it. He puffed a few times and sat silently staring at the wall of trees on the other side of the lake. "What about the rest of the tapes?"

Chris smiled. "You can have them, too."

"Do you have any idea what you're asking?"

"I sure do, Agent Camper. I'm sick of power and I'm sick of corruption. The higher you go in power, the more you can get away with, and I know what would happen if I turned this evidence over to you people. The grand jury would examine the tapes and videos, call 300 witnesses, and they would still find no evidence for indictments. And you know what I'm saying's the truth. Bud Joe and his mother hurt every day over the loss of their loved one, while the dirty bastard who's responsible walks around scot-free, pretending that he's a model government official. That's just not my idea of justice for all."

Agent Camper sat quietly for a moment. "I'll get back to

you as soon as possible, but it won't happen."

"Somebody had better do more than try, Agent Camper. I'm sitting on a keg of black powder, and you people could light a fire, if you're not real careful"

"I'll do my best. You have my word."

Agent Camper leaned forward in his seat and reached for Ashley's hand. "I'm very sorry about your car, but I'm awfully glad you weren't seriously hurt."

"Thank you, Agent Camper."

With a powerful yank of the rope, the outboard motor sputtered and roared. Chris spun the handle around to high speed and the small fishing boat lurched forward. Camper grabbed his hat and gripped the edge of the boat as they skimmed across the lake toward the dock.

CHAPTER NINETEEN

"Granny...."

His words were cut short by a blast of fire and brimstone from the other end of the telephone line. "Dr. Christopher Burns! Where are you? Is Ashley all right? I've been worried out of my mind."

"Ashley's okay, she's with me, but it'd be too dangerous to tell you where we are."

"I read about the car bomb in the morning paper. I feel sorry for the boys who tried to steal it, but I'm glad it wasn't Ashley who opened the door."

"Yes, Granny, it was a close call, too close."

"Are you okay?"

"For the moment, but I need a favor."

"Just name it, Chris."

"When you go to work in the morning, explain the situation to Dr. Stubblefield. Tell him I'll be taking a few days off until this thing's settled. He's a good man and he shouldn't have any problems handling everything."

"Sure. Is there anything else I can do for you?"

"Yes, call my father in the morning, if you don't mind."

"You don't want me to call him today?"

"No, wait and call him at the office. I don't want to upset my mother. She'd worry herself sick, and there's nothing she can do. Tell him we're safe and not to worry. If anyone else should call or come by the office asking questions, you don't know anything."

"Well...what else can I say? I am totally in the dark."

"Good girl, and be careful yourself."

"Okay, Chris." There was a brief silence. "Louis Hamilton called early this morning from South America."

"What'd he want?"

"He wanted to know what was going on, if anything had happened."

"What'd you tell him?"

"I told him about Ashley's car. He almost went into shock. He also said he still had a few things to take care of but he hoped to be back by late Wednesday."

"I'm hoping this situation will be over by then."

"God, I hope so too, Chris. A person can only stand so much."

"I've got to go now, Granny. I don't want to stay on the phone too long."

"Take care, Chris."

It was after 1:00 p.m. when Agent Camper called a cab from the YMCA building, having been left on the same corner by Bud Joe.

The skinny little taxi driver sat sideways, with his right arm planted across the back of the seat, and talked a mile a minute during the entire drive back to the FBI office about two teenage boys who tried to steal a car. "Yeah." He talked as if the conversation was two-sided. "Got the daylights knocked out of 'em. Bet they think twice before they try that again. Wonder just what went through their minds when the dang thang blew? Yes, sir, if they're lucky enough to pull through, they'll wear the scars the rest of their lives. I'll be hanged if I can figure these kids today. Used to think I was being punished 'cause me and the missez never had any kids, but lately I thank the good Lord every day for his mercy. Yes, sir, my daddy caught me trying to smoke when I was 13, and he literally tore my butt up. You married, son?"

"No, sir." A muzzle would be nice, he thought, tossing a 20 in the front seat two blocks before they reached the office. He opened the door and stepped out of the taxi before it came to a complete stop. "Keep the change," he said over his shoulder and shook his head violently as he darted into the office.

He walked without stopping, his head down, until he reached his office and shed the dusty sport jacket. He sat down in his chair, placed his hands behind his head and raised his feet to the top of his desk. He got up again and walked out into the large room usually occupied by six desk clerks and secretaries. He glanced at the various plaques and portraits of past and present FBI directors, one or two hanging slightly lopsided, on the dark gray walls. He stared at Director Russom's flattering picture and wondered who would fill his shoes if he should die or retire. He smiled as he thought about the long line of possible successors who would break their buns for the position to uphold law and order and serve their country to the best of their ability. Bull, he frowned, pure bull. They all loved the limelight and prestige that went with the title. In the past ten years as an agent though, he had to admit, Director Russom had been a very dedicated man, leaving his predecessor pale in comparison.

Tony Camper planted his hands deep in his pockets and walked slowly back to his office. He glanced at his watch; 1:30 p.m. It was an hour later in D.C. He closed the door, picked up the phone and hoped the director would be home by now. On Sundays, he and Mrs. Russom attended church, then dined out. This was always the maid's day off and Mrs. Russom's day to cook.

The phone rang three times. Director Russom answered, "Hello."

"Director, Tony Camper here."

"Yes, Tony."

"Sir, the situation here in Austin is very serious."

"What do you mean?"

"The senator's son has in his possession all the videos and tapes we discussed."

"How much does he want to turn them over?"

"He says they're not for sale."

"Then what the hell is it?"

"He says he wants justice."

"What the hell does that mean?"

"He wants the vice president to resign and admit his involvement with April Crafton."

"Does he realize he's asking for the moon?"

"He doesn't seem to, sir, but I don't think he'll give in."

"And what if Ramsey doesn't resign?"

"He says he'll give them to the press and every tabloid magazine in the country."

"Then we do have a problem. Where is Dr. Burns, now?"

"I'm not sure. I met with him this morning on Lake Travis."

"Where is Lake Travis?"

"Thirteen miles west of Austin."

"Have some of the local agents stake the place out."

"I'm working on that right now. I have a couple of agents on their way to the office."

"Good. I'll set up a meeting with the president and Nesbitt as early as possible in the morning. After the meeting, I'll catch a flight out to Austin. I'll be there sometime early tomorrow evening. Meantime, if anything else comes up, call me."

The director hung up.

Mrs. Russom entered the study with a cup of hot coffee. "You look worried, dear. Is there something I can do for you?"

"Yes, you can pack me a bag. I'll be leaving for Austin in the morning."

"It must be serious to pull you away from Washington."

"Believe me, my love, it's very serious. This situation could go down in history books."

"That serious?"

"That serious and then some."

Director Russom flipped the cards on his rolodex. "George Bivens," he muttered, "Where are you, George? Ah, here we go."

He dialed the number. One ring. Two rings. Three. "Oh, for Pete's sake, George, answer the phone." No answer. He slammed the phone back into the cradle and checked the number again.

Mrs. Russom entered the study. "Are you talking to me, dear?"

"No, Pumpkin, I'm talking to myself."

She smiled, shook her head and went back to her business. Ten minutes had passed. He vigorously punched the buttons on the phone as though he were killing ants on a picnic table. After the fourth ring, George Bivens answered.

"Hello."

"George, this is Director Russom."

"Good afternoon, director, what can I do for you."

"Arrange a meeting for me with the president, first thing in the morning."

"Can't do that, director. The president's calender is full all week long."

"George, this is a matter of life and death. Do you hear me?"

"I don't have a problem with my hearing, director, but that doesn't change a thing. It's always a matter of life and death with you and Director Nesbitt."

"Listen to me George and pay attention, I don't intend to repeat myself. I'll be there at eight-thirty in the morning, and if you don't want an embarrassing situation on your hands, you'd better do as I tell you. Arrange for me to see him at 8:30 a.m. Director Nesbitt will be with me, and we WILL see the president."

"Okay, okay, you don't have to get nasty, 8:30 a.m. it is."

"Thank you, George, you're always very cooperative. That's what I like about you." There was a click on the end of the line.

The director picked up his coffee and walked to the window. The air was dead still and the dark clouds had begun to roll in. "Severe thunderstorms coming in," the Mrs. had commented on the way home from the restaurant. A tornado would be nothing compared to the storm brewing in Austin, he thought. The director's nerves tightened. He walked back to his desk and dialed the phone.

"Hello," Lionel Nesbitt answered.

"Lionel, Frank Russom here. Could you meet me at the White House, eight-thirty in the morning?"

"What's up?"

"I'll tell you in the morning."

"Come on, Frank, you know I don't like surprises."

Director Russom went into detail about the events in Austin. He observed the tone in Nesbitt's voice. There was no evidence of surprise. An uneasy feeling kept gnawing in the pit of his stomach. He had known Lionel Nesbitt for years, and since they had both become directors of the FBI and CIA, there had been numerous knock-downs and drag-outs. There was something missing in the conversation, something he had failed to mention. It wasn't his words that worried Director Russom, it was his lack of words.

"Thanks for calling, Frank, I'll see you in the morning," Director Nesbitt hung up.

The click of the phone at the other end of the line echoed in Director Russom's ears. He opened his bottom desk drawer and reached for a full bottle of whiskey. He filled his empty coffee cup with about three inches and gulped it down in two long swallows. He squeezed his eyes shut and held his breath. He seldom did this, being a coffee and tea man mostly, and after a few moments it seemed to sooth the gnawing in the pit of his stomach. "Damn you, Mr. High and Mighty Vice President."

Director Nesbitt picked up the phone and fingered the buttons. It rang only once before he heard an answer.
"Downs, here."
"Do what you have to do to find Dr. Christopher Burns. He has the videos and tapes. Get them."
"Yes, sir."

Sunday, 2:00 p.m., Austin time. Jeri Lynn kicked off her three-inch heels and dropped her church dress on the floor near the bed. She wiggled into a sexy swimsuit and stood sideways, viewing herself in the mirror. Not bad for 40-some-odd years, she thought. She liked the way men turned their heads when she swayed along the poolside.

She pulled her beach bag from the closet and crammed a towel inside, along with her sunglasses and a novel. She went into the kitchen, opened the refrigerator door and placed a cold Diet Coke beneath the beach towel.

Jeri Lynn stepped off the elevator and strolled along the poolside, enjoying a muffled whistle or two. She bent slightly and sat her beach bag down. After she had settled herself comfortably in one of the lounge chairs, facing the sun, she pulled the strings on the beach bag and reached for her suntan lotion. She popped open the Coke, took a delicate sip and sat it on the poolside table. Then she poured a palm full of lotion and began to spread it evenly over her arms and shapely legs. She opened her novel, propped up a shiny knee and began to read.

Totally absorbed in the book, she didn't notice the blond-haired man who had seated himself in the lounge chair inches from her own. He cleared his throat loudly, and she glanced around. She wondered how he expected to soak up any of the wonderful rays, dressed like a preacher.

She dismissed the thought and went back to her story.

He cleared his throat again.

She looked around with a blank expression and pulled her sunglasses down to the edge of her nose.

"Can I help you with something?" she asked.

"Are you Jeri Lynn McAfee?" he asked, smiling.

"If you're looking for Luther, I haven't seen him in days, and I don't intend to pay any of his past-due bills." She loved that answer and grinned broadly. Luther was history anyway.

The blond-haired man answered carefully, "I'm not looking for Luther."

"Then what's your problem?" she asked.

"I'm looking for Dr. Christopher Burns."

She gazed at him as he gave her another grin. "Why in the hell are you asking me? I don't keep up with Dr. Burns on his day off."

His grin faded. "Oh, but I think you do know where he is."

"Where'd you get that crazy idea?"

"Does the name, Granny, mean anything to you?" he asked sharply.

How could he possibly know that? Chris was the only person in the world who called her 'Granny.' Had the lab offices been bugged or had he used some high-tech equipment to listen to their phone conversation earlier? The question was what to say next.

"Well?" he grunted.

She spoke the first words that came to her mind, "I really don't know where Dr. Burns is."

The tall man stood and ran the tip of his forefinger down her cheek. "I do hope for your sake, you're telling the truth."

"Read my lips, cutie. I don't know where Dr. Burns is."

"You know," he smiled, "I don't believe you. Good day, Mrs. McAfee."

"Miss," she muttered.

She pushed her sunglasses back over her eyes and watched

as he disappeared down the sidewalk and around the corner, which led to the front entrance of the apartment building.

The apartment manager's office was located in the northeast corner of the bottom floor with two massive windows on both outside walls. Jeri Lynn's lounge chair was positioned at the right angle, allowing a clear view through the office to the east side of the building.

She bent her head in the pretense of reading and watched over the top of her sunglasses. She could see a reflection of his bright floral tie through the double glass. He was standing as still as a statue, watching her reaction to his visit.

After she was satisfied that he was no longer watching, she got up, smoothing her swimsuit, and packed her towel, sun lotion and empty Coke can back into her beach bag.

She casually walked into the building, pushed the button for the elevator and nervously looked around. The door opened and she waited as two of her neighbors stepped into the hall. She was so frightened, she could hardly respond to their greeting.

She unlocked her apartment door, stepped inside and paused a moment by the closed door. What should she do? She was afraid to use her own phone, and who would she call? Then the thought came to her; the FBI agent who had come by the office to see Chris.

Minutes later, she had dressed and called a cab. She walked out to the curb and stood there for a moment, then began to walk up the street. She turned and began to walk back, just as the cab pulled to the curb. She stepped in, "Arboretum Mall," she said as she closed the door. She leaned back against the seat fingering her purse strap and tried to remember the agent's name as they moved through heavy traffic towards the mall.

She ambled through three department stores, watching over her shoulder. The tall, blond man was nowhere to be seen. A young sales clerk yawned and smiled wearily.

"Is there a pay phone, somewhere close?" Jeri Lynn smiled and asked.

"Yes, ma'am, go through children's wear and take the short hall to the right. It's close to the ladies' restroom."

"Thank you."

It was just past 3:30 p.m. when she dialed the phone.

"Federal Bureau of Investigation," the desk clerk answered.

"Sir, this is Jeri Lynn McAfee. I work with Dr. Christopher Burns at the State Crime Lab. A few days ago, one of your agents visited Dr. Burns, and I need to know his name."

"Yes, ma'am, that was Agent Tony Camper."

"Oh yes, that's his name. Is he there by any chance?"

"Yes, ma'am, one moment and I'll transfer your call."

"Mrs. McAfee," he said at last. "What can I do for you?"

"Agent Camper, a tall man with blond hair approached me at my apartment swimming pool this afternoon wanting to know about Dr. Burns."

"Who is this?"

"I'm sorry. I'm Jeri Lynn McAfee. I work with Dr. Chris Burns."

"What did the man want to know?"

"He wanted to know where Dr. Burns is today."

"What did you tell him?"

"I told him I didn't know, and that's the truth."

"Have you heard from Dr. Burns?"

"Yes, he called early this morning, but didn't say where he was. I'm scared, Agent Camper. This man threatened me."

"How?"

"He ran a finger down my face and told me he hoped, for my sake, I was telling the truth. What should I do?"

"What's your address?"

"I live in Spicewood Apartments, out close to Arboretum Mall."

"I'll find it and have that area patrolled tonight; in the meantime, if you should see him again, call the office here.

If I'm not in, the desk clerk will know where to reach me. Okay?"

"Thank you, sir."

She replaced the telephone and shut her eyes, stroking her forehead. "Damn," she whispered, wondering what the hell she was supposed to do now.

She placed another quarter in the slot and dialed.

"Hello," her friend answered, free of emotion and sounding tired.

"Mary Jane, this is Jeri Lynn, would you do me a favor?"

"Sure, kid."

"I'm stranded at Arboretum Mall. Would you be a dear and pick me up?"

"Sure, meet me at the front entrance in 20 minutes."

"Thanks, Mary Jane. I need a friend."

"Has Luther split again?"

"Luther's history."

CHAPTER TWENTY

Mary Jane Buckner stopped in front of Arboretum Mall and Jeri Lynn slid into the front seat of the grey Lincoln, buckled herself in and crammed her purse between her feet.

"Good Lord, Jeri. If I didn't know better, I'd think you've been on a three-day drunk. You look pukey and hungover."

"I'd probable feel better if I could kill a fifth or two."

"What'd Luther do to you?"

"It's not Luther. I wish it was. It's worse."

"You're pregnant."

"At my age?"

"Why do I get the feeling you don't want to tell me what's going on?"

"I'm scared."

"Of what?"

"You won't tell?"

"How long have we been friends, Jeri?"

"I know, I'm sorry." Jeri Lynn began to blurt the whole story, from day one. She was able to maintain her composure, except during the part about the visit from Blondy. He meant business, she could tell. She'd seen movies with thugs like him. They'd stop at nothing, and this man hadn't believed her story. She felt doomed. Her voice trembled as she talked about him. She began to sob and fumbled in her purse for a tissue to blot the tears that hung from her heavy eyelashes.

Mary Jane, weaving in and out of the Sunday sightseers,

reached over and patted her friend on the leg. "Get a grip, Jeri. Maybe you should leave town for a few days."

"And go where?"

"Just pick a place and go."

"That wouldn't help. He'd find me."

"Then buy you a gun."

"I'm afraid of guns."

"Did you call the police?"

"No. I called the FBI."

"What are they going to do?"

"They said they'd send somebody over to my apartment."

"There you go. They'll make sure nothing happens to you. Besides, they'll probably need you for a witness when it's all over."

"I hope you're right." Mary Jane had made a good point and she felt better. Much better.

Jeri Lynn rode the elevator to her third-floor apartment. It stopped on the second floor to let off two male tenants, with whom she had exchanged pleasant nods.

She unlocked the door, stepped inside and sat her purse on the small table in the short hall.

She scurried through the bedroom, into the bathroom and began filling the bathtub. A long hot bath would soothe her aching, tense muscles. She undressed and put one foot into the water. The phone rang. She dried her foot and walked to the phone beside her bed. "Hello."

Nothing. Another one of those heavy breathers, she thought.

She went back to the bathroom and lowered herself into the bathtub. She released a loud sigh of contentment and slid down, leaving only her head above the water. The phone rang again.

She tried to ignore it and let it ring. After the fifth ring, she got out of the bathtub, wrapped a towel around herself and went back to the phone, leaving a wet trail across the bedroom carpet.

"Hello," she answered breathlessly, toweling herself dry as she spoke.

"Miss McAfee?"

"Yes, this is Miss McAfee."

"I have someone here you might like to talk to."

"Who is this?" she asked.

Then she heard a familiar voice on the other end of the phone. "Jeri Lynn, this is Luther. Please, baby, tell this man what he wants to know. He means business."

"Luther? Where are you? Luther?"

The other voice came back on the line. "Where is Dr. Christopher Burns?"

She clenched her fist. "I don't know. I'm telling you the truth, I don't KNOW."

In a low angry tone, the voice replied, "Okay, Miss McAfee, if that's the way you want it."

"Whoever you are, please don't hurt Luther. If I knew where Dr. Burns was, I'd tell you, but I don't."

"Sure," he said and hung up.

She dropped the towel and quickly dialed the FBI number, bugs or no bugs. Agent Camper answered almost immediately.

"This is Jeri McAfee. They've got Luther," she blurted out.

"Who's Luther?" Camper asked.

"An old friend of mine. They're holding him hostage to make me tell where Dr. Burns is."

"Did you recognize the voice or any familiar sound in the background?"

"No, there was no sound at all except for the man who called, and I've never heard his voice before."

"I'm going to send a female agent over to spend the night with you, just in case he should call back. She'll bring a recorder, and if you get any more calls, we'll have something to go on. Okay?"

"Thank you, Mr. Camper," she said as she hung up and stared at the phone. Her knees suddenly felt weak as she began to dress.

FBI Agent Rachel Tanner stood on the corner waiting for the light to change. She touched her hair lightly, assuring herself that the black wig was still in place.

She crossed the street briskly, her flat-heeled shoes snapping on the pavement. She glanced again at the SPICEWOOD APARTMENT sign and compared it with the address Agent Camper had given her. It was the same. She'd expected a run-down little place over a bakery, but this high-rise was something else.

She casually walked into the lobby and spied the off-duty agent sitting in the television area. His cotton shirt was opened three buttons down, and he was sitting with one leg thrown over the arm of the chair. He glanced down at the beach bag sitting in front of the chair. She walked in front of him and looked down. "Is this everything I need?"

"Everything."

She picked up the bag and called up to Jeri Lynn's apartment from the telephone in the lobby. She stepped into the elevator when the doors opened, pressed the button to the third floor and rode quietly upward.

The doorbell rang. Jeri Lynn closed her eyes, fighting the feeling of tension in her body as she walked to the door. She peeped through the security hole and saw a black-haired woman. She turned the locks, leaving the safety chain in place, and said, "Yes?"

Agent Tanner flipped open her badge and smiled. "Jeri McAfee?" she asked.

"Yes, I'm Jeri."

"I believe you're expecting me."

"Your ID shows blonde hair. How do I know you're who you say you are?"

Agent Tanner peeled back the wig and nodded. "This is just an extra precaution. May I come in?"

The frown on Jeri Lynn's face relaxed, and she replied, "Please do, you had me worried for a minute."

The sun was almost down, and a cool breeze had begun to blow in from Lake Travis. The sky in the west was deep orange, and in a few minutes, the sun would be gone. The air smelled as if the breeze had filtered through the middle of the bluebonnet and wild honeysuckle vines.

Chris and Ashley walked along the edge of the sandy beach, Savannah and Bud Joe following a few steps behind.

Jacob had stayed behind to chat with Marty and keep an eye on the resort office. He was uneasy and paced back and forth until Marty insisted that he take a seat in the easy chair behind the counter.

Chris removed Bud Joe's old fishing hat from his head and brushed his hair back with his hand. The lifeless hat had matted it down, and it lay stiff against his scalp.

Ashley found his new hairstyle amusing, picked up a handful of water and sprinkled it on his head. "This would be a good place to spend a vacation," she said.

"Let's just pretend that's what we're doing," Chris murmured as he pulled her close and stole a kiss.

A few steps behind, Bud Joe walked with Savannah, telling her stories of his childhood. He chuckled and she laughed with him. Suddenly, Chris said softly and firmly, "Get down."

Realizing the seriousness in Chris's voice, Bud Joe pulled Savannah to the ground.

The semi-darkness was broken by the bright lights of a car that had pulled down on the sloping bank in front of *The*

Elizabeth.

They could see the shadows of a man and woman who had gotten out of the car and walked out onto the pier. The soft breeze blew gently through the leaves of the oak trees, and between gusts, they could hear muffled voices.

Chris pointed to the bushes a few feet up the bank's incline and whispered, "Ashley, you and Savannah stay here. Bud Joe, come with me and let's get a closer look."

They crawled on the wet sand to within 20 yards of the yacht, where Bud Joe stopped behind a bush covered with honeysuckle. Chris crawled a few feet farther and crouched behind another bush.

Suddenly, without warning, Bud Joe felt a piece of cold metal press against the back of his neck. He turned his head slightly to greet a flashlight shining in his face.

"What the hell is this?" the man asked.

"If you'll take that gun away, I can explain," Bud Joe said.

"All right. But you'd better make it good."

"I own this resort."

"This is your resort?"

"That's right," Bud Joe answered. "I saw the car pull down here and thought I'd better check it out."

The man lowered his flashlight, and Bud Joe could see him for the first time. "Who are you?" he asked.

"I'm Blade Henderson, part owner of this yacht."

"I thought it belonged to a lady by the name of Beth Wagner."

"She's the other part owner. We're engaged to be married."

"How long do you plan to keep the boat down here?"

"Two or three days, but that's none of your business."

"Mister, how 'bout pointing that gun someplace else. It's making me nervous."

"I'm sorry, man." Blade stuck the butt of the gun in his armpit, clamped down and extended his hand. "I appreciate you keeping an eye out down here for us. There's so much crime going on, you just can't take any chances. Know what I mean?"

You're a fine one to talk, Bud Joe thought. Then he chuckled in his friendly way. "I'm Bud Joe Crafton."

"Glad to meet you. Sorry I scared you." He looked again in the direction of the yacht. "Guess I'd better get back to the little woman. See you around, Bud Joe."

"Yeah, see you around."

Bud Joe stood silently as he watched Blade Henderson's flashlight flicker across the ground and disappear onto the deck of the yacht. Then he said, "You can get up now, Chris."

The woman standing on the deck of the yacht rummaged through her large purse and emerged with a key to the door. She opened the door and turned on the exterior, then the interior, lights. The yacht lit up like a gambling casino.

Chris and Bud Joe watched in awe. They heard giggles and the sound of glasses clicking together coming from the yacht. Shortly afterwards, Blade left the yacht and walked back up the slight incline to the car. He unloaded three boxes of what appeared to be assorted canned goods, two boxes of wine, three armloads of clothes and the two green file boxes Chris had seen before. He walked around the deck to the back of the yacht making last-minute checks.

Hurriedly, Beth left the yacht and ran back to the Corvette, where she retrieved a black briefcase from the back seat. Then she ran back onboard and disappeared into the cabin. Moments later, she rejoined Blade on the deck and the lights of the yacht went black. The two figures returned to the car, which pulled out and headed back toward the city limits of Austin.

Bud Joe and Chris approached the two girls, still crouched low in the bushes, perspiration rolling down their faces and burning their eyes. They glanced up quizzically.

"It's okay now," Bud Joe said, "They're gone."

Their muscles tense and aching, they all ran stiff-legged back to the air-conditioned office. Jacob and Marty were seated behind the counter watching the news on the local television channel. Jacob looked up with a blank expression and asked. "Well...what have you two been doing, wrestling alligators?" He pointed to Bud Joe's and Chris's wet, sandy clothes and smiled.

Bud Joe was breathing heavily from the excitement and the 100-yard run. "Something funny's going on down at the boat," he wheezed.

Jacob raised his eyebrows. "Like...what kind of funny?"

"Looks like that feller Blade Henderson and that Wagner woman's planning a trip. Told me the boat would probably be leaving in two or three days. That was after he took the gun away from my head."

"Gun? What gun?" his mother barked.

"He thought I was a burglar. Slipped up on me and put a gun to my head."

"Did he mean to shoot you, Bud Joe?" his mother barked again.

"Well, Mama...I didn't ask, but you have to think when somebody puts a gun to your head, he's thinking about it."

"The last two boxes he unloaded were the two green file boxes we saw at his apartment," Chris added.

"Well...won't they be surprised if they try to cut a deal with them," Jacob commented. "Where are they now?"

"They went back to town," Chris answered.

"They didn't see you, did they, Chris?"

"No, just Bud Joe."

Jacob began to pace the room in an irregular route. "I don't have a good feeling about all this." He began to pace again, combing the side of his mustache with his thumbnail. "Bud Joe, let's take a look around the campgrounds."

They left the path and walked through the grass behind the

cabins. From one of the cabins came the sound of a door slamming.

"Is someone staying in that cabin, Bud Joe?" Jacob whispered.

"Yes, sir, folks from St. Louis. They're okay."

They walked on through an area of short grass to a clump of trees and turned away from the edge of the lake. Beyond the trees was a row of shoulder-high bushes. In the blackness of night, they began walking in the direction of the pavement.

Suddenly, they heard someone cough. They stopped and looked in the direction of the lake. Near the road, about 100 yards in front of them, was the vague outline of a car. They retraced a few steps and crouched down in the underbrush.

The tall man, who had been standing in front of the car, opened the door and seated himself sideways. He turned his head to the driver and muttered something, then he turned, lifted his feet into the car and closed the door.

A frown crept over Jacob's face, and his lips puckered under his mustache. "Bud Joe, I'm afraid we've got some real problems. I'd hate to guess who those men are."

"You want me to go up there and ask 'em, Mr. Hughes?"

"No, Bud Joe, that'd be too dangerous. Let's just watch them awhile and see what happens."

After an hour, the tall passenger opened the door and stepped out of the car. He looked in all directions, then opened the back door and made himself a bed on the narrow seat.

"Well, Bud Joe, we might as well go back to the office. Looks like they're planning on staying all night."

"Sure looks that way, Mr. Hughes."

Jacob stood with one hand braced against a tree for a few seconds, then he bent forward and began walking in a crouched position through the bushes toward the resort office. Bud Joe followed a few steps behind.

They walked with increasing speed, but when they noticed a

man moving around the side of cabin one, they slowed their pace and watched as he crossed the pavement and disappeared into the trees that lined the banks of the lake.

When Jacob stepped into the resort office, he turned to Bud Joe and asked, "What time do you normally close the office?"

"Eleven o'clock, Mr. Hughes."

Jacob looked at his watch. "It's 10:30 p.m. now. Is there another way out of here besides the main road?"

"No, sir, Mr. Hughes," Bud Joe replied.

"What's going on, Jacob?" Chris asked.

"This place is crawling alive with suspicious people, and I don't have any idea who they could be."

"Maybe Blade found out we have the videos and tapes."

"I don't think so. Maybe since you talked to Agent Camper out here, he may have staked out the place."

"What should we do?"

"There's nothing we can do but wait it out." He turned to Savannah, who was standing behind the counter with Marty, and said, "You'll need to call Beth in the morning and tell her you're sick and can't come in. We don't want to arouse any more suspicions than we have to."

"What about me?" Ashley asked.

"I think she already knows you won't be there."

Jacob looked at his watch again. He lit a cigar and stood at the window, a cloud of smoke drifted lazily over his head. He turned to look at Bud Joe, his teeth crushing the end of the cigar. "Lock up and turn out the lights as usual, Bud Joe. It's going to be a long night."

CHAPTER TWENTY-ONE

Monday, 8:30 a.m. George Bivens opened the door to the president's office and motioned to the directors. "The president will see you now," he said.

The president was sitting at his desk, knees crossed, tapping his pipe into a large crystal ashtray. He said nothing, but merely motioned to the two grim-faced men.

"Mr. President," Director Russom began. "We have a situation in Austin that could blow the White House and the election out of the water. Dr. Christopher Burns has in his possession videos and taped conversations of Vice President Ramsey with one of the Hamilton girls whom Director Nesbitt spoke to you about earlier."

"I remember," the president replied. "Give him whatever he wants for the tapes."

"It's not that simple, Mr. President. He's not asking for money."

"Well...what's he asking for?"

"Justice, sir."

"Pardon me?" The president frowned.

"They want the vice president to resign and take full responsibility for his involvement with the girl," Director Russom said.

"Oh, hell!" The president leaned forward in his chair with a sudden lurch. "You know damn well he has ambitions to be the next president after this term. So, how are you going to get him to resign? Any suggestions?"

None. Silence prevailed.

The president packed his pipe with cherry tobacco and stuck it between his teeth without lighting it. "What are our chances of finding Dr. Burns and getting this evidence?"

"Our chances are pretty slim. There's really not enough time," Director Russom said.

With a look of disgust, the president rose. "I'm tired of hearing about this crap. Work it out and handle it yourselves." He abruptly left the office, leaving the two directors staring blankly at each other.

"Well...Nesbitt, you seem to be overloaded with knowledge today. Any suggestions?"

Director Nesbitt looked at Frank Russom and gave him a friendly, go-to-hell look.

"The two of us could talk to Ramsey and persuade him to resign," Russom said.

The thought amused Lionel Nesbitt. He slapped his knee and laughed facetiously. He stood, his long arm reaching out and his hand palming Russom's shoulder. "Forcing Ramsey off the ticket would be about as easy as pushing a rope uphill," he said. "Have a nice day, Frank, and don't take any wooden nickels."

Thunder rumbled and the sky had turned dark gray as Director Nesbitt left the White House. He glanced up at the flag hanging limply at the top of the pole. A gust of wind came as he held his eyes on the red, white and blue. The flag jerked and unfurled. The wind died, the flag popped and fell limp again. He loved his country and his president and would do whatever he had to do to protect them both. He stood for a long moment, snapped his heels together and saluted. He lowered his hand and began walking, glancing over his shoulder in time to see the flag being lowered and removed. Seconds later, raindrops began to fall, slow and large at first.

He sped across the Potomac hardly noticing the downpour and entered the CIA building. He opened the top drawer of his desk, removed his credentials from his pocket and placed them inside, then slowly closed the drawer.

He drove back to D.C. and parked his car at one of the busy malls. Deep in thought, he walked six blocks in the blinding rain and stopped at the first telephone booth. He wiped the rain from his face and dropped a wet coin into the slot.

A deep voice answered.

"Put Benjamin on," the director said.

"Just a moment."

"Yes?" Benjamin Sarrelli answered.

"Nesbitt here. Do it. Three o'clock this afternoon."

"Consider it done."

The telephone ringing close to Dr. Mel Vincent's head awakened him. He opened his eyes and looked around the room. He nudged his blond wife, who was sleeping soundly on her stomach with her head buried in the feather pillow.

The phone continued to ring. He groaned and squirmed until he had freed his arm from under her body. He picked up the phone with his right hand and looked at his watch. Nine o'clock in the morning.

"Hello," he answered dully.

"Mel, Benjamin Sarrelli here. Were you still asleep?"

He lit a cigarette. "Sorta. Just dozing in and out."

"Listen, I want you to go over to Baltimore and pick up our boy today. How soon can you be ready?"

"Give me 20 minutes."

"Good. I'll have my driver pick you up in my limo and drive you over there."

He jumped up and jerked the covers from the bed. His wife's blue silk gown had gathered up around her waist exposing her round plump hips. He chuckled and said, "Now haul ass you beautiful creature, I've only got 18 minutes left."

"Where're you going?"

229

"To Baltimore."

"What for?"

"What is this, *Unsolved Mysteries*?"

"Just wondering. You've got the day off, and I thought we could do something together. But if Baltimore is more appealing, just go on. Don't mind little ole me."

"I'll take you out when I get back. I won't be very long."

Mel stepped out of the shower, dried himself and lathered his face to shave. His wife sat the coffee on the vanity. He gulped it down and brushed his teeth vigorously. He poured a capful of Scope into his mouth and tipped his head back. He gagged and choked, popped some toilet tissue from the roll and wiped his face.

She peeped around the door frame and asked, "You okay?" He smiled and nodded, still coughing as he stepped into his dark grey trousers. His chest moved with his breathing as he buttoned his crisp white shirt.

Five minutes later, he was walking from the elevator of the apartment building down a long corridor toward the front entrance, where Benjamin's chauffeur waited.

"Dr. Vincent?" he asked.

"Yes, I'm Dr. Vincent."

"I'm Jud Armstrong," he said. He was a tall, muscular black man with his black chauffeur's hat perfectly balanced on his head. "I'll be driving you to Baltimore to pick up a passenger for Mr. Sarrelli."

He walked proudly to the car and opened the back door of the limousine.

Dr. Vincent shook his head sharply from left to right. "Jud, if it's all the same to you, I'd rather sit up front. I hate riding in the back alone."

"That's fine with me, sir." He closed the back door, opened the front door and waited for the doctor to seat himself. He walked around to the driver's side, opened the door and folded his masculine body, gripped the steering wheel and pulled himself in. He started the motor and pulled out into traffic.

It began to rain and they rode in silence, listening to the wipers pop and groan from the heavy downpour. For 20 minutes Jud maneuvered the long limo through the crowded streets and congested traffic of Washington. As he approached the last intersection, Jud took off his chauffeur's hat, placed it in the seat and patted the sides of his short hair. The top was more than short; he was on the brink of baldness. He forced his speed to the limit and set the cruise control. Then he adjusted his pant legs, relaxed and released a long sigh. The black limo seemed to float as they headed down Interstate 95 toward Baltimore.

"How long have you worked for Benjamin?"

"Ten years, sir. Ten wonderful years. Mr. Sarrelli is a fine man to work for. We have dinner two or three times a week and talk about our problems. When it comes to the color of a man's skin, Mr. Ben's colorblind. He just sees a man as a human being, no more or no less."

Dr. Vincent wrinkled his face. "Benjamin, with problems? I can't imagine that."

"Yes, sir, he's human. Very much human."

"Benjamin looks tired. Is he sick, Jud?"

"No, sir. His wife left him five years ago. Just like mine, she couldn't take his lifestyle, and she's the only woman he's ever loved. He's just about grieved himself to death."

"Why doesn't he just go get her?"

"He tried that, and tried to do better, but a leopard can't ever change its spots."

As the rain began to slack, Mel and Jud stared straight ahead in dead silence. After driving a few minutes, Jud asked, "What street will we be looking for, sir?"

Mel fished in his shirt pocket and withdrew a small piece of paper. "Market Street, house number 637."

Twenty minutes later, Jud tapped the brakes and the big limo rolled into downtown Baltimore. The rain had stopped, and the clouds began to break up as they turned at the corner of Spruce and Market. Three wine beggars sat on a concrete bench, looking hot and hungover, waving as if they were familiar with everyone.

Market Street was wide and curving, lined with large, old and neglected houses. Each home was set apart by large trees, chain-link fences and overgrown lawns.

When they approached 637, a tall, frail man, dressed in an Air Force colonel's uniform, emerged from the front door of the large stucco house and came around the back of an old battered station wagon parked in the driveway.

Mel hesitated a moment, then opened the limo door and stepped out onto the graveled driveway. "Don Forester?"

"That's me. Didn't recognize me standing up and wearing a uniform, did you?"

Jud got out of the limo and opened the back door. "Are you ready, sir?"

"I'm ready."

Dr. Vincent seated himself in the back seat with Forester. They fastened their seatbelts as Jud started the engine and backed out of the driveway. Vincent handed Forester the necessary identification cards and documents. In less than an hour, they would arrive at Andrews Air Force Base, Maryland.

The vice president's plane, Air Force Two, began its final approach for Andrews. Vice President Drew Ramsey, accompanied by three Secret Service men, one seated on each side and the other sitting in front, glanced at his watch. "What time will we be landing?"

The Secret Service man seated to his right answered, "Less than five minutes, sir. We had a 30-minute delay to avoid the thunderstorms."

"Good."

Drew Ramsey was confident he would be president after the next four years had been served. He glanced at the three men sitting straight and silent in front of him and was enormously flattered. Their lives were dedicated to his safety and protection.

The Sarrelli limousine stopped at the security gate and Jud handed the officer Donald Forester's identification card. He looked at the card, saluted, then motioned them through, no questions asked.

Jud parked in the VIP parking space as Forester leaned forward reading the thin black letters, UNITED STATES OF AMERICA, gleaming and stretching the entire length of the Air Force helicopter.

Donald Forester saluted the security guards standing at the base of the pad and walked up the ramp of the Air Force helicopter. He paused, looked around and stepped inside. He stared at the roomy cockpit and proceeded back toward the rear. His legs were weak and his torment was visible.

Dr. Vincent sat in the back seat of the limo, chain smoking, as he waited. Jud started the engine, rolled down his window for some fresh air and left the motor running.

After several minutes, Forester stepped from the helicopter and walked slowly down the ramp. He saluted again and walked briskly back to the waiting limo.

The security guards saluted as Vice President Ramsey and the pilot walked up the ramp and took their places in the helicopter for the flight back to Washington. They grasped the inner handles and secured the doors. They adjusted their headsets and fastened their seatbelts. The pilot leaned down, fingered the controls and the helicopter blades began to turn, spewing a cloud of dust as it lifted gracefully from the pad.

Members of the press waved, some saluted, pens and pencils scribbled frantically on a dozen note pads as reporters scrambled to their cars for the short ride, following the Secret Service men, back to the White House.

CHAPTER TWENTY-TWO

"Mr. Vondonitti."

"Yes, Stefano."

"Telephone, sir."

"Who is it?"

"Beth Wagner, sir. She says it's urgent."

Sal Vondonitti reached for the phone, releasing a long obscene sigh. "What can I do for you, Miss Wagner?"

"Mr. Vondonitti, there's something you need to know."

"Well...what is it?"

"Blade Henderson has tapes and video movies of his transactions with you that could put you and your family behind bars for the rest of your lives."

Vondonitti's face became red from anger, and his eyes bulged. "Is this some kind of joke? How do you know this?"

"I have no reason to lie to you, Mr. Vondonitti. I know exactly how many trips he's made out of the country for you."

"What does he plan to do with the tapes?"

"Cut a deal."

"Cut a deal? With whom?"

"The highest bidder."

"That son-of-a-bitch! Has he lost his mind?" Vondonitti shouted and jumped up from his plush sofa.

"He got awfully upset over the last shipment. Said you cheated him out of a million dollars."

"That crazy bastard. Who the hell does he think he is trying to blackmail? Me? Where is he now?"

"Out on his yacht. I thought you ought to know he's planning to leave Austin tomorrow."

Vondonitti paced a moment, then stopped. "What's the name of this damn yacht and where is it?"

"*The Elizabeth*, and she's docked on Lake Travis, 13 miles...."

"I know where Lake Travis is. What time's he planning to leave?"

"He's getting the yacht ready for a buyer who's supposed to meet him at Cypress Creek at eight o'clock in the morning. He's leaving with it around midnight tonight."

"You did the right thing by calling, Miss Wagner. I won't forget you."

"Thank you, Mr. Vondonitti."

Sal Vondonitti slammed the phone back in its cradle and screamed, "Stefano!"

"Yes, Mr. Vondonitti."

"Get my sons in here!"

"Yes, sir."

"Call my pilot and tell him to get the Lear ready to go to Austin. Find out what time he'll land and call Max Naylor in Austin. Tell him to meet the plane at the airport."

"Will that be all, sir?"

"That's all for now."

Beth hung up the public phone at the service station smiling to herself. Mr. Vondonitti, you stupid old son-of-a-bitch.

Shortly after 10:00 a.m., the Greyhound bus pulled into the Austin bus terminal, its destination...Dallas. Beth handed her large suitcase to the attendant, and he placed it in the baggage compartment of the bus. She handed her ticket to the driver, who was standing next to the opened doors. He smiled, admired her beauty, cancelled her ticket and handed her the stub. "Going to Dallas, are ya?"

"Yes, sir, going to visit my mother."

He smiled back and held her arm as she climbed aboard. She thanked him and covered his tall masculine body from head to toe with her eyes.

The bus was almost deserted for the moment, except for two older ladies with blue-gray hair, seated three rows from the rear, enjoying a private conversation.

Seated one seat in front of them, on the opposite side of the bus, was a young blonde mother with a four-year-old who was screaming and running up and down the aisle, squeezing by each passenger trying to take a seat. His mother sat oblivious to this behavior, powdering her nose and patting the tight ringlets that hung loosely on her shoulders.

Beth chose a seat in the rear of the bus behind the two older ladies and waited nervously as it began to fill to capacity. She began to worry. What had gone wrong?

She opened her large purse, found a mirror and studied the black wig and rose-tinted glasses which she was now wearing. Not bad. She might consider a dye job.

She carefully observed the passengers who were standing in the aisle waiting for a seat. There was no one resembling her beloved Arnold Leitzen. The driver closed the door and the last passenger, a tall, broad-shouldered man with a beard and gray hair, ambled toward the back.

"May I sit down, beautiful?"

She lowered her tinted glasses and stared, then a broad smile swept across her face. "Arnold, you handsome old man. I didn't recognize you."

"Well...wasn't that the whole idea?"

"How'd you recognize me?"

"I'd recognize those gorgeous boobs anywhere." He winked.

"Arnold, you're an idiot. I don't know why I love you."

"I'm awfully glad you do."

"Does your wife know you're leaving?"

"Hell no, she's in Europe. I guess she'll figure it out sooner or later."

He kissed her lips gently. "We're going to have a wonderful life, lying on the beach in the sun, day in and day out, drinking the best wine money can buy and sleeping after we've had sex all night. And, of course, you can shop and buy loads of expensive new clothes. We'll just do anything that strikes our fancy."

"You wonderful fool."

The bus driver watched patiently through the rearview mirror for the mother of the unruly brat to seat her son. When she tried coaxing, he pointed a grimy little finger in her face and yelled, "No, I'm four years old. I don't have to mind you. My daddy said so." Loud and clear.

Arnold snorted. "If I had my way, he wouldn't see number five."

"Oh, Arnold, don't you want to have four or five kids?"

"Not no, but, hell no. Kids wreck your sex life."

"Arnold, is that all you think about?"

"Only when I'm near you."

All eyes were now on Little Richie. He turned, jerked from his mother's grip and fled up the aisle. On the last leg of his trip back her patience snapped. She snatched him by the arm and slammed his plump little fanny down in the seat next to the window.

For the next 20 minutes, Little Richie made loud noises through his stubby little nose and spoiled everyone's mood. Five minutes later, he surrendered to Mr. Sandman and collapsed in his mother's lap.

"Did you put the briefcase on board the yacht?" Arnold asked.

"Yes, it's on board."

"Timer?"

"Yes, the timer's set for midnight."

"Good girl."

"Did you call the airlines in Dallas?" Beth asked smiling.

"Yes, all the arrangements are made. What about the

money?"

"Everything's done. I made the last transfer and destroyed the computer code. We now have all we'll ever be able to spend, ready for transfer to anyplace we want to put it."

"I love you for your brain, you know."

"And I'll kill you if you're ever unfaithful, Arnold Leitzen."

"No problem, my dear Elizabeth."

She shot him a startled look. "How did you know that?"

"I know everything there is to know about you, and don't you forget it."

"Don't get cute."

He rested his head on the back of the seat, closed his eyes and smiled.

At 1:55 p.m., the attendant unloaded their luggage at Dallas Greyhound Bus Station, and they hailed one of the Yellow Cabs sitting across the street.

"Where to, sir?" the driver asked.

"Dallas-Fort Worth International Airport."

"Yes, sir."

The driver pulled west into the traffic, flipped on the meter and pushed heavily on the gas pedal. He glanced in the rearview mirror and asked, "Newlyweds?"

"Yes, as of four hours ago."

"Congratulations. Going on a honeymoon?"

"Uh-huh."

"Where to?"

"Australia."

"Oh, man! That's a wonderful place to spend a honeymoon. I've never been there, but I've read a lot about it."

The driver pulled to the front entrance of the airport and unloaded the baggage. "That'll be $22, sir."

Arnold handed him $30. "Keep the change."

"Thank you, sir. Hope I can bring you back in 20 years for your second honeymoon."

"I'll see that you do." Arnold smiled.

"Fine, sir. The fare'll be on me, and you two have a nice trip."

Beth worked her way to the Delta ticket counter and bought two tickets to Montreal, Canada.

"Any luggage?" the friendly, dark-haired agent asked.

"One," Beth answered and set the suitcase on the ramp next to the counter.

The luggage was tagged and the agent placed it on the ramp behind her. She placed the baggage claim and airline ticket in an envelope and handed them to Beth.

Beth scanned the sparsely crowded airport and ambled into the ladies' room. She ripped the tickets into small pieces and flushed them down the toilet.

Arnold Leitzen took his turn at the American ticket counter and purchased two one-way tickets to Jamaica.

The obese ticket agent, with a crew cut, spoke through his porky-looking nose, "Any luggage?"

"One," he answered and set the luggage on the ramp beside the counter.

The ticket agent tagged the luggage and sat it behind him on the ramp. He placed the baggage claim and airline tickets in an envelope and handed them to Arnold. He stuffed them inside his suit coat and went to the snack shop to join Beth.

They ordered coffee and a BLT, ate and nervously waited for the countdown to board at 2:55 p.m.

The last call for flight 903 was called as the flight attendant lowered the rope to the boarding ramp.

The turbines on the sides of the jet whined softly at first, then built up to an ear-torturing roar. The ground crew unhooked the long umbilical cord that linked the cabin to the air-conditioning truck and pulled away. The young man on

240

the tractor, pulling the luggage wagon, wheeled in a circle and bounced off behind two other jets parked along the gate wall.

The jet rumbled slowly down the taxiway to the runway and paused for final clearance. In less than five minutes, they had lifted off, and the enormous plane had become a mere blip on the radar screen.

Arnold Leitzen, former professor of political science at the University of Texas, leaned back against the seat, unfastened his safety belt and stretched his long legs. At 42, his face was still remarkably pubescent-looking, along with the rest of his lean, but well-muscled anatomy. His brown eyes seemed almost concealed behind his dark tan. He still ran three miles and swam two every day of his life.

He had married a college sweetheart, and their union was never blessed by any children. He had been a successful high school coach in his earlier years. His wife, who persistently maintained that he had a future in public service, urged him to go back to school, get a degree in political science and involve himself heavily in politics. After receiving his degree, he ran for governor of their home state and was miserably defeated by the incumbent. He returned to teaching and continued to work as Texas party chairman every four years for presidential elections.

Beth had picked up a copy of the *Dallas Morning News* and sat calmly reading the society page. She leaned over and kissed his fake beard. "Happy?"

"Very." He smiled and his thoughts returned to what he envisioned as his perfect future.

The airport in Miami was packed elbow to elbow with people. It was noisy and the air was hot and stuffy, smelling like a wet poodle. People were pushing and shoving, speaking profanities in unknown languages; a perfect place to fall victim to a pickpocket artist.

D.J. POLLOCK

Beth stepped inside the crowded restroom that contained ten johns designed to accommodate 70 slow-moving ladies with slacks, girdles and pantyhose. "Thoughtful engineering," she muttered.

Her turn for the overworked john finally came. She stepped inside the stall, relieved herself and tore the two tickets to Jamaica into small pieces and flushed them down the toilet.

Arnold stuck the two tickets to their final destination in his suit coat pocket, worked his way through the crowd and joined Beth in the American Airlines waiting area. And then the elation came...so wonderful and intensely overwhelming it left him breathless; a quiet world in a deserted, remote haven of rest.

CHAPTER TWENTY-THREE

Senator Burns grabbed his phone and barked at his secretary, "Get me Director Russom."

He put the phone down and waited. Several seconds, he waited.

His secretary buzzed him back. "Director Russom is on his way to Austin, senator."

"Austin! What the hell's he doing going to Austin at a time like this?"

"His secretary didn't say, sir."

"Call his secretary back. I want to talk to her."

He put the receiver back and waited silently another 30 seconds.

His secretary buzzed him back. "The director's secretary is on the line, senator."

He snatched the phone and barked again, "When did the director leave for Austin?"

"I'm not sure, Senator Burns. He left the office about 11:30 a.m."

"Well...why in the hell didn't he call me?"

"I wouldn't know that, sir; it was an unexpected trip."

"Well, hell, does he know...." He slammed his fist on top of his desk and pulled the phone away from his ear. "Hello...Hello. That stupid girl. She hung up on me. She just flat hung up on me," he muttered. Then he noticed the small lamp that had toppled over the phone. "Oh, hell," he muttered. "I cut myself off." He slammed the phone back in its cradle so hard several sheets of paper blew off the top of his desk.

He stood and kicked the roller on his chair, then cursed the pain it caused. He buzzed his secretary again. "See if you can find my wife. If she's not at home, she'll be playing bridge at Mrs. Russom's."

The secretary buzzed him again. "Mrs. Burns is on the line, sir."

"Mama, pack a bag, we're going to Austin."

"Brandon, has something happened to Chris?"

"Yes and no. His secretary called me a few minutes ago and said they had a problem Saturday night, and they're hiding out someplace. I don't have time to go into the details."

"When will you be here?"

"I'm leaving the office right now. Our flight leaves in two hours. I'll explain on the way to the airport."

"I'll be waiting, dear."

Wearing a blue summer suit, Director Russom deplaned at Austin's Robert Mueller Airport at 7:30 p.m.

Every available press agent and television crewperson had been jerked from their desk and sent to the airport. Several reporters clamored for answers as Director Russom emerged from the front entrance. "Director Russom, word has it the helicopter carrying the vice president was sabotaged. Is there any truth to that rumor?" one reporter asked. "What about the rumor that the Mafia was involved?" another snapped. A third reporter forced his way through the crowd and shoved his microphone in the director's face. "Was the vice president assassinated?"

"I have no comment at this time," the director replied. He hated to be rude, but he had no other choice except to abruptly leave the press standing with unanswered questions.

They hurried to Agent Tony Camper's car and two

motorcycle policemen began to guide them through the traffic.

"What the hell was that all about. Sabotage and the vice president. Has something happened?"

"Yes, sir. I was trying to get to you before the press did. I don't know how they found out you'd be on that plane."

"What's happened?"

"The vice president was being transported from Andrews to the White House and the copter went down."

"What do you mean...went down?"

"The helicopter exploded over the Potomac and burned before it hit the water."

"No possible survivors?"

"No, sir."

"Oh, my God!" The director slumped in his seat and began to recall his thoughts at the early morning meeting with Director Nesbitt and the president. He was not a violent man and having wished something would happen, he felt remorseful. He asked his God for forgiveness and said a prayer for the vice president's wife and two young sons.

"Are you all right, sir?"

"Yes, Tony, I'll be okay. It's just quite an unexpected turn of events."

"To say the least, sir."

The director sat silently for several moments, staring straight ahead. "Has the White House called a press conference?"

"Yes, sir. The White House spokesman confirmed the vice president's death at 4:00 p.m."

Agent Camper and the director stepped from the car and hurriedly walked the 20 steps to the FBI office to avoid the press. One of the secretaries handed a telephone message to Tony. Without stopping, he snatched the paper from her hand, followed the director into his office and closed the door.

Agent Camper read the message and smiled. "Angela and Little Richie are in Miami waiting to board the plane for San Juan, Puerto Rico. She says Beth Wagner and Arnold

Leitzen are playing it cool. They don't suspect that the young mother, with the noisome child, is about to make the biggest bust of her career. Angela is almost certain that the money Beth Wagner has embezzled from Louis Hamilton, along with the drug money, has been placed in the banks on the island. She will alert the authorities there and have them in custody by tomorrow at the latest. She's done a superb job on this case."

"Is she taking Little Richie?" Director Russom asked.

"Yes, her husband will be joining them there in a few hours for a week of R and R."

"Good."

The director set his briefcase on Tony's desk, snapped it open and withdrew a folder. At that moment, the desk clerk knocked on the office door.

"Yes, Melinda?"

She stepped in, smiled and spoke to the director. "Excuse me, Agent Camper. You have a call waiting on line two from Dr. Chris Burns. This is the third time he's called."

"I'll take it. Thank you." He nodded at the director and picked up the phone. "Dr. Burns, Tony here. What can I do for you?"

"I understood you to say you'd be going to Washington to speak to the director."

"My plans changed, the director's here."

"Director Russom's here in Austin?"

"That's right, Dr. Burns."

"I heard the press conference from the White House on the news a few minutes ago, and it's unbelievable about the vice president."

"Yes, it's a terrible tragedy, and we need to talk. Can we meet somewhere?"

"I'm staying in cabin one at Lake Travis Resort. Be here at 11:30 tonight."

"We'll be there."

Sal Vondonitti's oldest son, Elton, along with two body guards, deplaned at the Austin airport at 11:00 p.m. Max Naylor backed the van up to their Lear jet, and they quickly stepped into the side door. They pulled slowly away, turned west into the traffic and, minutes later, drove through the last intersection that led to Lake Travis Resort.

"Why you drive so slow, Max?" Vondonitti asked.

Max was sweating and his fingers were a frozen curl of flesh around the steering wheel. He tapped the brakes for the last stoplight, and Vondonitti's lean, straight body tilted forward. Max caught a glimpse of his flat-eyed face in the rearview mirror.

"It's only 13 more miles west of here, Mr. Vondonitti. About ten more minutes worth." Max could tell his excuse went over like a lead balloon. Elton Vondonitti, like his father, was not a patient man.

Max slowed the van and began to watch for the lights of *The Elizabeth*. Suddenly he could see a large yacht heaving up and down as the waves rolled against the bank of the lake. The yacht was dark and appeared deserted. He pulled to a stop, and they stepped out on the pavement a few hundred yards away.

Suddenly Vondonitti whispered, "Hold it." The men froze.

"The yacht," he whispered. "Someone's turned on the lights. Max, where are you?"

"Right here."

"Get up here. Can you tell who it is?"

Max walked up even with Vondonitti. "Yes, sir, that's Blade Henderson. Get down, some lights are coming," Max whispered.

Agent Camper parked his car behind the resort office and went inside where Bud Joe was working.

"Agent Camper," Bud Joe said.

"Bud Joe, there was a van parked back down the way, pulled slightly down in the trees. Would you happen to know who it belongs to?"

"No, sir. There's no reason a van should be parked anywhere down this way."

"Thanks, Bud Joe. And Bud Joe...."

"Yeah, Mr. Camper?"

"Lock up and warn your mother. There could be a little trouble."

"Trouble?" Bud Joe's eyes snapped.

"Please, Bud Joe. Do as you're told."

Bud Joe locked the resort office and warned his mother. Then he went out the back door of the apartment and walked rapidly to cabin one. He brought Savannah and Ashley back to the apartment, grabbed his hunting rifle and ran back down the winding path behind the cabins.

Chris answered the knock on his door. "Agent Camper, Director Russom, come in," he said.

"Dr. Burns, I think we have company down the way," Camper said.

Agent Camper turned to Jacob, who by now was standing behind Chris. "Mr. Hughes, would you call the locals and have some backup sent out here?"

"Gladly."

Chris turned off the lights in the front room, and they all stepped out onto the screened porch.

"What about the tapes?" Agent Camper asked.

"They're here. I'm ready to turn them over to you."

"I'm sorry it all ended this way, Dr. Burns."

"I was a fool to think one man could make a difference."

Tony looked out across the lake and started to speak.

He squinted his eyes and stepped outside the door. He motioned for the director. Chris and the director joined him in the shadows.   Just at that moment, Bud Joe and Jacob stepped silently from the porch.

Camper led the way as they crouched low and ran across the asphalt road until they reached the bushes on the far side. There they watched silently as four men walked briskly toward *The Elizabeth*.

"That's one of the Vondonitti boys," Camper whispered. "What's he doing here?"

At 11:55 p.m., Elton Vondonitti and the three men swarmed aboard *The Elizabeth*. The motors began to roar, and the yacht pulled away from the bank, slowly at first. Then as the motors roared louder, the yacht began to speed away.

Three gunshots were heard as Agent Camper, the director and the others ran to the lake's edge. The yacht stopped momentarily in the middle of the lake, then after a few moments, began to move slowly back toward the shore.

"What's that beeping noise?" Camper asked.

"It's my watch," Chris replied. "It's midnight."

Suddenly a thunderous explosion lit up the sky. Director Russom and the others began to move back. Fire and debris filled the air. They stood motionless as they stared at the flames and listened to the dim and distant screams from the burning yacht. It seemed like hours before the crackling and popping stopped and a small cloud of black smoke drifted silently upward.

The director turned and spoke softly, "Well, my friends...I think it's all over."

Agent Camper and the others stood motionless, their faces shiny with sweat. They turned and walked without speaking back to the cabin.

As they approached the cabin, Director Russom spoke. "I'd like to get the tapes and videos now, Dr. Burns."

"What will you do with them?"

"They'll be sealed and not be opened for 75 years. There is the welfare of two young sons to consider."

When Agent Camper and Director Russom entered the FBI office at 1:00 a.m., the desk clerk handed the director a telegram.

Russom smiled and read the telegram aloud, *"Arnold Leitzen and Beth Wagner are now in custody. Boy, were they surprised! See you in a couple of days. Angela."* They all laughed.

"Director, Senator Burns and his wife are here in Austin trying to reach you," the desk clerk added. "Please call him at the Marriott, room 216. He's very anxious."

Director Russom turned to the desk clerk. "Get Senator Burns on the phone. Tell him I'm on my way over to see him."

"Yes, sir."

"Well, director," Agent Camper smiled and said, "we saved the government a bundle tonight."

"How's that, Tony?"

"We didn't have to fire a shot."

"You're right. Wouldn't it be nice if all the thugs in the world would square off and kill each other."

Tuesday, 2:00 a.m. Director Russom knocked softly on the door to room 216 of the Marriott and waited.

The senator had already picked up the phone and jiggled the hook four times to arouse the night switchboard operator. Hearing the knock on his door, he replaced the receiver.

He opened the door, his brows narrowing into an expression of concern. "Frank, are my son and Ashley alright?"

"Yes, Brandon, they're safe and sound; it's all over."

"Where are they?"

"Lake Travis Resort."

"Did he turn over the videos and tapes?"

"All but two, and I'll get those as soon as I can assure their safety."

"I still can't believe the vice president's dead."

"Well...his death will probably go down in history as another unsolved mystery."

"What about that young girl, April Crafton?"

"We'll never know about that. I'm afraid the truth went down in the helicopter. As of now, it's a closed case."

"Do you think the first Hamilton girl who died was connected to any of this?"

"No. After a lengthy discussion with Savannah Page, I'm convinced she actually committed suicide. Her father, Jacob Hughes, thinks there was a connection, so I didn't dispute his theory. There are some things that are better left unsaid. It's never easy to deal with a suicide, so we'll just leave it alone."

"When Chris and Ashley told me what was going on, I would've never dreamed so many people would wind up being involved. What about Blade Henderson and Beth Wagner?"

"Henderson was involved with the Vondonitti family. We've been trying to indict them for several years, but just never could get the goods on them. After the FBI revealed the contents of the tapes and videos to the Vondonitti family, they surrendered without resistance, pled guilty and it looks like they will be serving sentences in the Federal Penitentiary in Joliet, Illinois.

"One of the sons, along with Henderson, was killed in an explosion a couple of hours ago. He and three of his henchmen went out to Henderson's yacht on Lake Travis and apparently someone had placed a bomb on board."

"My goodness!" Laurel Burns said.

"Beth Wagner and Arnold Leitzen ran off to Puerto Rico, and they'll be in custody as soon as they're brought back to Austin. She'd embezzled quite a large sum of money from the Hamilton firm. I don't know, at this point, what Leitzen's involvement was. He sure picked a loser this time," Russom chuckled. "Their trial date will probably be set for mid-December. The embezzled money that had been deposited in Puerto Rican banks will be impounded pending the outcome of the trial."

"What about Dr. Sulcer. Was he murdered?" asked Senator Burns.

"We don't know for sure. His children wouldn't give us permission to exhume his body. We may have to get a court order to find out exactly what happened to him."

"Laurel and I really appreciate your taking the time to come by here to tell us this tonight. We're grateful for all you've done for us, Frank."

"We owe your son a great deal, Brandon, and I intend to do whatever's necessary to ensure his and Miss Denton's safety."

"Thank you. We owe you so very much."

"No, Brandon, if you hadn't been concerned enough to tell me about these problems, they would have gone unnoticed and unsolved. You have a good, honest son to be proud of."

CHAPTER TWENTY-FOUR

Tuesday, 8:00 a.m. Frank Russom walked into the Austin FBI office just as the desk clerk answered the phone. "Telephone, sir. It's Director Nesbitt."

He walked into Camper's temporary office and picked up the receiver. "Russom, here."

"Frank, this is Lionel. What's going on down there?"

"I have the videos and tapes...now, are you going to call off your hounds, or will it be necessary for me to call a press conference."

"What hounds?"

"Come on, Lionel, the two agents you've had on Burns's and Denton's tails for so long."

"It's done. What else?"

"I want Burns and Denton left alone. Understand? No more agents in Austin. No more, Lionel."

"You have my word, Frank. What do you plan to do with the videos and tapes?"

"Put them in cold storage for the next 75 years. We'll be dead and gone by then."

"You're a good man, Frank. I owe you one."

"One?" he asked and hung up.

Jacob Hughes parked in front of the Austin airport, reached into the glove compartment and popped open the trunk lid.

Louis Hamilton placed his suitcase inside, seated himself in the front seat and fastened his seat belt.

"Welcome home," Jacob said.

"Fill me in on everything, Jacob."

"We may have to drive to Dallas and back before I can finish," he said. "It's all so unbelievable."

"I was shocked to hear about the vice president. Any details yet?" Louis asked.

"No. The morning news hinted that the president will be holding a press conference today to announce his appointment of a new vice president who will be his running mate in the upcoming election. That reminds me, Louis, you'll have to appoint a new executive officer and chief of security."

"Why?"

"Well, Beth's in jail for embezzling from your company and Blade was killed in a boat explosion on Lake Travis." Jacob talked as fast as he could and related the events of the past few days. He finished just as he pulled into a parking space at the Hamilton Building.

"I can't believe it!"

After pausing a few moments, Jacob asked, "What do you plan to do with your business now?"

Louis hesitated. "I called the surgeons in Houston before I left and delayed our meeting, but I'm still planning on selling out."

"I'd like to discuss that with you, Louis. I might be interested in buying. I've done quite well for myself in the past few years, but I'm getting close to 50, and that's a little too old for detective work. I'd have to find someplace for Lena, my secretary. She's a good typist, but wouldn't know how to turn a computer on."

"I just might know where she could get a good job, Jacob."

"Where's that, Louis?"

"Come on in and we'll talk about it. I'm really pleased you're interested in buying my business. You're an intelligent man and I'm sure you'd do well with it."

Before long, Jacob Hughes was the new owner of Hamilton Medical Services and agreed to keep the firm under that name.

Within hours after the transfer, a striking change had come over the Hamilton Building. All existing strict rules that had been enforced by Beth Wagner were abolished, and the mood settled into a more relaxed one.

Savannah Page was named the new executive officer and Ashley agreed to work until a replacement could be found for her position.

On her last day of work, Ashley entered the Hamilton Building with mixed emotions. It was the beginning of a new life and the end of an old one. She had made some wonderful friends, and it had all been worth it. She turned on her computer, for the last time she thought, and walked slowly to the breakroom for a cup of coffee. It was deserted. She poured herself a cup and ambled down the long hall, passing all the offices. No one spoke or looked up from their computers. Why was everyone so cold? She finally persuaded herself it wasn't that important.

Five o'clock in the afternoon. All her accounts had been entered and balanced. She turned off the computer and picked up her purse. For a few moments, she gazed around the room, taking that last look as tears welled behind her eyelids.

She turned off the light and stepped into the hall. There was no sound as she passed through the last security door and stepped into the foyer. The cubicle was locked and dark.

As she stepped outside, she noticed the empty parking lot. She shrugged, jumped into the car and for five full minutes drove aimlessly, overwhelmed with sadness.

It was five minutes past six in the evening when she pulled the key from her purse and unlocked her apartment door.

Chris was waiting, watching the evening news as she sat her purse on the hall table. "Hi Carrot Top. How'd your last day at work go?"

"Horrible."

"What happened?"

"Everyone avoided me like I had the plague or something. I'm really hurt. Jacob wasn't even there this afternoon."

"Well...I wouldn't read too much into that. Maybe they hated to see you leave and just didn't want to say goodbye."

"I don't know, Chris," she sighed.

"Where would you like to eat dinner?"

"It doesn't matter," she answered sadly.

Chris parked his new Cadillac in front of the Candlelite and opened Ashley's door. As they approached the front entrance, he took her by the hand and led her inside, where they stood in front of the folding doors to the private dining room. "I'm afraid I have some bad news, Ash."

"Is it about Jacob?"

"Yes, Ash. He wasn't at work this afternoon because ..."

The doors were opened and Ashley stared inside.

Chris smiled broadly. "He wasn't at work this afternoon because he was here, getting ready for your going-away party."

"Surprise!" the entire staff of Hamilton Medical Services yelled in unison.

Ashley stood spellbound. Her mouth widened into a canyon, and her hand covered her eyes. "Oh Lord!" she squealed. "I should've known."

Chris pulled her close and waved a hand. "Ladies and gentlemen, I have an announcement to make. Six weeks from tonight, Ashley and I will be married. And of course, you're all invited."

"I can't believe you people," Ashley said.

"Who's going to give you away?" Jeri Lynn asked, standing arm-in-arm with Louis Hamilton.

Jacob walked close to Ashley smiling broadly. "I am. I'm the lucky man."

Savannah reminded Ashley that her wedding was only six weeks away. "Are you going to be able to do everything you'll have to do in six weeks?"

"With your help, I will," she said smiling. "Chris's mother will be staying the last two weeks with us to help out."

At that moment, the doors of the private dining room swung open. Everyone stood silently for a moment. Who was the handsome man in the double-breasted suit standing in the middle of the doorway with the short, black-haired woman? Was there a new lawyer in town?

Jacob walked up close to them and blinked his eyes several times. Finally, he spoke, "Bud Joe?"

"Yeah, that's me, Mr. Hughes."

"Well, you clean up right nice, Bud Joe."

"Thank ye, Mr. Hughes."

Jacob patted him on the arm and said, "You're a damn good man, Bud Joe. Don't you ever change."

"Where's Ashley?" Marty asked.

"Here I am, Marty," Ashley said, pushing her way through the crowd.

"What's this I hear about you and Chris getting married?" Bud Joe asked.

With a broad smile, Ashley held up her left hand.

Bud Joe's eyes bulged. "Good Lord, mama, look at that rock. It's as big as a headlight on a Volkswagen."

"I'm so proud for you both, Ashley. I know you're going to be real happy," Marty said.

Chris motioned to Jacob and they stepped outside the

folding doors. "What is it, Chris?"

"Do me a favor."

"Sure, what is it?"

"Jeri Lynn's worried about Luther. Would you call your friend in homicide and see if he's heard anything?"

"Sure, I'll be right back."

Jacob walked into the lobby and placed a coin into the pay phone.

"Police Headquarters."

"Is Detective Barron in?"

"Yes, sir, just a moment."

"Detective Barron here."

"Hank, Jacob Hughes. Have you had an accident report, or anything at all, on a man named Luther Whitfield?"

"Funny you should ask. A man who identified himself as Luther stumbled into the station here, acting like a gorilla that had sat down on a bumblebee, mumbling something about being kidnapped and asked me what the hell I was going to do about it."

"When?"

"Oh...about three or four weeks ago."

"What did you do with him?"

"I put him in the holding tank until he sobered up. Why do you ask--do you know Luther?"

"No. Just doing someone a favor. Thanks, Hank."

"Anytime, Hughes."

Jacob went back to the party and motioned to Chris. "Luther's been in jail," he said.

"What for?"

"Public drunkenness."

"But Luther doesn't drink, Jacob," Chris whispered.

"He does now."